THE INCURABLES

THE RICHARD SULLIVAN PRIZE IN SHORT FICTION

editors

William O'Rourke and Valerie Sayers

1996 *Acid,* Edward Falco

1998 *In the House of Blue Lights,* Susan Neville

2000 *Revenge of Underwater Man and Other Stories,* Jarda Cervenka

2002 *Do Not Forsake Me, Oh My Darling,* Maura Stanton

2004 *Solitude and Other Stories,* Arturo Vivante

2006 *The Irish Martyr,* Russell Working

2008 *Dinner with Osama,* Marilyn Krysl

2010 *In Envy Country,* Joan Frank

2012 *The Incurables,* Mark Brazaitis

THE INCURABLES

Stories

MARK BRAZAITIS

University of Notre Dame Press

Notre Dame, Indiana

Published by the University of Notre Dame Press
Notre Dame, Indiana 46556

Manufactured in the United States of America

Library of Congress Cataloging-in-Publication Data

Brazaitis, Mark, 1966–
The incurables : stories / Mark Brazaitis.
p. cm. — (The Richard Sullivan Prize in short fiction)
ISBN 978-0-268-02231-0 (pbk. : alk. paper) —
ISBN 0-268-02231-3 (pbk. : alk. paper)
E-ISBN 978-0-268-07564-4
I. Title.
PS3552.R3566I53 2012
813'.54—dc23
2012018053

∞ *The paper in this book meets the guidelines for permanence and durability of the Committee on Production Guidelines for Book Longevity of the Council on Library Resources.*

For Yael

and for my family

CONTENTS

ACKNOWLEDGMENTS

The author is grateful to the editors of the journals in which stories in this collection first appeared.

Notre Dame Review: "The Bridge," "This Man, This Woman, This Child, This Town," "Afterwards," and "Classmates"

Confrontation: "Security"

Post Road: "If Laughter Were Blood, They Would Be Brothers"

The Sun: "The Boy behind the Tree"

Ploughshares: "The Incurables"

Cimarron Review: "I Return"

The author is also grateful to his colleagues, fellow writers, and friends who have supported his work throughout the years: John Coyne, David Hassler, Katy Ryan, William O'Rourke, Valerie Sayers, Howard and Karen Owen, James Harms, Mary Ann Samyn, Kevin Oderman, Ethel Morgan Smith, John Ernest, and Felisa Klubes.

THE INCURABLES

THE BRIDGE

1

Standing at the north end of the Main Street Bridge, Sheriff John Lewis saw, no more than fifty feet in front of him, a man and a woman hoist themselves from the pedestrian walkway onto the bridge's topmost guard-rail, grasp each other's hands, and leap as if they were intending to dance into the sky. It was 6:13 on what was otherwise an ordinary April evening.

Sheriff Lewis immediately formulated an explanation: *They're bungee-jumping*. And a consequence: *I'll have to arrest them*.

Even when he reached the smooth, round rail from which they'd jumped and saw no bungee-jumping equipment attached, he held firm to his understanding of what had happened. He allowed a moment to pass before he placed his hands on the rail and stared over the side of the bridge. On the bicycle path 165 feet below lay the body of the man. A few feet from the path, in the overgrown grass, dandelions, and Queen Anne's Lace beside Celestial Creek, was the woman's body. He pulled back and shook his head, as if to clear the pair of images from it. But when he looked again, the scene was the same.

He reached to his hip, lifted his cell phone from its case, and dialed what he thought was headquarters. "I've got two suicides off the west side of the Main Street Bridge," he said to the woman who answered.

"John? What's going on? Are you all right?"

He realized his mistake with her first syllable. "Marybeth, I've just seen two people kill themselves." He told his wife where he was. He asked her to call 911 and have them send a car and an ambulance. His hands were shaking too much now for him to dial his cell phone.

He leaned over the rail again. A woman in electric lime jogging shorts and an Ohio Eastern University T-shirt was standing a few feet from the bodies, her hands covering her mouth. "Please step away," he shouted down to her. "This might be a crime scene." He didn't know if he was using the right language. "Please step away."

She looked up at him, her face contorted in what looked like disgust or agony.

"I'm the sheriff," he explained, "and I'm coming down."

By the time Sheriff Lewis labored down the stairs at the northwest corner of the bridge, he was winded and red-faced. He was sixty-four years old, and he'd been sheriff for less than a month.

When Sheriff Lewis reached the bike trail, he moved first to the man's body and put his thumb on the man's wrist. He felt a strong heartbeat but was sure it was his own. He lumbered over to the woman and did the same, but the drumming pulse he felt was also doubtless his. He looked up at the woman in the lime jogging shorts. She seemed frozen.

"They're dead," he said. When he heard the ambulance's siren, he added, "I think."

The ambulance and the police car arrived simultaneously, driving from opposite ends of the bike trail, which was just wide enough to accommodate the vehicles. The two well-toned men in the ambulance confirmed Sheriff Lewis's hesitant pronouncement. Sheriff Lewis glanced over at Officer Mark Highsmith, who had joined the Sherman Police Department only two weeks earlier. He was the only employee in the department with less time on the job than Sheriff Lewis.

"What do we do now?" Sheriff Lewis asked him.

It wasn't Officer Highsmith who answered, however. "Pray," said the woman in the lime shorts.

— "You acted in a completely professional manner," Marybeth assured him. It was a few minutes before one in the morning. They were in their queen-sized bed, in their dark bedroom, their air conditioner rattling in the window. "You did what was necessary. You handled the situation with grace."

"I called you," he said.

"But you told me exactly what to do," she said.

"So that *you* could handle the situation with grace."

Marybeth, who was nine years older than Sheriff Lewis, had had two strokes in the past eighteen months. She used to mountain-climb and go white-water rafting, but now she left the house only to attend physical therapy sessions. Sheriff Lewis used to be the inactive one. Before he became sheriff, he was an English professor at Ohio Eastern, where he'd worked for thirty-two years. His specialty was detective fiction, psychological thrillers, and true crime, and he liked nothing more than sitting in his study and tinkering with the commas in articles he'd written for *Studies in Popular Fiction* and other scholarly journals.

"They were a married couple, both forty-two years old," he told Marybeth. "One of their neighbors said they'd been trying to have a baby for years. They tried every procedure University

Hospital offered. A week ago, their adoption of a Korean child fell through."

"How sad," she said.

"I don't even know what drew me to the bridge. On my way home, I dropped off our letters to the boys at the mailbox in front of the post office. But instead of walking straight back to my car, I walked down to the north end of the bridge. If I had reacted quicker, I might have saved them."

"It's not your fault," Marybeth said, her voice softer now. He knew she wanted to sleep. She'd waited up for him to come home, which had cost her.

"We'll talk tomorrow," he said, and he kissed first her hair, then her cheek, then her lips. Everything tasted dry and powdery, almost dust-like. Lately he'd begun to fear that their next kiss would be their last.

Two years ago, Marybeth had expressed concern about his impending retirement from the university. She didn't know what he'd do without classes to teach, students to advise, and meetings to attend. Or she did know: He'd disappear into his study and emerge hours later smelling of decay.

In the late 1960s, Sherman had made its top law-enforcement position an elected one and had changed the authoritarian title "chief of police" to the friendlier "sheriff," even though there was already a county sheriff. In running for sheriff of Sherman, John Lewis hoped to upend his wife's idea of him as someone in danger of remaining in a holding pattern until his heart stopped or cancer called. He gauged his chances of winning at somewhere shy of 1 percent. But when the incumbent refused to distance himself from his best friend, a man who, in a psychotic break, murdered his wife and two children, and the other candidate was found to own land planted with enough marijuana to keep every high school student in the state high for a year, he became everyone's fallback choice. It helped, too, that Marybeth tapped into her family inheritance to buy television, radio, and newspaper ads, which emphasized her husband's service in the army and his long-standing participation in a Neighborhood Watch program.

During the last ten years, Sheriff Lewis's hair had turned gray and his waist had expanded like an inflatable ring at a swimming pool. If he was going to acquire a nickname in his new job, he was sure it would be "The Marshmallow." His wife, by contrast, was slimmer than she'd ever been—too slim. After her first stroke, she'd given up dyeing her hair, which was a ghost-like white. Her skin, which usually had a golden hue, had lately looked dishwater gray. When he expressed his concern to her doctor, a young woman as brusque as she was competent, she said, "There's no returning to Go, but we'll do the best we can."

Sheriff Lewis waited until he heard Marybeth's smooth, deep breaths before he left the bed and walked up the stairs to his attic office. From his window, he could see the bridge, its south end no more than a few hundred feet from his house. If he had been here, he would have shouted down a warning to Richard and Rachel Henderson. Would they have heard him? Would they have listened?

Sheriff Lewis sat down at his desk, clicked on his computer, and typed the words "suicide," "prevention," and "bridges" onto Google. He told himself he would investigate every site that came up. He had 2,050,000 to read.

— The next morning, Mayor Bloom sat at his desk, doodling with a blue pen on the sole of his right shoe. Sheriff Lewis sat in the hard-backed chair to the side of the mayor's desk. The mayor's office was on the second floor of City Hall, across the redbrick plaza from the clock tower. Sheriff Lewis had arrived at exactly eight o'clock. The mayor hadn't come to work until twenty of nine. At nine, he had to attend a ribbon-cutting ceremony at a bridal store at the Sky Lake Mall, which was why he asked Sheriff Lewis to speak as fast as he could.

"We need to secure the Main Street Bridge against additional suicide attempts," Sheriff Lewis said.

"I'd like to," Mayor Bloom said, "just as I'd like to redesign the Sky Lake East exit off Interstate 77 so people stop flipping their cars on the hairpin turn. Six people flipped their vehicles last year—and one of them is still in a wheelchair. And if we're dreaming about safety now, I'd go ahead and close all the bars and restaurants on the days of Ohio Eastern football games. And on game days I'd also prohibit every store within a sixty-mile radius from selling alcohol. We've had no deaths on football Saturdays during my watch, thank God. But the number of close calls makes me wonder when our luck is going to run out."

The mayor, who was Sheriff Lewis's age, was well over six feet tall and weighed no more than 175 pounds, but he moved in the world like a short, fat man—with languidness and suspicion. It looked like the mayor was drawing a flower, with large, looping petals, on his shoe. "Anyway, if we put up fencing or netting now, it might be seen as an admission of guilt. We might as well mail the families of the dead couple—the Hendersons, right?—the millions of dollars they'll sue us for."

"Excuse me?"

Mayor Bloom signed his name below the flower doodle before depositing the pen behind his right ear. Gazing at Sheriff Lewis, the mayor said, "When I was young, I wanted to be an artist. My mother wanted me to be the Jewish FDR." He gestured around his office, the walls crowded with the mayor's landscapes and self-portraits. "Here you see the result. Mediocrity is the offspring of compromise." He gave a resounding laugh.

Out of politeness, Sheriff Lewis nodded, although he suspected this wasn't the response the mayor wanted.

Mayor Bloom said, "We don't have the money to settle a lawsuit, so let's not provoke one. And to get approval to add safety features to the bridge would call for a vote of the city council. I can tell you right now what two members of the council would say: 'Whoever is desperate enough to jump off a bridge is desperate enough to find some other way to die. So why waste the money?' The Main Street Bridge may be a convenient portal to the next world, but it isn't the only one, and we can't police them all."

Sheriff Lewis saw the Hendersons holding hands, saw the sky embrace them, saw the sky let them go. *I was an eyewitness,* Sheriff Lewis thought to say. But he checked himself, knowing that his having seen what happened didn't strengthen his argument to secure the bridge.

"Besides," the mayor said, "before the Hendersons, how long had it been since anyone had jumped off the Main Street Bridge? Half a century? Maybe longer."

Sheriff Lewis's cell phone rang. Although he had a police radio, which he wore dutifully around his waist, his subordinates, in acknowledgment of his struggle with police codes and radio frequencies, usually called him. Sheriff Lewis began an apology to the mayor, but the mayor was on his feet and heading out the door.

"Sheriff," said the voice on the phone, "we've got another jumper."

— The jumper was Harriet Smith, who lived on Prairie Street, which ran perpendicular to the south end of the Main Street Bridge. She was eighty-six years old. She'd brought a stepladder to assist her in climbing onto the railing. A graduate student from Costa Rica, Hector Márquez, who had been walking back to his apartment, helped her set up the ladder. He assumed she wanted to observe the two beavers who were swimming in the narrow creek below.

"One minute, I was showing her where the beavers were," Hector said, "and the next, I was watching her leap off the rail and fall to the bicycle trail like a bird without wings." He shook his head and said "Very, very sad" so many times Sheriff Lewis put a hand on his shoulder.

Sheriff Lewis thought: *I should have had an officer on the bridge as soon as I saw the Hendersons jump. I should have anticipated copycat behavior. This is my fault.*

And so he had Officer Highsmith take the first shift on the Main Street Bridge. "I want an officer here twenty-four hours a day," Sheriff Lewis said to Highsmith, as if the new officer had the authority to enforce such an edict.

Sheriff Lewis had left his car in the parking lot of the Dollar Store on the north side of the bridge. As he walked to it, he heard a voice behind him: "Sheriff Lewis, may I have a word with you?"

Sheriff Lewis turned to find a short, red-haired man with a palm-sized tape recorder in his hand. Looming behind him, his arms stretched as if to grab him, was Officer Highsmith.

"I don't think he's planning to jump," Sheriff Lewis assured Officer Highsmith. "Better see what that family has in mind down there." Sheriff Lewis pointed to the south side of the bridge, where a man and woman were pushing two children in a double stroller. Officer Highsmith retreated.

"Would you call this an epidemic?" the red-haired man asked. His name was Otis Allen and he was the owner, editor, and publisher of *The Horizon,* a weekly print newspaper with a daily Web update. He was also, as far as Sheriff Lewis knew, the paper's only correspondent. He'd done a flattering profile of Lewis during the sheriff's race, although toward the end of the profile, he didn't fail to mention that Lewis's experience with crime fighting had been mostly theoretical.

"I don't think three suicides make an epidemic," Sheriff Lewis said.

Allen countered: "In a town of fifty thousand people such as Sherman, three suicides is the equivalent of New York City having five hundred and forty."

In his old job, Lewis would have engaged Allen in a debate about the value of such statistical extrapolations. Instead, he said, "The situation is sad and disturbing, but we will do our best to prevent additional misfortunes."

"How?"

Sheriff Lewis glanced over the bridge, which was a step or two more than one hundred yards long and accommodated two single lanes of traffic as well as pedestrians on elevated concrete walkways on both the east and west sides. Officer Highsmith was running toward a teenaged boy in ripped blue jeans and a white T-shirt. The boy had been walking across the bridge but now appeared fixed in place like an animal on the highway, a beaver or groundhog waiting to become road kill. "Stop where you are!" Officer Highsmith yelled.

Officer Highsmith's words achieved the reverse: The boy turned and ran in the opposite direction.

Here's our solution, Sheriff Lewis would have said if the scene hadn't struck him as ludicrous. He knew enough about his new job to say nothing at all.

— "She was eighty-six years old," Marybeth assured her husband in their dark bedroom. The air conditioner was on again. It had been an unusually hot April. "She had terminal cancer. And I wouldn't be surprised if the coroner finds she had a heart attack before she even hit the bike path."

"If I had put an officer on the scene immediately, it wouldn't have happened."

"You can't know that. Instead of the student from Costa Rica, it might have been one of your officers who helped her up onto the stepladder. No one expects an old woman to throw herself off a bridge."

"I'm thinking of closing the bridge," Sheriff Lewis told his wife.

"To foot traffic?"

"I'd like to close it to all traffic, at least temporarily. But I realize this wouldn't be a popular decision."

"I suspect it wouldn't," said Marybeth, her voice cracking from fatigue. "People will resent being punished for what three desperate people did. How many vehicles travel over the bridge on an average day?"

"Five thousand."

"So what's wrong with keeping an officer on the bridge all the time?"

"It means leaving another area of town uncovered. Tonight, for example, the officer on the bridge would ordinarily be patrolling Partytown."

"Is it still a fire trap? It's amazing what students will agree to live in."

"I have to hope the students behave," Sheriff Lewis said. The moment he finished speaking, he heard the wail of a fire engine. He heard his cell phone ring in his pants on the floor.

Three minutes later, he was driving to Partytown, where two houses were blazing.

— Sheriff Lewis's cell phone woke him up at 6:14 the next morning. "Are you crazy?" Mayor Bloom said. "You can't pull an officer out of Partytown, especially now. Ever heard of spring fever? Ever heard of graduation? If these kids aren't screwing each other blind, they're setting fire to each other's bunk beds. And the landlords—I prefer to call them scumlords—of all of those tinderbox houses in Partytown are furious. Three of them called me after midnight last night. Talk about a bunch of litigious assholes! They're already talking about a recall election for both of us. They want no less than four officers patrolling Partytown at all times."

"What about the bridge?" Sheriff Lewis mumbled in his half sleep. He hadn't come home until three in the morning.

"I told you: Let them jump. No one cares when a depressed geriatric flings herself over a bridge. But when the star cornerback of the football team runs out of his house with his ass on fire, that's a catastrophe!"

"I thought he was a linebacker."

"I don't care if he's the punter," the mayor said. "If he plays football, his butt better not be burning."

"I'll do what I can," Sheriff Lewis said. "I have to weigh the—"

"No, no, no," Mayor Bloom said. "There's no weighing involved. At least two officers in Partytown. We have to keep these assholes happy or the party's over for us."

— Sheriff Lewis thought to crawl back into bed beside his wife but he knew he wouldn't be able to sleep. So he slipped upstairs to his office, where he clicked on his computer and read the morning's *Horizon*. The top story was, of course, Harriet Smith. There was a sidebar to the main story, a commentary written by Otis Allen. It began, "In his decades as a university professor, Sheriff John Lewis saw death every day—in the pages of the mysteries and true crime accounts he read. Now he's seen death in reality, and he looks at once befuddled, scared, and guilty."

He heard his wife call him. She wanted water.

"There's a glass beside the bed," he said.

Her voice was faint, as if he was hearing it from across the street: "I can't move."

After he helped her sit up and brought the water to her lips to drink, he told her he thought he should take her to the hospital. "So I can sit in their bed instead of ours?" she replied. "I've earned this bed, John. Don't take it away from me."

Dorothy, a retired home health-care aide they'd hired to look after Marybeth during the day, was coming in an hour, and this thought brought Sheriff Lewis immense relief.

"What were you doing?" Marybeth asked him.

He told her.

"Don't worry," she said. "I bet there are only fifteen people in the whole world who read that thing."

— "*The Horizon* is calling it an epidemic-in-the-making," said the young woman in a yellow summer dress and pigtails who was sitting in his office when he arrived at work. Her name was Clementine Crowe, although everyone called her CeeCee, she said. She was a junior at Ohio Eastern and the president of the Delta-Delta-Delta sorority. She was chewing what Sheriff Lewis initially thought was gum but was now certain were sunflower seeds. "By executive order, I've already formed the Main Street Bridge Safety Brigade—Bridge Brigade, for short."

CeeCee's dyed hair was so blond it was almost white, and her skin radiated from what Sheriff Lewis could only imagine was the most intense artificial tanning session available without a prescription. He was sure it would be possible to warm his hands by the glow of her face.

After CeeCee explained how the Bridge Brigade intended to operate—Tri-Delt volunteers would be posted at the four corners of the bridge from eight a.m. to midnight in order to escort pedestrians across—she confessed to what she hoped to achieve beyond stopping would-be suicides: "We have the personnel and, to be honest, the leadership to be named Tri-Delta Sorority of the Year. Until now, we didn't have a project by which to prove our worthiness." In a whisper, she added, "The president of the winning sorority gets to visit the White House *and* Disney World."

"Let me make this clear: There's no epidemic here," Sheriff Lewis said. "If we'd had two automobile accidents in two days, we would call it unfortunate and move on. And what we've had the past two days is unfortunate."

"So you don't like my idea?"

Sheriff Lewis sighed. "I do," he admitted.

"So it's a go?" she asked, and she flicked her right hand as if she was turning the ignition in a car. He nodded.

Seconds later, she was on her cell phone, speaking so quickly he couldn't understand her.

"When will you start?" he asked when she was off the phone.

"Five seconds ago," CeeCee said. "You'll know who's in the Bridge Brigade by our pink T-shirts and our shorts with three pink triangles across the derriere."

It was the speed at which the Bridge Brigade had reported for work that caused Sheriff Lewis to stare at her with his mouth open, but she must have ascribed another cause to his befuddlement. "Derriere is French for rear end," she explained. "You know, posterior. Buttocks. Butt. Caboose. Back door. Personal floatation device. Booty. Groove thing. Piggly wiggly."

"I understand," he said.

"Helicopter pad. Fantasy Island. The Final Redoubt of Desperate Men. Bottom. Bum. Two Mountains and a Long, Dark Valley."

"Thank you," the sheriff said, chuckling. "I'm fully informed now."

After CeeCee left, Sheriff Lewis tried to busy himself with the other obligations of his office. But he couldn't stop thinking about the bridge. So he stepped out of his office and walked the six short blocks to the bridge's north end. He saw girls in pink standing like radiant soldiers at each corner. Officer Highsmith was at the south end, talking to a sorority girl whose hair was even lighter than CeeCee's but whose tan wasn't in the same league.

This might work, Sheriff Lewis allowed himself to think. *We'll guard the bridge for a week or two. People with copycat ideas will have time to cool off and think twice.* He expelled a large breath. It was as if he'd spent the last couple of days under water and had only now reached the surface.

Although Sheriff Lewis would have preferred to keep Officer Highsmith on the bridge all day, he dreaded another early-morning call from Mayor Bloom. Besides, it looked as if the Bridge Brigade could handle the situation as competently as any police officer. He told Officer Highsmith to remain on the bridge another hour before heading over to Partytown.

Sheriff Lewis returned to his office, located on the first floor of City Hall. His office was no larger than the average prison cell, and its only window looked out onto Main Street and its idling busses. He had yet to decorate the walls, and they remained an industrial gray, but he had transferred most of the books he'd kept at his office at the university to bookshelves here. If someone ever asked him to give an impromptu talk on Sherlock Holmes or P. D. James's great poet-detective, Adam Dalgliesh, he was prepared.

From his main desk drawer, Sheriff Lewis removed a bound copy of Sheriff Peter Marcello's *Reflections and Suggestions,* which Marcello had left him as a welcoming gift. He opened his predecessor's book at random: "One persistent problem you will encounter is motorcyclists who make use of the six straight stretches of road in town, especially Airport Avenue, to show off both the power of their bikes and their suspect ability to control them while kneeling, standing, and even fornicating."

If people screwing on Harley-Davidsons were the worst problem he faced from now on, Sheriff Lewis thought, he'd be the happiest law-enforcement official in America.

He couldn't have been daydreaming for more than five minutes when his cell phone rang.

— Officer Mark Highsmith and Alice Emerald, a member of the Bridge Brigade, lay face up on the bike trail below the east side of the Main Street Bridge. It was likely that every bone in their bodies was broken, yet Sheriff Lewis found something disconcertingly serene in their expressions. They looked like lovers who instead of gazing into each other's eyes had chosen to stare together at the sky.

The ambulance arrived, attended by the same pair of efficient weight lifters. The bodies were soon swept up, shut inside the vehicle, and borne off.

"I should have been suspicious," said CeeCee, who'd come silently to his side. It was obvious she'd been crying.

"Suspicious of what?"

"Of the pendulum. Last month, it was all I could do to get Alice out of bed. This past week, she has been ecstatic. The pendulum was bound to swing back."

"What about Highsmith?"

"Maybe he was trying to save her. Maybe he thought it would be like jumping into a river after a drowning person. Or maybe . . . maybe . . ." She looked up at him, her face streaked with tears and so bright it almost obscured her somber brown eyes. "Maybe I have no idea."

"I don't know how you could."

There was a pause in their conversation before Sheriff Lewis said, "I'm afraid we're going to have to retire the Bridge Brigade."

"I was going to propose doubling our numbers," CeeCee replied. "And from now on, I'll require each member to sign a pledge not to jump off the bridge." As she looked at his skeptical face, she added, "Please?"

Otis Allen appeared quickly, as if he'd risen from the dank brown creek beside them. His red hair was wet with sweat, and he carried a white towel over his shoulder like a boxing corner man. He put his palm-sized tape recorder in front of Sheriff Lewis's lips. "Are you ready to call this an epidemic?" he asked.

"I'm ready to call it hell itself if that's what it'll take to stop people from jumping."

Sheriff Lewis's last word hadn't yet completed its journey from his mouth to the tape recorder when, behind him, he heard a terrible thud.

— "I'm sorry, John," Marybeth said in what used to be the comfortable darkness of their bed. But no place felt comfortable since the suicides began. Or was it since Marybeth had her first stroke? The latest victim was Stanley Halbert, a forty-eight-year-old convenience store owner who had claimed to be crossing the bridge in order to deliver lemonade to members of the Bridge Brigade. (He carried a jug of lemonade and a stack of paper cups to support his claim.) In his brief look into Halbert's background, Sheriff Lewis found nothing to explain why he would commit suicide. His business, located a block from the Ohio Eastern campus, was thriving. He and his wife had celebrated their twentieth wedding anniversary the previous month with a Caribbean cruise.

With Mayor Bloom's swift consent, Sheriff Lewis had assigned two officers to patrol the bridge at all times. Officers working in eight-hour shifts would keep both sides of the bridge under twenty-four-hour surveillance. Every pedestrian would be treated as a potential jumper.

In selecting officers for bridge duty, Sheriff Lewis had chosen the six who seemed least likely to imitate Officer Highsmith, whose life story, alas, yielded few clues about his motivation for killing himself. Meanwhile, with the sheriff's reluctant blessing, CeeCee had doubled the number of Bridge Brigade patrollers. There were now eight on the bridge at one time. Sheriff Lewis had asked her to have them keep an eye on his officers. He had asked his officers to keep an eye on the sorority girls.

With his force stretched thin, he could only pray Partytown wouldn't burn to the ground. He also had had to remove an officer from Spanishville, which was named after the Guatemalans, Hondurans, Mexicans, Nicaraguans, Panamanians, and Salvadorans who had come in the mid-1980s to be the manual labor in the construction of the university's twenty-thousand-seat indoor coliseum and afterward had settled in a neighborhood north of it. Although Spanishville was a low-crime area, its residents were inevitably blamed for the unsolved murders, rapes, assaults, arson, and burglaries in town.

"I'm sorry, John," Sheriff Lewis's wife repeated, her voice so soft he had to put his ear next to her mouth. "It's like a plague of irrationality." Her head seemed to have melted into the pillow. He was amazed to see again how gaunt and wasted she looked. She was once his Scandinavian princess, but her beauty had been trumped by old age and infirmity.

"I think we need to have your doctor look at you again," Sheriff Lewis said.

"So she can tell me I'm seventy-three-years old and in failing health?" she managed in a weak voice.

When there was a long silence, his wife said, "Would you like to talk about the bridge?"

"No, thank you," he said, and he kissed his wife on the cheek and waited until she fell asleep before going upstairs to his office. He looked out of his window at the bridge, illuminated by its eight gold lights. It was past midnight, so all the pink-clad members of the Bridge Brigade were gone—all save one. She might have been five hundred feet from where he stood, but he recognized her from her pose, one hand on her hip, the other in motion in front of her as if she was conducting an orchestra rather than merely speaking to one of his police officers.

He reached for his phone and dialed her number, which he had memorized without intending to. When she answered, he said, "I think we have it covered now, CeeCee, although of course I'm grateful for your help."

"I'll give it another half an hour," she replied. "By one o'clock, I'd like to think that even the most desperate will have gone to bed."

"It would be nice to think so."

"And shouldn't you be in bed, too, Sheriff?"

"I suppose I should." He told her he could see her from his attic window, and when she waved, he waved back. He doubted he was anything more to her than a shadow, but she acknowledged him all the same.

— Sheriff Lewis woke up before his newspaper was delivered. He had a cup of coffee in his kitchen, which overlooked his back yard. Thirty years ago, it hosted a swing set and sandbox. His two boys were now grown and gone, his older son in Hong Kong, his younger in Paris. Before the suicides, he had never felt especially sentimental, at least as far as he noticed, but as he recalled his boys playing in the yard, child raising seemed an easy and ever-joyful task. He could secure his children's happiness simply by giving them a push on the swings. He could secure their safety, a bruised knee or scrape on the arm notwithstanding, by building a fence around their play area or, in the absence of an enclosure, by being a moveable fence, keeping them contained.

Now this, he thought. *This out-of-control death lust. This madness.*

He clicked on the TV on the kitchen table. On its twelve-inch screen, he recognized the scene immediately: the south end of the Main Street Bridge. A woman with buttercup-blond hair was on live, interviewing people about why citizens of Sherman were throwing themselves off the bridge. Because it was six thirty in the morning, her subjects were either old people who, having gone to bed before eight the previous evening, were alert and coherent or Ohio Eastern students who had stayed up all night, perhaps in expectation of seeing another jumper, and were delirious.

There were a large number of people in the background. *Like spectators at a high-wire act without a net,* Sheriff Lewis thought.

"I think people in this town and in towns everywhere across the country have turned their backs on Jesus," said a white-haired woman. "What they're left with is the devil or self-destruction. Maybe self-destruction is the better choice."

"I think it's like the Bermuda Triangle," said a young woman, half of whose black hair was dyed bubblegum pink. Her eyes darted around as if they were viewing a frenetic tennis match. "The bridge is haunted, and I bet when people cross it, they hear voices saying, 'Jump, jump, jump.' I'm telling you, there's an evil presence here."

"I'm willing to bet there are very strong gusts of wind that are lifting people off the bridge," said a young man who may have been sporting a goatee or may have forgotten to wipe his chin after eating chocolate pudding. "If the mayor of Sherman was willing to put up some windbreaks, I'm sure we would see a decrease in the number of so-called suicides."

The last person interviewed was CeeCee, who, after spitting out a couple of sunflower seeds, said she couldn't explain the suicides. "My only concern is to stop them," she said. "Today, I'm meeting with the director of mental health at University Hospital, and I'm hoping to have two volunteer counselors down here by noon. Last-minute therapy might be exactly what people need to keep living."

As the anchorwoman asked a question of the blond correspondent, the camera showed Sherman police officers escorting groups across the bridge. After they'd crossed, some people chose to recross. The bridge, Sheriff Lewis could see, was becoming an amusement park ride.

As the blond correspondent summed up the situation, using words such as "strange," "disturbing," "mysterious," "weird," and "wacky," Sheriff Lewis saw a blue van drive slowly past her and onto the bridge. The color and design of the license plate weren't ones he recognized.

Over the correspondent's shoulder, in the middle of the bridge, he saw the van stop. He wondered if it was about to release a pack of what he'd heard referred to as "disaster tourists," people who traveled to the scenes of floods, tornadoes, earthquakes, and the like.

The van's two back doors spread open. Out raced at least eight people. The driver's-side and passenger doors also expelled several people. Whoever was manning the camera stepped past the correspondent to focus on the van's passengers. The scene was shot in wide-angle: six people on the east side of the bridge, six on the west side, men and women, all of them ascending the black guardrails. Sheriff Lewis's police officers were at the far ends of the bridge, out of the camera shot.

"Stop them!" Sheriff Lewis shouted at the screen. "Please, God, stop them!"

Standing on the topmost guardrails on each side of the bridge, the van's former passengers held still a moment, like a flock of birds on a pair of telephone wires, then, in unison, jumped.

“I saw them!” shouted the blond-haired correspondent into the camera. “What you saw on TV, I saw live! I can prove it was real!” It was as if she was trying to convince herself.

As Sheriff Lewis continued to shout, “Stop them! Stop them!” his cell phone rang against his hip.

— Via telephone, Sheriff Lewis ordered the bridge closed to both automobile and pedestrian traffic. As he arrived on the scene, concrete roadblocks were positioned at both ends of the bridge. Orange barrels were employed to block pedestrian access. Police tape was strung like yellow tinsel over both the roadblocks and the barrels. People and vehicles were soon jammed on either end of the bridge.

Occasionally, someone would shout, “I want to jump!” Sheriff Lewis didn’t know whether the voices were serious or only full of morbid humor.

Journalists—television, radio, print, Internet—had descended on the scene with ambulance-like speed. Some were gathered on the bridge’s north side; others were on the trail by the creek, hovering near the twelve bodies.

Mayor Bloom had called Sheriff Lewis to tell him he’d be down as soon as he could think of a reasonable answer to the inevitable questions, one of which was, “Do you think you’re capable of stopping this insanity?” and another of which was, “Will you resign?” Mayor Bloom thought Sheriff Lewis had better prepare his own answers.

Sheriff Lewis saw all twelve bodies into the ambulances, two of which had come from Sheridan, the town thirty miles to the west. He couldn’t stand to look at any of the faces, however. If he saw one of them, he was certain he would throw up, an act the reporters would feel no remorse in publicizing. He was losing too much already; he refused to lose his dignity.

When the bodies had been driven off, Sheriff Lewis climbed up the stairs and walked onto the middle of the bridge, to where the blue van was parked. No one had bothered to turn off the engine. "We hear the FBI is sending agents," said Officer Reinaldo Cruz, who stood cross-armed at the back of the van.

"I haven't heard anything," said Sheriff Lewis, who would have welcomed intervention by any higher authority. The influx of jumpers from out of state—the twelve latest victims had come from California, Mississippi, Montana, Nebraska, and Oregon as well as Alaska, which was where the van was registered—proved that the Main Street Bridge was the nation's problem.

The sheriff's cell phone rang. It was the mayor again. "The governor said he would of course send in the National Guard if it wasn't occupied digging trenches in the sands of the Middle East. He's sure this mess is going to cost us all our jobs unless we come up with a dramatic solution. He's talking about destroying the bridge."

"And putting what in its place?"

"Hell, I don't know. Maybe a suicide theme park. In the meantime, I've ordered netting put up. There's an outfit in Columbus that specializes in that sort of thing. And I can tap into Sherman's emergency fund without consulting the city council. The fund is meant for fires and floods and other disasters. I think this qualifies."

"I'll keep the bridge closed until the netting goes up."

"It should be up by tonight. This Columbus outfit prides itself on how fast it can make bridges suicide-proof. They put up one in Ithaca, New York, in two hours and fourteen minutes. And their work is supposedly indestructible. The Ithaca bridge collapsed before the netting did.

"Rush hour will be hell. River Run will be clogged up like no toilet any plumber's ever seen." The mayor grunted. "Did I hear right that that van isn't local?" he asked.

"Uh-huh."

"Where's it from?"

Sheriff Lewis told him.

"Well, they found the last frontier all right."

— There were other people who had traveled from long distances to end their lives. Sheriff Lewis could distinguish the would-be suicides from the people who'd come to witness a suicide because of how little the would-be jumpers brought with them. One man from Austin, Texas, had only an old baseball mitt and an apple. A man from Orono, Maine, had brought a photograph of his Dalmatian and a water pistol.

CeeCee had succeeded in persuading University Hospital to send psychiatrists, psychologists, and social workers to the scene. Four people who'd come to jump off the bridge agreed to be admitted to the hospital's psychiatric ward.

On the bike path below the bridge, a "Live In" had begun. First a couple of dozen, then hundreds, of people gathered to sit on blankets on the concrete bike trails or in the neighboring brush. Two fishermen had motored up from the river, their boats looking huge on the thirty-foot-wide creek. A performing space with a microphone was set up directly under the bridge. For the most part, the musicians played old protest songs, although one of the acts was a newly formed acoustic punk group called Beast of a Bridge. All their music, announced the lead singer, would be composed on the spot. To Sheriff Lewis, what they played sounded like tin cans falling from a kitchen shelf. Somewhere in the noise he recognized the word *lonely*.

Sheriff Lewis remained on the scene until three thirty, when he realized that his dizziness was likely the result of having unintentionally fasted since last night's dinner. His weakened condition made him think of his wife. He called Marybeth, but reached Dorothy, who told him Marybeth was sleeping.

"How's she doing?" he asked.

Dorothy, who was always direct, told him she thought Marybeth needed twenty-four-hour care, especially if he was going to be keeping irregular hours. She spoke without accusation, but he worried he was letting Marybeth down. At the same time, to take a leave of absence or resign as sheriff now would doubtless be seen as cowardice. He thought, too, that it would be an admission of culpability over what had happened on the bridge. He did feel culpable, but he knew he would feel less so—perhaps he would even feel exonerated—when the suicides had stopped.

"I hope you don't mind my forwardness," Dorothy said, "but I've talked to a couple of women already. They could start today, if need be."

"Well, good," Sheriff Lewis said softly. He added, "Go ahead, then. Thank you."

As Sheriff Lewis was about to say goodbye, Dorothy said, "I hope you'll permit me an observation."

"Of course."

"I don't know how much of what ails her is her body and how much is her mind."

"What do you mean?"

"You said she used to be active—an adventurer, you said?"

"She talked about climbing Mount Everest," Sheriff Lewis said, and he wondered why she hadn't; money wasn't the issue—what she'd inherited from her parents would have covered it. Was it because he never expressed much interest in her most outrageous adventures, which weren't so much outrageous as they were simply out of the country? He'd always told her: I can travel the world in the pages of a book and I never have to leave my armchair. "She's climbed a number of mountains in the States," he added, although he couldn't remember the name of a single one.

I didn't support her the way I should have, he thought. He said, "This . . . this condition of hers is another kind of adventure, another mountain to conquer."

"Is that how she sees it?" Dorothy asked.

"I'm certain of it," he said, speaking with all the confidence of a man who was feeling the earth shake, who was seeing the ground split beneath him.

"I'll make sure someone's looking after her all twenty-four hours of the day," Dorothy said.

Sheriff Lewis thanked her again and said goodbye. He tried to recall what Marybeth had said about any of her mountain-climbing experiences, and now he remembered her speaking of one climb, how being on the top of this particular mountain was like "being alone with the sky."

Walking to the north side of the bridge, Sheriff Lewis saw CeeCee instructing a quartet of her sorority sisters in what to do on the now closed bridge. They were to give people interested in crossing the bridge the option of proceeding to River Run or talking with one of the mental health professionals available in the yellow tent in the parking lot of the Dollar Store.

When she was done, Sheriff Lewis said to her, "I think you need lunch even more than I do." He offered to treat her to a pizza or a hot dog or whatever she wanted. She chose tofu curry at One Night in Bangkok, a Thai restaurant next to the Sherman Public Library, three blocks from the bridge. Sheriff Lewis appreciated the restaurant's dark red décor, its dimness, its feeling of seclusion. He was tired of being in the sun, on the bridge, exposed.

Yet soon after Sheriff Lewis and CeeCee ordered, Otis Allen appeared at their table. He looked as tired as both of them combined, but he doggedly held out his tape recorder.

Sheriff Lewis told Allen all he knew about plans to make the bridge suicide-proof.

"And when people turn to other means to end their lives?" Allen asked. "What's the long-term solution, Sheriff?"

It was CeeCee who answered. Sitting straight in the red-cushioned booth, she said, "We need to discover how to ask each other for help—without fear of ostracism or ridicule or judgment."

Allen turned to Sheriff Lewis, who nodded his agreement.

"And how do you encourage people to turn to each other for help?"

"You let them know you're here and you care," CeeCee said. "You let them know you want them in the world. You let them know you won't judge their condition, only try to ease their pain."

"Anything to add, Sheriff?"

"I think she said it all."

When Allen left, Sheriff Lewis turned to CeeCee. "What you said was perfect."

"It applies to you, too."

"So I seem in need of help?"

She didn't hesitate: "Yes."

He laughed. "I won't be one of the jumpers," he said.

"How can you be sure?"

"It's called knowing yourself. It comes with age."

"Now you're patronizing me," she said.

"I'm sorry." He looked at her, her pink face glowing like a desert mirage, her hair as blond as desert sand.

He said, "And you? Can you be sure?"

She answered quickly: "No."

"Why not?"

"Because I've tried before."

When he didn't respond immediately, she said, "Don't worry—it was pills, not a bridge. And I was young—eighteen."

"How old are you now?"

"Nineteen." She amended, "Nineteen and a half."

— By a quarter of eight, when the sun was a red spot two inches above the horizon, netting twelve feet high shot straight up from the black railing on the Main Street Bridge. It was supported by a thick wire attached to poles at the bridge's four corners. The weave on the netting was tight and the material was slicker than plastic. Aesthetically, however, the netting was ghastly; its height and mud color gave the bridge the dark, claustrophobic feel of a tunnel with a skylight.

Mayor Bloom and Sheriff Lewis stood at the center of the bridge. "This ought to do it," said the mayor, patting the sheriff on the back.

"I hope so."

"It better," the mayor said. "I'm so anxious I've started doodling all over my body—with both hands!" He pulled back the sleeves of his white dress shirt to reveal naked women with Barbie-sized breasts on each forearm.

"If Otis Allen gets a peak at them, I'm doomed," the mayor said. "But I'm too fond of them to wash them off." He sighed. "I've heard people say that there's a reason for everything. In my darkest hours, I fear that the reason for the Suicide Bridge is to send me into retirement."

"I don't think it has anything to do with us," Sheriff Lewis said. "There are larger reasons." He thought of war in the Middle East and the panic-inducing threat of terrorism; he thought of the polluted, overpopulated, boiling world. He thought of the everyday troubles of illness and heartbreak, of work (or lack of work) and dreams defeated. At the same time, he thought, *The bridge could be my punishment. But for what? For being a hermit and dampening Marybeth's worldly dreams? Or it could be an opportunity. For what? For what CeeCee wants to do—confront our isolation, reattach ourselves to each other?*

Hundreds of people were still assembled at the bridge's north end, and the mayor excused himself to speak to them. After a five-minute reflection on recent events, the mayor inaugurated the new, suicide-proof bridge with the words "No more madness," a chant the crowd picked up and amplified.

Presently, the concrete barricades were removed from both ends of the bridge, and people rushed onto the elevated pedestrian walkways. Soon after, the bridge was opened to automobile traffic, and the cars crawled across it so their passengers could stare at the imposing netting.

"It looks like a spider web," someone next to Sheriff Lewis said. He turned and found his predecessor, Peter Marcello, rubbing the netting with his right hand. "And it feels like a wet sliding board."

Sheriff Lewis informed him, with a degree of pride, about the reputation of the netting manufacturer.

Marcello, a man with a weight lifter's physique and receding black hair cut to near baldness, didn't seem to care. He asked, "How are you holding up, Professor?"

Sheriff Lewis didn't know whether Marcello's last word was meant to mock or console. He attempted a joke: "Well, I haven't jumped off any bridges."

"But I bet you've thought about it," said Marcello.

Sheriff Lewis readied a denial, but Marcello spoke again: "Too late now."

Marcello removed his hand from the netting and, in a softer voice, a voice Sheriff Lewis wouldn't have recognized as his predecessor's, said, "I would offer you my help. But I'm not sure I'd have any to offer in this situation. And maybe you won't need it now."

"Thanks anyway," Sheriff Lewis said.

"You're more than welcome," Marcello said, and Sheriff Lewis thought he was going to add, "Professor." Instead, Marcello said, "Goodnight, Sheriff."

About five minutes after Marcello left the bridge, Mayor Bloom called Sheriff Lewis on his cell phone: "I think we're viable again. We're FDR after Pearl Harbor. A crisis occurred on our watch, but we soldiered on and now we'll reap the benefits."

Sheriff Lewis thought to remind Mayor Bloom that FDR had had tangible adversaries. And what were he and Mayor Bloom fighting? Nothing they could point to with certainty. Nothing they could be sure of stopping.

— Although CeeCee expressed only qualified faith in the netting's ability to prevent more suicides, she had given the Bridge Brigade the night off. She, however, joined Sheriff Lewis at nine, and with two police officers, they each covered a corner of the bridge. Sheriff Lewis planned to withdraw one of the officers in the next hour. Sometime after this, he would make a decision about leaving the bridge without a police patrol.

After their celebratory burst onto the bridge, people had gone home, and there had been no pedestrians since. An occasional vehicle drove by. On one occasion, a bearded man in a red Toyota pickup shouted at Sheriff Lewis: "Thanks a lot, Sheriff." From the man's tone, Sheriff Lewis didn't know whether he was being genuine or sarcastic. The driver of the next pickup to pass, who looked like the brother of the previous driver, slowed down to shout: "You ruined the fun! Now we'll have to go kill ourselves with shotguns and razor blades!"

Several times, Sheriff Lewis turned to place his palms against the netting. The bridge had the look and feel of a cage. The people of Sherman, he thought, were locked in to life.

At ten thirty, Sheriff Lewis sent one of the officers to patrol both Partytown and Spanishville. He decided he would send the other, Officer Cruz, to join him in an hour.

To CeeCee, Sheriff Lewis said, "I think it's bedtime."

"Why do I think you won't fall asleep yet for hours?" she asked.

He smiled. "For someone who doesn't know me, you know me too well."

"I'll buy you a drink," she said.

"All right," he told CeeCee, "but let me make a phone call first."

He dialed his home number. "Dorothy?" he asked the voice on the other end.

"Close. I'm Millie, her sister-in-law. This must be Sheriff Lewis."

"Yes."

"Marybeth is sleeping."

He asked how his wife was doing, and Millie said she was fine. She'd had a small snack an hour and a half before, had watched a television program, then had fallen asleep. He told

Millie he'd be home in an hour—providing nothing happened on the bridge or elsewhere.

Sheriff Lewis and CeeCee walked into town, to Don's Underground, whose six middle-aged male patrons looked up from their beers, surprised to see a college-age woman in the bar. There was an old poster on the wall celebrating one of Sherman's local bands, the No Exits, the four young women attempting to look both jaded and sexy. The red-haired guitarist had taken one of his classes when she was in high school. He'd heard she'd gone on to study at Harvard and then at Tufts Medical School. So often Sherman's most talented, most intelligent, most industrious, and most inventive left and never returned. This wasn't only Sherman's story, he supposed.

The song playing in Don's Underground was twice as old as CeeCee.

They ordered drinks at the bar and brought them to a booth, its wooden table sprinkled at the end near the wall with peanut shells. CeeCee asked him what he would have been doing on a night like tonight when he was in college.

"You're assuming I can remember so long ago," he said, and he drank from his Killian's.

She held him with a patient smile, and he understood she didn't want a facetious answer. "You want to know a secret? I met Marybeth when I was in college, at Ohio Eastern."

"That qualifies as a secret?"

"She was my professor—my instructor, I should say. She was a grad student in environmental sciences and was a teaching assistant in a lecture course called something like 'Flora and Fauna from Coast to Coast.' The class met some kind of requirement, otherwise I wouldn't have been anywhere near it.

"We were dating before the end of the semester. And she still had the nerve to give me a 'C.'"

"Ouch," CeeCee said.

"Well, I deserved it, I guess." He sighed. "I was a senior, living off campus on the second floor of a house in Sherman's

First Ward, which was even more run down than it is now. A married couple, the Wrights, who might have been in their mid-thirties, or maybe they were younger, lived below me. I didn't know them well. Sometimes I heard them at night having loud, bitter arguments. The words they yelled at each other—I couldn't imagine using them in any context, much less shouting them at someone I loved, although for what it's worth, I did see them on occasion walking back from town, holding hands.

"Several years after this, after I was married, after I'd been in the army, after I'd finished grad school at Ohio State even, I learned that Mrs. Wright—Allison was her name—had killed herself. She'd done it a few months after I'd left the house. No one contacted me at the time. I guess they didn't have to. It was supposedly an open-and-shut case. But I wondered."

"Because of the arguments you overheard?"

"Yes," Sheriff Lewis said. "And because there was so much passion in her side of the arguments. She gave as good as she received. And because on the occasions I saw her returning from town hand in hand with her husband, she looked happy.

"I looked up the case on my first day as sheriff—that's how interested I was in it. I was sure I'd find out that Mr. Wright, Jason, was the sheriff's cousin or the stepson of the mayor—exonerated because of his connections. But Jason wasn't even in town when his wife killed herself. He was in California."

He paused to wipe peanut shells onto the floor. "This seemed illogical—unfair even. Allison seemed so much alive."

CeeCee put her hand near his on the table. He moved his hand to wipe more peanut shells to the floor.

"Have you always been this sad?" she asked.

His first instinct was to tell her he wasn't sad at all, merely disturbed by recent events, as anyone would be. His second impulse was to tell her she didn't have the right to pry into his life. But his sense of propriety felt rusted and obsolete, hardly worth holding on to in the presence of someone who was, despite the short time he'd known her, a friend.

He told her about the last two years, the changes in his life, in Marybeth's health.

"And you?" he asked her. "What possibly could have prompted you to make such a serious attempt on your life?"

CeeCee sipped her Sprite before saying, "I wish I could tell you I'd found out I had cancer or my father had been abusing me or my mother had died when I was four and I had begun to feel an overwhelming grief over her loss. But none of this would be true. My life isn't perfect. I mean, my parents are divorced, I've had an abortion, my brother is a Republican, but added up, they aren't exactly a recipe for suicide."

"So why try to kill yourself?"

She sighed. "Have you ever looked at the rest of your life and asked yourself, 'Why bother?'"

He was about to answer when his phone rang.

"Sheriff, Officer Cruz reports shooting a would-be jumper on the Main Street Bridge."

— When Sheriff Lewis reached the scene three minutes later, the deceased, a man in his late twenties or early thirties, was lying face up on the pedestrian walkway on the bridge's east side. He wore shorts and a T-shirt but no socks or shoes. Sheriff Lewis would learn that he'd coated his feet and hands with a homemade epoxy in order to scale the slick netting.

Sheriff Lewis's cell phone rang. It was Mayor Bloom: "I think the Sherman police department should have a new motto: 'We kill 'em before they can kill themselves.'" He puffed into the phone. "Let's follow this strategy to its logical end. If we murder everyone in town, we'll be assured of being number one in suicide prevention."

There was a long pause before Mayor Bloom punctuated what he'd said with a single, un-mayor-like word.

— When Sheriff Lewis returned home, at so late an hour he couldn't bear to see what time it was, Millie was sitting on the couch in the living room, watching a documentary about World War II prisoners. Grainy black-and-white footage revealed pale, shirtless men standing against walls, as if waiting to be executed. After Sheriff Lewis introduced himself, Millie said, "She called out once, and I rushed upstairs, but she was only talking in her sleep." Millie's white hair was in two pigtails on her shoulders. She looked like Pippi Longstocking as a senior citizen. "She said the name Billy several times."

"Billy," Sheriff Lewis repeated.

"I'm sorry," Millie said, and he thought she might be blushing. "I hope Billy isn't the name of some ex-sweetheart of hers."

Sheriff Lewis felt something open inside him. It was a box full of everything he'd hidden from his wife, and although its contents were mostly trivial—the names of girls he'd had crushes on in high school, the times he'd skipped his office hours in order to watch action movies at the Sky Lake Mall—it made him sad to think he might never share them with her.

"Billy was one of her brothers," Sheriff Lewis said. He'd died when Marybeth was ten years old. She had three other brothers, all living. She'd mentioned Billy maybe twice in the last decade.

Excusing himself, Sheriff Lewis walked upstairs to check on his wife. He stood at the foot of the bed for ten minutes before he could at last make out her breathing, which seemed to come from a far place. He wondered if she was giving up, if she was talking to Billy because she thought she'd soon be with him.

Presently, he ascended the stairs into the attic. He crouched in front of the window and stared at the bridge. The gesture was superfluous. Wherever he looked, he saw the bridge. Whatever he thought about was connected to the bridge.

He turned to his computer and read Otis Allen's latest entry in *The Horizon*. "To blame Mayor Bloom, who once aspired to be the next Picasso, and Sheriff Lewis, who came to his current office straight from the scholarly seclusion of Ohio Eastern University, for what has occurred on the Main Street Bridge might, on first glance, be exactly what we should do. Both men's lack of expertise surely is part of the reason why Sherman seems so hopeless as it attempts to halt a suicide epidemic.

"But are we completely unhappy with what has unfolded over the last few days? Even as we have professed sorrow for the families of the deceased, haven't we privately thrilled in seeing or hearing about our fellow townspeople—indeed, our fellow countrymen (and next, no doubt, our fellow citizens of the world)—hurling themselves off the bridge? We delight because we think that another person's weakness means we're strong, another person's disease means we're well. We delight when we can say, 'Better him, better her, than me.'"

Sheriff Lewis resumed his place at the window, staring at the bridge. He tried putting Otis Allen's last sentence in his mouth, tried uttering it to the bridge in the distance. But the words began to trade places with each other. And so in the end, he was saying, "Better me than him, than her. Better me than them."

Perhaps the bridge wanted me all along, he thought in sleepless delirium. *Perhaps I am the sacrifice it sought from the beginning.*

— At half past six the next morning, a van painted in rainbow colors and a black pickup truck with a pink cannon in its bed stopped in the middle of the Main Street Bridge. The back door of the van opened and out popped six happy-faced clowns. They wore everything a clown usually wears, right down to the giant, polka-dotted, pointed shoes. The drivers of the van and pickup truck, a pair of bouncer-sized men in black T-shirts and black cowboy hats, stepped out of their vehicles and raised the semiautomatic rifles they were holding. One of the men pointed his rifle at Sheriff Lewis, who had taken three steps onto the south end of the bridge. The man fired two shots over Sheriff Lewis's head.

Crouching, Sheriff Lewis retreated to the end of the bridge, his heart pounding so hard he thought he'd throw it up. He'd walked to the bridge this morning with no other purpose than to verify how secure against death it was.

Two clowns jumped onto the back of the pickup truck. One stepped into the mouth of the cannon, the other ignited it. There was an ostentatious sizzling sound followed by a gargantuan boom. The clown in the cannon shot over the netting on the west side of the bridge like a football sailing over a goalpost.

Sheriff Lewis stood, rushed forward, and shouted, "Stop this immediately!" A bullet sizzled past his ear, and he crouched and backed up.

Sheriff Lewis was 150 feet or so from the pickup and its cannon. He was armed, but he didn't trust his marksmanship; he might shoot one of the two television reporters who were standing, microphones in hand, on the north end of the bridge. There were no police officers anywhere, and Sheriff Lewis remembered, as if in a dream, ordering the bridge's police detail suspended after what Officer Cruz had done.

Boom! Another clown flew from the cannon and over the netting. It was an extraordinary thing to witness, Sheriff Lewis thought, but only until the clown reached the peak of his flight. When gravity proved supreme, it was sickening.

By now, dozens—no, probably more like a hundred—people had gathered at the ends of the bridge to witness in person what they'd seen a moment before on TV. Some had scribbled messages on poster boards, urging the clowns to return to the circus or come to Jesus. One poster board said, "Hi, Mom."

If death alone had been the clowns' aim, they could have done a neater job by turning the semiautomatic rifles on themselves, Sheriff Lewis thought. This was suicide as entertainment. This was suicide as public spectacle, as comedy, as circus.

Boom! Out of the cannon flew another clown. He soared into the sky. He waved and wiggled his feet. He met an invisible wall and plummeted.

Sheriff Lewis saw CeeCee on the north side of the bridge. She must have pushed her way to the front of the crowd. Now she was walking with haste across the bridge. Sheriff Lewis saw one of the black-shirted men turn his rifle on her. "No!" he shouted, and the next time he shouted the word he did so in full stride. He ran toward CeeCee like the halfback he'd never been.

A moment later, Sheriff Lewis heard the sound of blades. He looked up and saw a military helicopter approaching the bridge like a giant dragonfly. A man in fatigues inside the open cargo hold, carrying what looked like a bazooka, fired canisters onto the bridge. They released a thick, purple smoke.

Sheriff Lewis stopped, and as he was about to cover his eyes, he saw the helicopter's windshield explode. The helicopter careened before skimming over the netting on the east side of the bridge and smashing into the netting on the west side. For a moment, the helicopter looked like a fly caught in a spider's web or a fish trapped in a net. But both helicopter and netting soon disappeared over the side of the bridge.

Another helicopter approached, but it, too, took fire. The helicopter slammed into the netting on the east side of the bridge and exploded, debris shooting into the sky and flying everywhere. In seconds, fire melted all but a few strands of the netting.

Boom! Another clown flew toward the sky. But with the netting now gone, the cannon seemed superfluous, needless theatrics.

"CeeCee!" Sheriff Lewis yelled. He'd lost her in the purple smoke. "CeeCee!" He coughed and yelled and coughed.

Boom!

He couldn't see much beyond the end of his nose. And now he heard a different noise from the sky. It wasn't from a helicopter, he was sure, but from an airplane. Or two. He heard a sound like certain fireworks make before they explode. *It's a bomb,* he thought. A second later, an explosion filled his ears and the bridge trembled so violently he fell to his knees.

Are they bombing the bridge? he wondered. *Bombing the bridge to save us from it?* He laughed and coughed and coughed again. "CeeCee!"

He was terrified she was dead. "CeeCee!"

Boom! Another clown shot from the cannon? Or was it another bomb dropping?

Sheriff Lewis rose and stumbled against something—someone. It was one of the van's drivers, his black T-shirt as tight around his muscled chest as skin. "Are you interested in a cannon ride?" the man said, and he gestured behind him. When Sheriff Lewis didn't answer, the man put his arm around Sheriff Lewis's shoulders and led him deeper into the smoke. A moment later, they'd reached the back of the truck. The man said, "Can you climb up yourself or do you need a boost?"

Sheriff Lewis thought. *This is a dream and I am powerless to stop it.* He put his right knee on the back of the truck and felt the man hoist him.

"Don't you dare!" The voice was so familiar that, in another life, it might have belonged to his daughter.

"CeeCee?"

Sheriff Lewis freed himself from the man's grip and stepped down from the truck. There was the crushing boom of more explosions. "CeeCee?"

Sheriff Lewis moved forward, but found himself in thicker smoke. When he heard footsteps behind him, he turned around. A rush of wind cleared the purple tear gas and permitted him to see, standing side by side, the two drivers, who had removed not only their black T-shirts but all their clothes. Holding hands, the men raced to the west side of the bridge, climbed up to the topmost rail, and jumped, kissing in midair.

"Why?" asked a voice he failed to recognize as his own.

— Due to the government's errant bombing, a third of Spanishville was destroyed. In the days that followed, residents complained that they had been intentionally targeted. No one was willing to risk a lawsuit against the government, however, for fear of retaliation against the community's undocumented members. But with help from the Amish who lived on the west side of Sky Lake, Spanishville was rebuilt in fourteen months.

City Hall was destroyed, and Mayor Bloom was buried under his desk, under rubble, for two days. When he emerged, he spoke of the "strangely satisfying" experience of being marooned with "limited but sufficient art supplies": a ream of white office paper, a pen, and the blood that occasionally oozed from the glass cuts in his body. He composed more than a hundred sketches, mostly of what he remembered of his childhood home and yard. "When there's no serenity to be had in the present," he said, "the past is the only retreat."

There were five fires in Partytown, although none of them could be linked to the bombing. Half of the university's twenty-thousand-seat coliseum was destroyed, however. It was now a ten-thousand-seat amphitheater.

No bomb ever hit the bridge.

But swamped in tear gas and feeling vibrations from bombs that seemed to be exploding all around him, Sheriff Lewis thought he was at ground zero. It would be only a matter of time, he was convinced, before he was killed. His life had been, on the whole, good, he thought, although lately he'd lost contact with the good. There was no carryover of happiness from one day to the next, no reserve of joy one could tap into. Each day brought the likelihood of despair as much as happiness. And unlike happiness, despair did seem to accrue, to pile onto itself from one sleepless night to the next until the thought of meeting it again in the next moment was intolerable, was like an earthly damnation.

Boom!

In the smoke, a body collided into his body. Sheriff Lewis felt her hair against his chin, her breasts above his belly. Her bright face pierced the purple tear gas like the sun.

"CeeCee!" he said, and being able to state this as fact rather than wish seemed as remarkable as anything he'd ever seen or done.

"You," CeeCee said softly and with relief. "You're still here."

Boom!

Boom!

"Stop it!" CeeCee shouted at the sky, which neither of them could see. "Stop it, please! There are only two of us left, and we both want to live!"

She turned to Sheriff Lewis and grabbed his hand. Her hand was hot; he could feel her blood pumping through it, wild with life. "I'm telling the truth, aren't I?" she asked him. "You do want to live, don't you?" She squeezed his hand, as if to prod him toward the right answer.

He prepared to mimic her optimism, but as his eyes blurred, succumbing to the tear gas and more, he saw a landscape of loss. He wondered when the concrete and iron he was standing on would dissolve beneath him. He feared to what degree he wanted it to.

"Keep holding my hand," he told her.

THIS MAN, THIS WOMAN, THIS CHILD, THIS TOWN

The teachers have left the front of the two-story brick building, where they'd gathered to greet students and parents on the first day of classes. Only Martin Williamson—Mr. W. to everyone at the Tree of Knowledge, a private elementary school—remains outside. He's the physical education teacher, and his first class doesn't begin until second period, at ten, but he came early today to be one of the greeters.

He turns to look up Wise Road, which dead-ends at the school, expecting to see nothing. Instead, as if from the mouth of a winter blizzard, from dust as white as snow, he sees a woman, running. Two steps behind her is a girl, her daughter no doubt, probably in kindergarten. The girl is wearing a yellow dress to match her yellow hair. She is shielding her eyes from the dust and is moving with the care and uncertainty, but twice the speed, of a blind person.

A minute passes before the woman, whose hair is a darker blond than her daughter's, stops in front of him, panting. A moment later, the girl catches up. Her panting is more severe. Clutching her stomach, the girl begins to cough, and Martin is sure she's about to throw up. He waits for the inevitable, but the inevitable doesn't come. When the girl ceases coughing and stands straight, he says, "Let me get you some water."

"She doesn't need water," says her mother with an accent he guesses is Russian or Polish. She ushers her daughter through the open green doors of the school. Martin has lost sight of the two when, from inside the dark building, as if from inside a whale, the woman calls out to him: "Thank you."

The woman returns three minutes later, and he wishes he had retrieved a cup of water in the interim. He has nothing to offer her except conversation. "Car broke down?" he asks.

She doesn't answer for so long that he thinks she hasn't heard him. But at last she says, "We don't own a car."

"You're taking the bus, then."

"No, I'm flying." She doesn't look at him, and his inclination is to take a step back and say, "Ouch." But she laughs, and he thinks her laughter is intended to include him.

"I'd give you a ride," he says, "but I teach next period. Of course, if you live near here, it wouldn't be a problem."

She glances at him before returning her gaze to the dust swirling off the road. "And who are you, if I could ask?"

Martin states his name and his position at the school. He wonders if he ought to give other vital statistics: his age (forty-two), his height (six-foot, three-and-a-half-inches), his weight (252 pounds). She says, "The famous Mr. W."

He asks her name (Katarina) and her daughter's (Mary). He is going to ask her more; he would be happy talking with her until his class begins, but Katarina looks at her watch, utters something in a language he doesn't recognize, and starts running. As she disappears into the plumes of white dust, he can hear the grumble of a city bus as it makes its way up Deer Hill toward the stop at the intersection of Wise Road.

When the dust clears, she is gone.

— Martin's mother is white. His father is black, or so his mother told him when he turned thirty-three. Before this, she'd told him his father was a professor of Romance languages at Ohio Eastern University who'd died—in a civil war, of a snakebite, in an earthquake, her story varied over the years—when, after Martin was conceived but before he was born, he returned to the country in Latin America where he was from.

Martin's real father is named James or Jason, his mother doesn't remember. "I thought he was the star of the basketball team, the center," she told him. "He made me believe he was. We were at a bar, a club. We went to his car. This was before I discovered the Lord. A day or two later, I saw a picture of the basketball team in the newspaper, and I knew I'd made a mistake. But it was too late."

His mother told him the true story when he turned thirty-three because Jesus had been thirty-three when he'd died. Martin didn't understand the connection.

"I guess I don't either," his mother confessed.

A few days later, his mother asked him if he was going to leave town.

"Why would I leave?" he asked.

She hesitated before saying, "Because you might want to find your father."

"I wouldn't know where to look."

After Martin's birth, his mother was hired as an administrative assistant in Ohio Eastern's history department, where she'd been liked as a student. She holds the same job today, two years shy of retirement.

In elementary school, Martin's classmates called him "Cuba" because of his father, although when his sixth-grade teacher, noting Martin's complexion, wondered if his father might be from Brazil, some of his classmates began to call him "Pele," after the soccer player.

He'd never liked his nicknames. They didn't seem as friendly as "Sparky" or "Polar Bear" or even "Mutt." His nicknames, he thought, implied foreignness. And his appearance already called attention to him in a town where most of the people with dark skin were the immigrants from Central America who lived in Spanishville.

After college, he had trouble finding a good job in town. Once he found one, he had trouble holding on to it. He had a tendency to become bored, to allow his mind to wander off his work. (He'd been the same in college, his C minus average proof.) Martin has been a city bus driver, the manager of the dairy section at Food World, a bartender and bouncer at the Above and Beyond Gentlemen's Club. He has held his current position at the Tree of Knowledge for four and a half years, his longest tenure at a single job and a sign, according to his mother, of his readiness to settle down. The next step, she says, is for him to find a wife.

His relationships with women have been as fleeting as his jobs, however. The last woman he lived with, Cora, from California, was a graduate student in political science. She moved in with him two weeks after they'd met, bringing with her her three-year-old son, Malcolm. Because his shift at the Above and Beyond Club didn't start until ten at night, Martin became Malcolm's primary caretaker. In this role, he reacquainted himself with all the public parks he'd visited as a boy. He made mountains of macaroni and cheese. He engaged in endless games of hide and seek.

Cora and Malcolm left Sherman immediately after she earned her master's degree. She might have said goodbye, but Martin can't remember the occasion. All he remembers is calling the boy's name one morning, as if Malcolm was only hiding behind the couch or under the kitchen table, and realizing he was gone.

— Martin is driving down Wise Road on his way to school, white dust billowing around his Toyota pickup, when he sees Katarina walking the opposite way. He slams his brakes so hard his truck skids. Katarina skitters to the side of the road like a bird. Martin hoped she would come at the same time she had yesterday. He planned to meet her at the door with a glass of water.

Without acknowledging him, she resumes her brisk walk toward the intersection and her bus. Quickly, he rolls down the window. "Katarina!" Her name comes out of his lips flat and in three syllables. She stops and turns around. He hops out of his truck. In the floating dust around him, his throat goes dry.

When it's clear she won't speak first, he says, "Are you all right? I hope I didn't scare you." He falls into a coughing fit.

"I should ask now if it's you who is all right," she says when his coughing has stopped. She takes a few steps toward him.

"I'm fine," he says.

"Would you like water?"

He tries to decline but begins another coughing spell. She jogs back to the school, which is only forty feet from where they are, and returns a minute later with water in a paper cup. He drinks it and imagines the water rinsing the dust from the walls of his throat.

"Better?" she asks, her smile large enough to allow him to see the gaudy dentistry on her lower teeth, a discordant clash of gold and silver.

He nods, holding up the empty cup.

Her teeth are an old woman's. But she cannot be older than thirty, he thinks.

"More?" she asks.

"No, no, I'm better," he says, although he cannot help coughing again. "I think I am."

"I missed my bus," she says, nodding toward the intersection, where her bus now sweeps past the empty stop. "You'll give me keys to your truck because I give you water?"

Martin doesn't know how to interpret her remark. Who knows how acts of kindness are repaid in Russia—or wherever she's from. But Katarina smiles again, a quick flash of white, gold, and silver.

With satisfaction, Martin realizes she is flirting with him. He's so pleased he misses her goodbye. She turns and resumes her march to the bus stop. "Let me drive you," he calls to her. "I don't teach for another forty-five, fifty minutes. Let me take you where you need to go."

She works downtown, as a housekeeper at the Hotel Sherman, which used to be populated by graduate students and visiting professors at Ohio Eastern who rented by the month. But it was bought and refurbished by the Marriott Corporation. Now the cheapest room rents for $100 a night. Katarina works at the hotel until Mary finishes school at three. She begins her second job, at the Book and Brew, a bookstore and coffee shop a few blocks from the Hotel Sherman, at four.

When Katarina is at the bookstore, Mary must stay with a babysitter or go to an after-school program, he thinks. But when he asks, Katarina says, "She comes with me to the bookstore. There is a children's section." And as if he accused her of something, she adds, "Mary is fine to play by herself."

"How long have you lived in town?" he asks her.

"We are new here. A month."

"And before you came here?"

"Yes, there was a before," she says, and she gives him a flat smile. They've reached the hotel, and he pulls in front, where a short, gray-haired man in a blue bellhop's uniform greets them as if they were arriving customers. When he opens the passenger door of the truck, he recognizes Katarina but is no less courteous. He takes her hand so she can step down. She is as slim as an actress.

Katarina walks toward the hotel's entrance before turning around and stepping quickly to her door, which the bellhop has closed. The window is halfway open. "I forget the kiss on your cheek—to mean thank you." She smacks her hand against her lips and blows him the kiss on it. "This will be all right to say thank you?"

Martin is about to answer but she is gone.

— Martin teaches physical education the way he drove buses for the city and the way he tended bar at the Above and Beyond Club, his body in one place, his mind often months or years into the past or future. He isn't especially nostalgic, but he'll find himself remembering the first time he saw a butterfly or the dresses his eighth-grade social studies teacher wore. And he isn't a planner, but he'll think about what he'll buy his mother for Christmas or what kind of job he might find if he moved to Cleveland or Columbus. Minutes will slip by, and he might as well be in a trance—as he must have been when, as a city bus driver, he drove off U.S. 40 and into a fence surrounding a llama farm.

Daydreaming comes with less of a price to a phys-ed teacher. A week after the start of the school year, he leads the first graders onto the soccer field, and he makes dividing the teams easy by pitting boys against girls. It's a fair match: The girls are quicker and have better footwork; the boys are stronger and more willing to throw their bodies around. But even if his eyes are focused on the field, he isn't paying attention to the game. He is thinking of Katarina, as he has been since he met her. He is thinking of her bottom teeth and their delightful assortment of colors. He is thinking of how, when he drives her from the Tree of Knowledge to the Hotel Sherman, she sits against the door, as if she might have to spring herself free at any moment. He is thinking of her accent and what she told him of her origins: She is a descendant of Lithuanian royalty. If history hadn't gone mad, she told him, she would be sitting on a throne.

This morning, he asked her when he could see her outside of the twenty minutes they spend in his truck every morning. "You can see me tonight," she said.

"But you work until ten."

"Do you go to sleep at ten?"

The truth is, he often falls asleep before nine. He likes to sleep; he likes to dream and remember his dreams when he should be umpiring a softball game or teaching the second graders how to play badminton. He often sleeps twelve hours a day. "I'm wide awake," he said.

"All right," she said, "meet me in front of the Book and Brew at ten."

— At the appointed hour, Katarina and Mary come out of the Book and Brew, and he helps Mary into the front of his truck. He offers the same service to Katarina, who declines, he thinks. But a moment before he steps away, she leans back onto his chest. He first feels the weight of her—a surprise, given how slight she seems, like a ballerina. Next he feels her warmth. And before she leaves his arms to spring into the cab of his truck, he smells her—like coffee beans and the fresh pages of unread books.

Katarina and Mary live in a third-floor walk-up in a building across from City Hall. Like much of downtown, the building is historic, having been constructed soon after the Civil War, but risks demolition from the wrecking ball of ambitious developers.

Katarina's apartment opens onto a small living room, which is furnished with a sofa and an easy chair, both of which must predate Katarina and Mary's arrival here by at least a decade. The white walls are bare, and Martin sees bold cracks in the ceilings. At the far end of the living room is an open door, which Martin guesses leads to the bedroom. To the right is a surprisingly substantial kitchen, including a breakfast nook with a round table and four chairs. This is where they sit as Katarina prepares Mary's "midnight snack" of applesauce and toast with strawberry jelly.

If Mary finds it strange to be sitting in her kitchen with her gym teacher at ten fifteen on a Friday night, she doesn't indicate as much in either word or expression. She concentrates on her food and doesn't say anything. He has heard her speak on only a few occasions. Her English is clearer than her mother's, but her voice is more fragile.

Mary receives a partial scholarship to the Tree of Knowledge because of how well she did on a pre-entrance test. Without the scholarship, Martin doubts Katarina would be able to afford the tuition. Martin tries to imagine Mary in an overcrowded public school classroom. He imagines her in a back corner, looking out a window.

After Mary eats her snack, Katarina takes her into the bathroom. Martin sits under the flickering bulb, wondering how long this building will stand and what will rise in its place.

Katarina isn't long putting Mary to bed. When she returns to the kitchen, she asks Martin if he'd like something to drink. He says, "I brought wine, but I left it in my truck."

"If you get it, we have wine," Katarina says. "If you sit here, we have water."

Martin rises as if having received an order, but Katarina is smiling in apparent acknowledgment of her joke. All the same, he guesses she was indicating her preference. She gives him her door key and he retrieves the bottle of Merlot from his truck.

She doesn't have a bottle opener, so Martin chips away at the cork with a knife before knocking what's left into the wine. He pours the wine into plastic cups. Katarina says, "Please make the toast."

Martin can't remember the last time he made a toast. "Welcome to Sherman," he says, and she smiles awkwardly. He senses she wanted something grander.

"Thank you, Mr. Mayor," she replies, and they tap their plastic glasses. His wine tastes distinctly of cork.

They talk about her apartment and his house. When he tells her he lives three minutes from his mother, she tells him she lives an ocean away from her closest relative, a second cousin who lives outside of Vilnius. He asks why she left her country, and she tells him it was too small for her dreams. "I have America-size dreams," she says, spreading her arms and smiling.

"And you and Mary moved to Sherman from Lithuania a couple of months ago?" he asks, confused about the chronology.

"Yes, I put my finger"—she holds up her right index finger—"on a map of the United States and Sherman is where it touches." She flashes a grin.

He doesn't know whether she's joking. According to *USA Today,* Sherman is one of the one hundred best small towns in the country. It isn't impossible, Martin thinks, that word has spread to Lithuania.

"Mary is an American citizen," Katarina says. "Red, white, and blue."

"Her father's American?"

"Yes, a red-blooded American."

When she doesn't continue, Martin asks if she's divorced. She isn't smiling now. "I was his mail-order bride. Bad to be such a bride, my friends tell me. Such a bride doesn't know what kind of man will be her husband. He could be the devil. And this man I married, he didn't want a wife. He wanted a slave. A slave to do his work, a slave to—" She stops abruptly.

Martin lets the silence gather before he says, "You left him a month or so ago?"

She shakes her head. "Mary was one year old when I left."

"Does he know where you are?"

She shrugs, and he thinks she shakes her head. She asks him whether he is divorced. He'd like to keep talking about her, but he guesses she is finished with this topic, at least for now. "I've never been married," he says.

She asks if he ever wanted to leave Sherman. He says no. "As my mom says, 'Why go a thousand miles to get what you can find around the corner?'"

"I see," Katarina says. "So around the next corner there is Hollywood and Pacific Ocean."

Martin laughs. "Well, we do have three movie theaters, including a multiplex at the mall. And, no, there's no ocean, but we do have Sky Lake."

"Yes, of course," Katarina says, and whether her smile is genuine or sarcastic, he can't tell. They have more wine, and she apologizes for her English, saying it is especially bad when mixed with alcohol; he tells her she speaks very well.

"I study since I was eight," she says. "I study extra hard when I realize I have no life in my country, when I realize I need to come here. But—" She looks down.

"But what?" he asks.

She looks up at him. "It was supposed to be easy."

He is about to say, If you do honest work, if you live within your means, it is easy—or at least it isn't difficult. You may not be rich and famous, but you will have enough in your life to be happy. But he guesses she's speaking about her husband and Mary. He feels like leaving his seat and crouching next to her so he can put his arm around her shoulder. But he doesn't know how she would respond to this gesture. So he takes another small sip of wine. He hasn't finished his glass yet. He doesn't think he should if he'll be driving home.

"I should have invited you into the living room, but now it's late."

He looks at his watch. "Yes," he agrees, "it's late." And thinking her comment was a signal to leave, he stands. "I enjoyed talking with you."

"Yes, and I with you." They move toward the front door. He opens it and takes a step into the hallway before turning around.

"You know, I could pick Mary up in the mornings and take her to school. It wouldn't be a problem. I live nearby and I have my truck and I have to go to school anyway."

"You don't have to say this."

Martin is confused. "Say what?"

"I accept. Of course. Thank you. But you don't have to say this."

Martin remains confused, and he wonders if the little wine he drank might have affected him more than he thought. A second later, she is in his arms, her lips against his. "This was waiting for you no matter how you said goodbye."

— Every Sunday, Martin visits his mother for lunch. Today, a month after he met Katarina, they sit in her front yard under a buckeye tree on the wooden picnic bench overlooking the cemetery to the south. Martin used to attend church with his mother on Sunday mornings, but this was before he got Saturn, an Irish setter–German shepherd mix, from the pound. He told his mother he'd have to get up too early in the morning to both walk Saturn and make it to church on time. It was a poor excuse, he knew, but she accepted it.

Although Martin and his mother see each other at least once a week and speak on the phone at least once a day, they always have a lot to talk about on Sundays. Over egg salad, beet salad, and lemonade, he talks to her about Katarina and Mary, and she seems interested, although he realizes she has heard him tell this kind of story, with the same intonations, several times. It occurs to him, as it has in the past, that while his relationships with women inevitably last longer than his mother's with his father, they have left him no keepsakes as enduring as what his mother retains.

For dessert, she has made apple pie. Because he would like to keep his weight somewhere shy of two hundred and sixty pounds, he knows he should refuse. But in order not to hurt her feelings, he agrees to have a small piece. When she drops another piece on his plate, he complains only mildly. He digs out the next two pieces for himself, quitting only when a single, small triangle of pie remains.

"Every time I leave here I'm qualified to be the fat man at the circus," he tells his mother. It's a frequent joke between them. So is her response: "There's nothing wrong with honest work."

Martin's mother is plump and always has been. All the pictures he's seen of her, including when she was a toddler, show her with a wide, round face and a potato-shaped body. Her short stature—she's only a little over five feet—accentuates her plumpness. She has strawberry blond hair, untouched by gray, and she knows how attractive it is. She goes to the Main Street Beauty College at least once a month to have it either cut or styled; she goes, too, because of how the students fawn over her hair.

Their conversation continues for ten minutes, then reaches a lull. "I know I've asked you this," he says, interrupting the silence, "but tell me again why you never wanted to leave Sherman?"

"Some people come from nomadic stock," she says, as if reading a speech. "They're comfortable flitting all over the world like migrating birds. My parents named me Rose for a reason—I was going to bloom in one place and one place only. And when I don't bloom anymore, I'll be in a place where people remember me blooming." She gestures toward the cemetery, where she long ago picked out her plot and headstone. One Sunday last spring, she brought him to the cemetery to show him what more she'd done: bought a plot and headstone for him. His name and year of birth were engraved in the gray marble. When he protested, she said there was plenty of room next to his grave site for his future wife and children.

"It takes a lifetime for a place to get to know you," she says, "and having lived all of my sixty-two years in Sherman, I'd be giving up someone who knew me and understood me and loved me in exchange for a dance with a stranger." She looks at Martin across the picnic table. "No one knows you the way people do in Sherman. Outside of Sherman, they'd see you for who they thought you were."

"They could get to know me."

"It's one thing to know a man from when he was an infant. It's another to know him only when he's a giant."

Toward the end of his sophomore year, Martin was in danger of failing a required composition course for the second time. In fact, he'd resigned himself to failing; he didn't think he was made to be a student. He'd graduated from high school, he thought, only because his teachers liked him—and the new math teacher in his senior year, a woman from North Dakota, was afraid of him. But his mother had found him two tutors, and one of them had written most of his final research paper.

Their grave sites are behind a pair of weeping willow trees, which he can see from his mother's yard. He notices, as he did the last time he was here, how the cemetery grass has become overgrown and clotted with weeds.

"I'll bring you more coffee," she says, plucking Martin's empty plate from in front of him and stacking it on top of hers. "I assume you're done with this?" she asks, gesturing toward what's left of the apple pie. "I'll wrap it up for you."

"All right, Mama," he says, vowing he'll save it for when he next visits Katarina and Mary, although he knows he'll finish it off tonight. He turns around on the bench and leans his back against the table. But he soon changes positions again so he can stare at the cemetery.

His mother returns, they talk and drink coffee, and the afternoon grows darker by degrees. He feels the way he usually does here. He guesses he would call it happy.

— Two weeks later, Martin is sitting in the well-worn couch in Katarina's apartment. Mary is in bed. Katarina puts a lit candle on the table in front of him and turns out the light. Lights from Main Street soften the darkness. Katarina disappears from the room.

Martin knows what she has in mind, and it is welcome, but as much as he'd like to anticipate it, to savor its newness, he is thinking about what he wants to tell her, turning it over in his mind as he searches for the right phrase, the right tone.

She comes to him wearing a red bow—the prefab, stick-on kind made to put on Christmas presents—and a midnight blue chemise nightgown. In the absence of a CD player, she has turned on the radio. The college station is holding a punk rock marathon. Between songs, students compete in a mock vomiting contest.

"What do you think?" She puts her hands on her hips and tilts back her head. Her bow falls out. She bends to pick it up, offering him a view of her naked behind.

He cannot hold back what he's been thinking since the morning he met her: "I'd like you and Mary to move in with me. I've got two bedrooms, and if you don't mind a dog—he's friendly enough, I hope Mary isn't allergic—and if—"

Katarina makes a sound somewhere between a sigh and a laugh. She stands and drops her arms to her side. "You haven't even touched me yet," she says. "I might be too hot and melt you like wax. I might be too cold and turn you into a snowman."

"No," he says, standing quickly. "You're just—"

She grabs his hands and puts them under her chemise, on her naked waist.

"Right," he says. "You're just right."

— On their drives to school, Mary speaks to him only if he asks her a question. And she answers in few words. If he didn't know her reputation at school, he might mistake her intense shyness for a learning disability. Academically, he overheard her teacher tell Katarina recently, she belongs in the fourth grade.

In his physical education classes, she doesn't stand out either for her ability or her lack of skill. What he notices is how little noise she makes during whatever game they're playing or whatever activity they're doing. She never smiles or gives any other sign she is enjoying herself. On the other hand, she doesn't mope, complain, or cry.

As Thanksgiving nears, and the silence in his truck on their morning drives continues, he asks her if she likes to sing. From the booster seat he bought her after Katarina agreed to let him drive her to school, she offers him a sliver of a smile. She is as pale and slight as Katarina. Sometimes he thinks she looks like a child model. Sometimes he thinks she looks like a refugee. He has the radio on, a true oldies station—music from the fifties, his favorite—but he clicks it off. "What songs do you know?" he asks.

She only shrugs. But he knows what songs they've been singing in Helen Carter's music class, and he starts with "This Land Is Your Land." He isn't used to singing, and his voice booms in the cab of the truck. He softens it as much as he can, but he has a naturally rumbling bass, like thunder in an oil drum.

He is halfway through the song when he realizes that Mary is singing too. She sings the next song with him and the next. They sing until they've pulled into his parking spot at the front of the Tree of Knowledge. As usual, she rushes out of his truck as if fleeing a burning building. This time, however, she turns back and opens her mouth. Because the passenger-side window is closed, he can't hear what she's saying. She smiles and disappears into the school.

— On Thanksgiving Day, Katarina has to work at the hotel, so Martin takes Mary to his mother's house. His mother has bought a packet of markers and three princess coloring books for her. When Mary wanders over to the African violets on the kitchen windowsill, his mother tells her how she grew them from seed under fluorescent lights in her garage. As usual, Mary is quiet to the point of muteness. Martin warned his mother to expect this.

Other guests arrive, including three of Martin's aunts, and his mother's small house is soon full of conversation. Martin keeps half an eye on Mary as he catches up with his aunts and cousins, most of whom live within ten miles of his mother's house.

After they've eaten turkey and pumpkin pie, and Martin has emerged from a daydream in which he imagined his father as the captain of a ship, he realizes Mary isn't at the table anymore. He finds her in the den, where his mother keeps her piano, although she hasn't played it in years. "Go ahead," Martin says, indicating the keys. She looks at him twice before placing her small fingers on the keyboard. A moment later, she is playing—at first tentatively, then with greater ease. When she finishes the short piece, she pulls her hands from the keys and stuffs them under her thighs. She looks at her feet dangling from the piano bench.

"Wonderful," he says. "Where did you learn how to play?"

From the kitchen, Martin hears his mother shout, "I knew those lessons would pay off eventually, Martin!"

"Where did you learn?" he asks again, this time with an urgency he can't explain.

Quickly, she answers, "Peter."

"Is Peter your father?" he asks. But he knows he can't be—Katarina left Mary's father when Mary wasn't even a year old.

"My father's dead," Mary says. And without pausing, she asks, "May I go color again? Please. Please?" She looks both bashful and afraid.

"Are you sure you don't want to play anymore?" he asks. When she nods and lowers her head and nods again, he says, "Sure. Of course."

As Martin and Mary are leaving the house, after all but one of his aunts have gone, his mother thanks him for coming and for bringing "the beautiful child" with him. (He guesses his mother has forgotten Mary's name.) As Mary walks out the door, his mother touches him on the shoulder and he backs up a step. "I remember the last child you brought here for Thanksgiving," she says, "the darling boy with the freckles."

"Malcolm," he says.

"And I remember how sad you felt when they left. Tears of a father as much as a boyfriend."

When she says, "Be careful with your heart," he cannot say of Katarina and Mary, "They won't leave."

He brings Katarina to his mother's house the Saturday before Christmas. They sit in her small living room, his mother on a couch with an orange flower pattern, Katarina on the matching armchair. They talk politely about Sherman, about Lithuania. They are about as far from each other as they can be while being in the same room. Yet Martin knows that if he kneeled between them, he would be able to touch each with his outstretched hands.

— A week before Christmas, Martin, Katarina, and Mary fit a small tree into the corner of his living room. Martin and Mary decorate it, singing carols; Katarina is tired from work, so she lies on the brown leather couch and watches them. Martin thinks, with pleasure, The tree will still be here when Katarina and Mary move in.

The same evening, after Mary has gone to bed, Martin suggests to Katarina that she quit one of her jobs. She was heading to the kitchen for a glass of water, but she turns around to look at him. She says she isn't the kind of woman to depend on a man's salary. Besides, she says, "You are no king of Wall Street."

He waits for her customary smile to undercut her comment. When she doesn't smile, he says, "Was Peter?" He immediately regrets it.

She approaches him across his living room with narrowed eyes. Her right fist is clenched, as if it held a knife. "Have you been playing inquisitor with my daughter?" When she is angry, her accent becomes less pronounced and sometimes even disappears.

He reaches out to stop her but she doesn't come any closer. "I don't know you," he says. "Who are you?"

"I told you."

"I don't believe you." She takes a step back, as if he pushed her. But if her face showed a moment's confusion, it resumes its looks of fury.

"All right," she says, "here is who I am. My blood isn't royal. I am a Jew. My mother was born in a camp. She remembered nothing, but her parents remembered everything and they told her everything she had forgotten. Is this why she kills herself when she is twenty-eight and the mother of a two-year-old daughter? And who become the guardians of the baby girl? The grandparents. The grandparents who are ghosts and are haunted by ghosts."

"I'm sorry," Martin says, and he moves to embrace her. He holds her in his arms, expecting her to cry. When she looks up, he sees her eyes are dry.

"And you?" she asks. "It is my turn to ask about you."

He hesitates, not because he hasn't told her the truth but because he has. He carries no revelation as dramatic as hers.

She steps back and says, "But I don't need to hear anything from you. There is nothing to hear I haven't heard. I see how you see yourself, and I know you believe what you see."

He doesn't understand what she's saying. She moves into his arms. "This is your sweetness," she says. "Sweet like the song of the bird who doesn't know winter is coming. Maybe if the bird keeps singing his song, winter will never come."

Martin says, "Some birds can live through winter."

"But their song isn't the same."

Before he can respond, she takes his hand and leads him to the bedroom, stripping him not hungrily but almost in sadness.

— On New Year's Day, Martin puts their two suitcases, both of them black and light, too light, surely, to contain their lives, into the back of his truck. He drives Katarina and Mary to his house and they enter it without ceremony. He has put a dozen red roses in a vase on his dining room table, which is circular and made of oak and was built by his grandfather, whom he doesn't remember. For a long time, Katarina doesn't notice the roses. When she does, she says, "Martin, you are so sweet, so sweet." And she makes a show of breathing them in.

At night, with Katarina in his bed, in *their* bed, he wraps his arms around her, knowing he'll only move them if she makes him. Eventually, she does shake them off—gently. Approaching sleep, she scoots toward the end of the bed and faces away from him. He places his hand as close to her naked back as he can without touching it.

He thinks, *This is it. This is the way life will be.*

The next moment, he thinks, *When will she and Mary leave?*

For a month of nights, Martin wakes up every couple of hours, checking to see if Katarina is still in his bed. He catches catnaps in the teachers' lounge between periods. Twice, he falls asleep during one of his classes. One time it is Mary who wakes him. She says, "You were snoring and it sounded like a rhinoceros."

"How do you know about rhinoceroses?" he asks.

"Steven," she says.

Mary is less shy with him now. She talks with him about her friends at school, music, what she would like to learn before she turns six—to swim and to ride a horse. She would also like to learn to fly, but she knows she will have to be older to do this—maybe eight or ten.

He doesn't ask her about Steven. He knows what the repercussions would be.

For several weeks, Martin presses Katarina to allow him to look after Mary when her school day ends at three. He has good reasons why she'd be better off with him: By ten o'clock, Mary is beyond tired, and eight hours of sleep isn't enough for a girl in kindergarten. Even Mary, who is more quiet in his house than she is in his truck, tells Katarina: "I would like it, Mother. I could play outside until dark or I could read like I do at the bookstore or I could go with Martin to play his mother's piano."

On a Sunday night, when Mary is asleep, Katarina relents, but she tells Martin, "If my husband comes for her when she is with you, and if you do not fight with your life to keep her by your side until I come home, I cannot forgive you ever and I will die." Lately she has worn her dark golden hair pulled straight back over her head. It gives her the severe look of a soldier. After her speech, she marches into their bedroom and closes the door. He thinks he can hear her crying.

After Mary finishes her school day, Martin plays badminton with her in the gymnasium that used to be a barn. She likes it when he hits the birdie into the rafters. A couple of times the birdie gets stuck and he retrieves it by throwing a volleyball or basketball at it.

When the weather turns warmer in the beginning of March, he plays soccer with her or they sit in the grass and she tells him stories she makes up about a princess named Mary who is lost and spends her time looking out windows—of cars, of buses, of trains—and wondering whether each house she passes is her castle.

One time after Mary's gym class, as he's shepherding the students back to their classroom, he hears a boy in front of him say to Mary, "You're lucky Mr. W. is your dad. You get to play games all the time."

Martin waits for her to set the boy straight about her father. But Mary says nothing.

Whenever Katarina comes home after working at the Book and Brew, she rushes to Mary's room, ignoring Martin's assurances that Mary is there, asleep. He learns to leave Mary's door open a crack so it doesn't creek when Katarina goes into her room. After Katarina sees Mary, she is always relieved and grateful, and often she'll come sit on his lap and they'll share a glass of wine and she'll call him "my sweet bear."

Martin doesn't ask about Peter or Steven or any other man in her life; he doesn't ask her why Mary thinks her father is dead, although he guesses death is the cleanest explanation, an explanation to end questions.

— During the Tree of Knowledge's spring break in April, Martin rents a two-bedroom bungalow on Sky Lake. Katarina is given only three days off from work, but during the five days of their vacation, she relaxes in a way he never would have thought her capable of. When they're sitting together on the flowered couch, she leans so far into him it seems like they've been melted together like two candles. And when she is lying on the shore in her one-piece, as he teaches Mary to swim in the heated pool outside their back door, he sometimes hears her laugh at the book she's reading or at the way a pair of butterflies frolic over her body.

On their last night in the cabin, with Mary asleep, they sit on the cushioned bench next to their back steps, staring at the small pool and, beyond it, the lake. He raises, as gently as he can, the possibility of her divorcing her husband. Immediately her face turns hard and suspicious.

He says, "I'd like . . . after a certain time . . . to ask you to marry me."

"So you think of yourself and not of me and Mary," she says. "You do not think how my husband will throw me from this country and I will lose my daughter forever to a hateful monster."

"We could hire a good lawyer—the best we could find. Maybe the decision about custody would be made right here in Sherman, where people know us—where they know me, anyway."

She laughs bitterly. "Please," she says. "What do you know about the law? You teach volleyball to five-year-old children. And what influence do you have? You are a black man."

He strikes her across the face so quickly he wonders if the sound he heard and the sting in his palm have sources external to him—a thunderclap and an insect bite perhaps. She reaches up to touch her cheek, as if she too cannot believe what has happened and is seeking confirmation.

"I'm sorry," Martin says, his voice heavy with remorse. "Katarina, I'm so sorry."

She is crying now, a fury of tears, although she remains as rigid as a statue. "No, I'm sorry," she says. "You are a gentleman from the start. A knight." She looks up at him. "Beautiful, brown knight."

"I never should have hit you," he says. Tentatively he reaches to hold her. She is stone. "I'll never forgive myself," he says.

She cries more, and the power of her tears surprises him and makes him afraid. But, as quickly, her crying ceases. "It's late," she declares.

By the time he joins her in bed, she is asleep. Or, because her eyes are closed and her breathing is slow, she appears to be asleep. But he believes she is awake, poised to leave as soon as she can be sure he won't hear her. He can still feel the sting on his palm.

At last, he surrenders to sleep. When he wakes and finds her next to him, sunlight streaming in the east window over which they failed to close the blinds, he considers it a kind of pardon.

When Katarina returns to work at the Hotel Sherman, he and Mary drop her off every morning. She will not hear of getting a driver's license. He doesn't ask her why because he knows: It will be only another record of her, a trail for her husband to follow.

— Martin maintains his vigil over her at night, exhausting himself with his suspicion, his fear, that she and Mary will vanish. Sometimes he'll catch her looking at him, as if she was the one worried about him leaving. On one of these occasions, he whispers, "How do you know when your husband is in the same town you're in?"

"Sometimes I see his car. Sometimes I am told by someone, a friend or someone who works at a shop where I go, that a man is looking for me. Sometimes I sense him."

Another night, he whispers, "What if I killed him?"

"Who?"

"Your husband."

She smiles. "I have thought of this."

"And?"

"I would probably shoot wrong the gun and hit only his finger or his toe and that would give them more reason to deport me."

"No," Martin says, "what if *I* killed him?"

"You are big and strong man, much bigger and stronger than he." She pauses. "But you are gentle, too gentle to be a killer." She pauses again. "But I know you love me. Thank you."

Martin pictures murdering her husband in clever, undetectable ways, removing forever Katarina's worries, her need to run. But he thinks she will run before her husband appears, before he, Martin, has the chance to prove to her the extent of his love, the profundity of his desire to make her and Mary his family. Martin knows the pattern of his life. To women he loves, he is like his town, only a quaint and welcome rest stop.

At Mary's graduation from kindergarten, Martin sits with Katarina and listens to Mary and her classmates sing a song about bunnies wandering lost in a field. The song reminds him of a time in high school when he missed a turn on his way to a friend's party and, five minutes later, found himself in a place he couldn't have imagined existed so close to Sherman. With its one intersection and its Ford pickup trucks parked in front of a shack-like building on his right, it looked like a scene from the Wild West. Stepping out of his car to ask directions, he noticed what decorated the bumpers of half the pickup trucks, and he sensed he should be afraid even if his mother had told him once that most people don't mean anything cruel by displaying the Confederate flag. The shack was a bar, full of smoke and music played by four men in jeans and cowboy hats, two with mustaches, another with a full, gray beard. In his memory, the music stopped the second after he walked in. He said thank you and goodbye to no one in particular before climbing in his truck and finding his way back to town.

Applause breaks him from his reverie. Mary and her classmates are bowing, curtseying. He wonders if the bunnies in the song ever found their way home.

— On the second Monday in June, Martin hears a knock on his front door. When he opens it, he finds a man of his age on his front stoop. He knows who it is immediately. Katarina's husband is at least five inches shorter than Martin, but although he is thin, his forearms, visible because he's wearing only a black, crewneck T-shirt, are well toned, as if he lifts weights. His brown hair is cut short, a near crew cut. He has a long, thin nose and a hard chin. He looks like a villain from the live-action version of a cartoon.

"Are they inside?" he asks. His voice isn't as deep as Martin expected.

"Who?" Martin asks.

"Come on, man," he says. And when Martin doesn't move, the man pulls a pistol from his khakis. "Please view this as friendly intimidation. It's been a long time since I've seen my daughter and I'd prefer to cut the red tape."

"They're not inside," Martin says. Although in his fantasies he anticipated the weapon, he finds himself trembling. Saturn, by his side, growls, and Martin quiets him.

"Let's check, all right?"

When Martin doesn't move, Katarina's husband shakes his pistol at him and says, "Turn around, buddy." When they're inside, he says, "I don't care about Kathleen or Karen or Katarina or whatever she's calling herself these days. You can fuck her till you go blind—be my guest. But no schizophrenic whore is going to keep dragging my daughter around the country. If I wasn't so tired of this chase, you and I could sit down and have a talk about what she's done to me and Mary. You'd see where I was coming from. But I'm out of patience."

When her husband is satisfied that Katarina and Mary aren't in the house, he orders Martin into Martin's truck.

"Couldn't you do this legally—contact police, lawyers?" Martin asks. "Make it more civil?"

"I can be plenty civil," the man snaps back. "And I *have* been civil, by-the-book civil. But I told you—I'm tired of the chase. By the time I get any law enforcement or judge to help me, that bitch has taken Mary a thousand miles away. I'll handle all the legal niceties once I get Mary back. And then you can be damn sure that crazy bitch will be back selling her cunt on street corners in Vilnius."

In the truck, the man leans against the door the way Katarina does. He props the gun on his left forearm. Martin sees sweat above his lips, a liquid mustache. "You know where they are," he tells Martin. "Drive there. If you drive somewhere else, I'll kill you. You can see how tired of this I am, can't you? So don't think I wouldn't kill you."

Martin does know where Katarina and Mary are: at a birthday party at the Grant Park pool. Katarina took the day off from work, and Mary was looking forward to showing off her swimming skills to her classmates. Ordinarily, Martin would have gone. But a storm the previous night had blown shingles off his roof and he wanted to replace them. Katarina and Mary had caught a ride to the pool with Faith, one of Mary's classmates, and Faith's mother.

Martin drives toward Sky Lake, toward its east end and Murderers' Cove, where in the twenties and thirties gangsters supposedly conducted assassinations. "Mary's school is having a picnic," Martin says. He hopes his voice is reasonable, matter-of-fact.

He leaves the two-lane road to drive down a dirt road. He goes six hundred feet before stopping at a dead end.

"Where are the cars?" the man asks, his teeth gritted.

"The bus dropped them. It'll be coming back to pick them up."

"If you're lying, you're dead, understand? I told you: I've lost patience." He half grunts, half sighs. "All right, damn it. Let's go."

They exit the truck, and Martin leads him down a narrow dirt path cut between pine trees. Martin knows Murderers' Cove well from when he was a teenager, when he and his friends came here to drink. A scattering of Old Milwaukee cans proves the tradition continues.

Martin stops. Over the next short hill is the lake. When Katarina's husband sees it, he'll know he has been deceived. There will be no one on the shore, no one in the water. Katarina's husband will think this a convenient, quiet place to kill him.

Katarina's husband is two steps behind him. "Why did you stop?" he asks. His voice is agitated, suspicious, nervous, even exasperated and desperate. For a moment, Martin allows himself to believe Katarina's husband, believe he's a frustrated father whose unstable wife kidnapped their daughter. But Martin pictures Katarina and Mary sitting at his dining room table, passing the mashed potatoes around, talking or saying nothing.

Martin says, "I don't want to be around when you see them. They'll know I betrayed them."

Katarina's husband holds his gun on Martin. "They'll know anyway. Keep walking."

Suddenly, Martin bends and grabs his knees. "Ouch!" he says. He slaps his left forearm. "Oh, shit! Shit!"

"What?" Katarina's husband says with alarm.

"Goddamn wasps!"

"What?" Katarina's husband looks around him, a wild turn of his eyes. This is all the distraction Martin needs; he pounces on him like a lion. Katarina's husband lands on his back and his eyes rattle. The ground isn't as hard as Martin would like, but with his knees pinning the man's arms to his sides, he grabs the sides of the man's head. He lifts his head and slams it down, lifts and slams—twenty, thirty times—until he is sure Katarina's husband is unconscious.

Still straddling him, Martin plucks the pistol from the man's limp right hand and shoves it into his mouth. He hesitates only long enough to assure himself of the silence, of their solitude in the cove. The gunshot is less an explosion than a loud snapping of fingers. Blood pours from behind both sides of the man's head.

Martin steps back from the body and contemplates it a moment, wondering if he could simply leave it here. He is suddenly tired, exhausted. And he wants to commence the joyous errand of going to the pool and telling Katarina that she and Mary don't have to run anymore, everything is all right now. He could come back for the body tonight. How likely is it that anyone would find it before tonight?

But if the body is found, the police would identify it. They would talk to Katarina. They would talk to him. He would be taken to jail, she might be deported. She would never forgive his clumsiness, his stupidity.

He removes the man's shirt and ties it like a bandana around his head. He pulls the body off the pool of blood and covers the blood with dirt and pine needles and other debris he finds on the side of the trail. As he is about to pick up the body and drag it to his truck, he hears voices from the lake. In a fury of strength, he drags the body off the trail and into the dense growth of pine trees on his left. The voices come closer. Martin turns and peers from behind a pine tree. He sees a man and woman—or a boy and girl, they can't be older than sixteen—spreading a blanket in a modest clearing a few feet from where he covered up the blood. No doubt they came by canoe from the other side of the lake. They're here to drink, smoke marijuana, screw.

They do all of this. Afterwards, the boy walks to within ten feet of where Martin is hiding behind a pine tree. *If he looks up,* Martin thinks, *I'll have to kill him. I'll have to kill them both*. But the boy, whose black hair curls like a wave over his forehead and into his eyes, is looking down, watching his stream of urine. A minute later, he returns to his girlfriend. They lounge on the red blanket, infuriating Martin with their talk about nothing important.

The boy and girl stay until dusk. When they fold up their blanket and stroll back to the lake, to their rowboat or canoe, he thinks again of abandoning the body. Katarina and Mary came home hours ago, Martin knows. Katarina saw her husband's car in the driveway. Martin tries to imagine her going to the police, telling them everything. But he knows what she did, and this is a relief and a curse.

He drags the body to his truck and, with no small effort, lifts it into the bed. He covers it with a green tarp he bought with such a far-fetched possibility in mind. He drives with unusual care to his house.

He parks his truck in his driveway. He pulls the man's car keys from his pocket and parks his Mercury in his garage. He goes inside his house, where his dog howls as if he's a stranger, and looks in Mary's bedroom. The drawers are empty. So are the drawers of Katarina's bureau.

He calls Patricia Knott, the mother of the birthday girl. "Oh, they left just after we had cake at around two," she says. In a softer voice, she asks, "Is something wrong?"

His "no" is quick and sounds so false that, to prevent her from asking anything else, he hangs up.

He calls the Greyhound Bus terminal. No one answers. He thinks to call US Airways, which flies four flights a day into and out of Sherman. He knows no one would tell him whether Katarina and Mary were on a flight. If they didn't take the bus or fly, they could have hired a van to drive them to Cleveland or Columbus. There are two such services in town, but no one answers at either.

He peels off his clothes, which he knows he'll have to burn or bury or dispose of in another permanent way, and shoves them into a garbage bag, which he puts in a closet. After he showers and puts on fresh clothes, Martin steps outside. He wants to begin his search now, but he knows he must deal with the body first. Martin didn't know, until he passed his mother's house on the way to his, how he would dispose of it. He throws a shovel next to the body in the back of his truck. Feeling feverish, he goes inside to drink water and eat something. He barely feels the food in his mouth, the water in his throat.

He knows he must wait until it's later and darker, when the chance of being seen is smaller. At a quarter to midnight, he drives to Shadow Hill Cemetery, to the spot where he is to be buried next to his mother, and digs. He finishes three hours later.

He forgot to bring water, and he thinks he might faint. He throws the body in. The body lands awkwardly on its side. Martin thinks about leaving it this way, but he climbs into the grave and turns it over, so its face is up. He hears Katarina's husband say, "I only want to see my daughter." After leaving the pistol at the dead man's feet, Martin climbs out of the grave and covers the body with dirt. This takes longer than he expects, but by the time he restores the grass in front of the tombstone, the place looks little different than when he came. The darkness and the willow trees have hidden him from the few cars that passed on the road two hundred feet above him.

Martin drives home and drinks three glasses of water. He lets Saturn outside and calls him back ten minutes later. He goes into his bedroom and sets the alarm, although he knows it's an unnecessary gesture. His sleep is shallow, and he is up two hours and forty-five minutes later, at seven.

He puts a note in his mother's mailbox. He is waiting for Dr. Andrews at her veterinary clinic when she opens at eight. He leaves Saturn to board with her. In his truck, he drives to the Greyhound station and accosts the clerk, who is sleepy and unshaven, with pictures of Katarina and Mary. Martin used to see the clerk, whose name is Frankie, all the time at the Above and Beyond Club. He even remembers Frankie's favorite drink: vodka and cranberry juice. And his favorite dancer: Becca Bishop.

Now Frankie looks at Martin as if Martin has just stepped off a bus from Mars. "Never seen them," Frankie says.

"They might have been on your three o'clock bus to Cleveland," Martin says. "Or your four-thirty to New York. Or your five-fifty to Columbus. You were working yesterday, Frankie. I know you work both shifts here."

Frankie isn't looking at Martin or the photos anymore but has returned to looking at something on his computer.

"Come on, Frankie," Martin says, "she's my woman, she's the woman I'm going to marry."

"I'm sorry," Frankie says, tapping on his keyboard.

Martin reaches across the counter and grabs Frankie by the collar of his blue golf shirt. "Damn it, Frankie, I know there's a very good chance they were on one of those busses."

"If you don't take your hand off me, I'm going to call the police," Frankie says. "I may call them anyway."

"Don't you know who I am, Frankie?" Martin says, releasing his collar even as he feels like breaking his neck.

Frankie picks up the phone. "It's obvious who you are," Frankie says. "You're someone who wants to hurt innocent people."

Martin isn't certain who he means by "people." Katarina and Mary? Frankie and whoever might come into the station? Frankie punches a 9 on the phone and Martin leaves.

The thin woman with the salt-and-pepper hair at the check-in counter at US Airways is the mother of one of his former students. Even if her name hadn't been printed on the tag above her breast, he would have remembered it. And although she shows no indication of ever having met him, he begins his query informally, "Rhoda, how are you? How's Cindy?"

He pauses, waiting for a response. There is none.

"I'm desperate here, Rhoda, and it would take too much explaining to tell you why, but I'd like to, I need to, know if there was a woman named Katarina or Karen or maybe . . . I don't know, I guess it could be any name . . . and her daughter, Mary. They might have caught a flight yesterday, and if they did, I need to know where they went."

"That information," Rhoda says slowly, as if she is speaking to a foreigner, "is confidential."

"I know, I know. But you know me, I was Cindy's phys-ed teacher—I taught her how to shoot a hook shot, remember? The woman, Katarina, she's my fiancée, but something happened—not between us but with her ex-husband."

Rhoda has taken a step back from the counter. He has the feeling she is looking for a button to press. He begins pleading again, and in the midst of his own quick, desperate words, he hears her say, "Security." He looks to his right. Down the hallway, a heavyset man in a blue uniform is approaching as fast as someone can without running.

It is Martin who runs. In his truck, he wonders if Frankie contacted Rhoda. He wonders if one of them might have, in fact, sold a ticket to Katarina, who might have begged Frankie or Rhoda to please keep her destination a secret because of the man who was following her. He can hear her say: "He wants to kill me. We are in danger. Please."

But they know me, Martin thinks. *They know I wouldn't hurt a woman or a child. But they looked at me like I was a goddamn stranger.*

When he's at a red light, he moves the rearview mirror so he can see his face. It stares back at him tired, desperate, and dark.

He stops at P.J.'s Rides. Even before he's two steps into the office, P.J., whom he used to play basketball against in high school, holds up his hand in a stop signal and says, "If she wants to contact you, partner, she will." (P.J. spent a summer in Texas when he was fourteen, and forever afterwards, when he has felt like he can get away with it, he has called men "partner" and women "cowgirl.")

"So one of your drivers took Katarina and Mary somewhere?" Martin asks. "Will you please tell me where, P.J.?"

"You're jumping to conclusions, partner," says P.J., who's standing behind a large oak desk. P.J. is barely point-guard sized, and with his goatee and his shining scalp, he looks like a Russian revolutionary from one of Martin's high school history textbooks. "I knew you were coming, thanks to an anonymous tip—well, anonymous to you, anyway."

Martin has never liked P.J., although he has never especially wanted to beat his face to dust. Now he rushes forward, his fist cocked. P.J. removes a black revolver from the top drawer of his desk and points it at Martin's chest.

"Don't think I wouldn't mind sending your pathetic ass into eternity," P.J. says.

Martin is still and silent.

"We always knew you had trouble in you."

"What the hell do you mean?" Martin says.

"You couldn't be Mama's angel boy forever. Daddy's black devil heart was gonna beat in you sooner or later."

"Come on, P.J." Martin finds himself feeling exasperated and sick to his stomach.

"Go on, partner." P.J. shakes the gun at him. "Go put some ice on it. It'll behave."

Martin wants to say, I've already murdered one man. What's another?

It takes all of his fortitude to turn and walk out the door.

The other car service in town, Gonzalo's Viajes, opened four months before and caters to residents of Spanishville. The man in the office, which is decorated with tourist posters of Costa Rica, Guatemala, Honduras, and Nicaragua, says he was working yesterday but he didn't see a blond-haired woman and her daughter.

Martin is grateful for the man's honesty. He is deflated by his message.

At noon, Martin drives out of town in the Mercury. He decides to go west, thinking Katarina might see it as offering the most possibilities, the widest space in which to hide. At a rest stop one hundred miles out of Sherman, he stuffs the clothes he wore the previous day, sprinkled with blood, into a trashcan. He knows he'll have to ditch the Mercury eventually, although he doubts anyone will be looking for Katarina's husband; he didn't seem the kind of man who would have relatives or a girlfriend who would care enough about him to call the police. On the other hand, he can't be sure. And he would hate to pull into a town where Katarina and Mary were staying only to have them see the car and flee again.

At his first stop, in Columbus, he goes to the Greyhound station. At the ticket counter, he holds up the photograph of Katarina and Mary. The clerk, who is white and at least sixty, says he hasn't seen them, but he wasn't working yesterday. Martin asks if he knows where someone might go to stay if they were new in town and didn't have much money. The clerk directs him to the YMCA four blocks from the station. At the Y, the woman behind the counter, whose skin is the same color as his, steps back when he approaches with the photograph.

"Have you seen them?" he asks.

She shakes her head.

"Are you sure?" he demands.

She takes another step back and looks around as if hoping to find someone to protect her.

He leans over the counter. If he wanted, he could grab the woman by her yellow blouse. "You don't even know me," he tells the woman. "I could be a prince, for all you know."

"A prince in the YMCA?" she asks. She seems calmer, as if she knows help is on the way. And it is: The door to Martin's right opens and in steps a man as tall as Martin but with darker skin, skin like ebony. His head is shaved and he has a large gold stud in his right ear.

"Is there anything I can help you with?" he asks Martin. The whites around his irises are luminous, hot.

Martin holds up his pictures and asks his question. His voice is a supplicant. He is so tired he wants to cry.

"I'm sorry," the man says. This is all he says, and Martin cannot tell whether he has seen Katarina and Mary and isn't saying or whether he's denying seeing them. He feels his blood rise. But he knows he would gain only trouble by threatening the man.

Both the man and the woman look at him without feeling. "Back home," Martin tells them, gesturing in the general direction of Sherman. But he doesn't complete whatever he wanted to tell them. Whatever he intended to say is no longer true. Tears flood his eyes, and he exits the YMCA before they see him cry.

— Over the course of the summer, Martin visits small towns from Bowling Green, Ohio, to Sunrise, Arizona. He places advertisements in dozens of newspapers—Katarina and Mary: The problem is solved. Please call me or come back. Martin—even though he has never seen Katarina read a newspaper.

The Mercury quits on him outside of Las Vegas.

In Santa Fe, New Mexico, the clerk at the Motel 6, a pale teenager with acne and body piercings everywhere, tells him with a shrug that his credit card isn't being accepted. Martin calls the company and is told he will not be extended more credit. "Our records show you haven't paid your last two bills."

It is August 6th. His mother allows him to use her credit card to buy a bus ticket from Santa Fe (via Dallas, Birmingham, and Columbus) to Sherman. He arrives not having eaten in four days. He is a year's salary in debt.

On the first Sunday of Martin's return, after he and his mother have finished egg salad and three quarters of an apple pie, his mother says, "I don't know if it was brave or foolish of you to run after her. If she left without a trace, she didn't want to be found."

He wants to tell her that Katarina wasn't like the other women he'd been with; her situation was different. But as he thinks what he'll say, the story sounds convoluted and preposterous, a scorned man's fantasy.

"And it sure was nice of Dr. Andrews to give you a break on boarding Saturn," she says. "Even so, you could have bought your dog a house for what you owe her."

"I suppose," he says. He decides to agree with everything his mother says. He is too tired for any kind of argument. Besides, winning the argument wouldn't bring back Katarina and Mary. And he's concerned, if only in a place in himself he would prefer not to acknowledge, that she, too, will turn on him, will come, like others in Sherman, to look at him with suspicion, displeasure, and fear.

Sometimes Martin talks to his telephone. He commands: "Ring!" He says, "Please, ring! Please? Please?" He holds out hope that even if Katarina, paranoid, perhaps, of her husband tapping his line, would never call, Mary might. But he wonders why Mary should treat him with any more distinction than the other men who have loved her and have been left, casualties of a madness Martin no longer believes was the sole domain of Katarina's husband.

And often he thinks: She's with another man. I've ended the threat to her safety, and another man will have what I want and deserve. Another man will have what is mine—my wife, my daughter.

Often, he cannot sleep. When he does sleep, he frequently wakes up late, missing his first class and sometimes his second. One day, he sleeps until noon, and when he calls the Tree of Knowledge to say he's on his way, the principal tells him to take the rest of the day off.

On another Sunday, over lunch, Martin agrees with his mother that while some towns have certain attractions and other towns have different attractions, Sherman offers as much, in its own way, as any of them. He agrees that people might be friendly elsewhere, but no friendlier than they are in Sherman, especially when they come to know you. Staying where you live, he agrees, saves you the headache and expense of realizing you were in the right place from the start.

And on another Sunday, Martin agrees with his mother that he has a sad tendency to fall in love with "mercurial women and their innocent offspring."

"Not that I haven't been guilty of some romantic foolishness myself—even after your father," she says. She reaches across the picnic bench and puts her hand on his. "Eventually, you accept a life of smaller pleasures—a lazy late summer day, a funny TV show, handing out candy and admiring all the kids' costumes on Halloween. Maybe they're the real signs of God's grace."

As usual, Martin nods, his mind in a future he'll never have.

Every Sunday after lunch, regardless of the weather, Martin walks down to Shadow Hill Cemetery and stops at his gravesite. He always wonders who he buried there. When he's fired from the Tree of Knowledge, when the owner of the Above and Beyond Gentlemen's Club tells him he isn't hiring despite the sign in the window, when the best job he can secure is custodial work at the Hotel Sherman, he comes to think it was himself.

A MAP OF THE FORBIDDEN

After his eulogy, after the last prayer, Tim Kovitch found himself alone in a corner of the Hotel Sherman ballroom. He was about to turn and look out the window, although he knew he'd see nothing more interesting than the brick façade of the failing movie theater next door, when he heard his name called, a song from the past. An instant later, Anna Appelstein was in his arms, the force of her embrace knocking him into the window's red velvet curtain. Dust poured from it, covering him and Anna like a veil.

"I met your wife," Anna said, gesturing to the other side of the room, where Patty was trapped in conversation with a pair of his father's old army buddies. "She's beautiful."

Anna had long, square teeth and the kind of pink cheeks, shy of burned, a person acquires by engaging in a healthy hour of gardening a day. Her breasts, large when she was a teenager, seemed more in proportion to her body now. Or perhaps their size was mitigated by the loose-fitting, white cotton dress she was wearing. Her eyes were the same startling blue.

He remembered a time he'd almost kissed her.

"Where are your children?" Anna asked. Tim and Patty had two sons, eight and six years old.

"At home, with a babysitter."

"Too bad. I was hoping to meet them."

Tim hadn't seen Anna since his senior year in high school, but she'd obviously caught up on his life. And thanks to his brother, who worked in the same office building in Cleveland as her brother, he knew something about hers. In the past twenty years, she'd dated men and women; she'd lived on a commune in Oregon where, it was said, the residents were married to each other and the earth; she'd contemplated medical school before becoming a certified homeopath.

He glanced at her hair, dirty blond and hanging around her shoulders; it had a trace of pink in it. He interpreted this to mean she hadn't stopped calling her life an experiment. Tim gazed at the ballroom, which was being cleaned and rearranged for a wedding reception, but it didn't hold his attention long. Twenty minutes after alluding to his father's infidelities in his eulogy, he wanted nothing more than to flood Anna's face with kisses. No, it was worse: He didn't think he could live if he didn't.

But he knew relief would come. Today or tomorrow—next week, in the worst case scenario—she would leave Sherman to return to where she was living—Boston, New York, Philadelphia, he couldn't remember—and he would resume his life as it had been and should be. "I'm so glad you came, Anna. How long will you be in town?"

"I moved back three days ago. I'm studying painting at Ohio Eastern."

"For the summer?"

"For the next three years."

He told her he'd like to invite her over to the house. She could meet his boys, he said. He asked for her phone number. He said he would call her. It was a promise he hoped to God he would break.

— After returning home at ten past three, Tim slipped into his office on the first floor of the four-bedroom house he shared with Patty and their sons. Three of the walls in his office were lined to the ceiling with bookshelves, all of them full; he'd even crammed books horizontally on top of books standing vertically. He had books in half a dozen boxes in other parts of the room. He had three stacks of books on his desk. He had books on the ledges of his four windows.

Why Tim needed such an extensive book collection was a mystery to Patty. He owned a bookstore, after all, the only independent left in Sherman or anywhere within sixty-six square miles. The Book and Brew sold new and used books, folk and world music CDs, and, for reasons Tim had forgotten, designer umbrellas. The eight-table, four-couch coffee shop, on the bookstore's second floor, was what was keeping the bookstore solvent. But Starbucks was supposedly coming to town any day.

Patty said he was imprisoned by books, and she was right. He worked twelve hours a day to keep the bookstore from going so far under that the coffee house wouldn't be able to support it. But he couldn't imagine his life, professional or private, without books. Family legend had him reading before he could walk.

Tim's father, during one of his romantic crises, had told Tim he envied his life of mere literary adventures. Remembering Anna in his arms, remembering both the firmness and pliancy of her body, he wondered if his father's words would remain true.

Tim sat in a canvas director's chair his wife had bought him for his thirty-fifth birthday, a period in which she hoped to tease him from his staid consistency. There was a gold star on the back of the chair and gold sparkles on the armrests. The chair was as uncomfortable as any he'd ever sat in, but a sense of obligation to

Patty, and a desire to show her he wasn't as predictable as the leather armchairs he favored, had stopped him from donating it to the Salvation Army. Now he thought: *I'll show her unpredictable*. At the same time, he thought: *I should talk to someone.*

But there was only one person Tim wanted to call. He had his hand on the telephone when the door opened and his six-year old, Isaac, stepped in. "You're naked!" Isaac exclaimed. Tim had discarded his white dress shirt on his desk; he often paraded around his house like this. Vain about his body, he spent forty-five minutes every other morning in his basement lifting weights and running on a treadmill. On the other mornings, he swam a mile in the YMCA pool.

As happened often when he saw his father bare-chested, Isaac removed his own shirt. Patty thought he and Isaac looked identical, from their curly black hair to their pale, smooth chests. Tim's father hadn't been blessed with similar attributes; he'd gone gray in his thirties and bald in his forties, and his chest was a gnarly forest. At his worst, Don Kovitch had looked like the heavyset older brother of the farmer in "American Gothic."

"Make a muscle, Daddy," Isaac said. When Tim did, Isaac grabbed hold of it with both hands and Tim lifted him up with his single arm. Eventually, Isaac's hands slipped off Tim's arm and he dropped to the rug.

"I win," Tim said.

"You cheated," Isaac said, which is what he always said when he lost. Today, however, the phrase seemed accusatory, foreboding.

A week before he died, Tim's father had said to him, "If I'd had your looks, I would have had five hundred lovers. Don't believe anyone who tells you that looks don't count. Compared with the good-looking man, the ugly man starts the race in quicksand. The only way he can catch up is to become a millionaire."

"But you're not a millionaire," Tim said, "and you haven't exactly been stuck in quicksand."

"Then I must be a magician," his father said.

"Will you come play Space Karate with me?" Isaac implored, closing his eyes and pursing his lips, as if waiting to receive a kiss. At the same time, Patty entered the room. At five-feet, eleven-inches, she was only two inches shorter than Tim. She had hair as black as Tim's and Isaac's, but it was long and straight. She was thirty-six, and her greatest concession to age was the slight puffiness around her eyes from years of too little sleep, every mother's burden. In other ways—her slim torso and legs, her toothpaste-commercial white teeth—she hadn't changed in the twelve years he'd known her.

So why did he keep feeling Anna's body against his? Why did tomorrow seem too long a time until he could see her again?

"Isaac, sweetheart, I think Daddy needs some time to be alone," Patty said.

"Why?" Isaac asked indignantly.

"Because he's remembering Grandpa Don."

Tim didn't want to be alone. If he were alone now, he knew he'd pick up the phone again. "I'll play with you, Isaac," he said. "Give me a minute." Isaac raised his fists in triumph, and, in the spirit of Space Karate, ran in slow motion from the office.

"You're welcome to take the rest of the afternoon off," Patty said. "I'll plop Isaac down beside Jacob in front of the TV. The meal won't take me long to make." They'd invited his father's two army buddies, one of whom lived in Idaho, the other in Oklahoma, to come for dinner.

"I hope our guests have early bedtimes."

"They're sweet men," Patty said.

"A couple of skirt chasers from the Greatest Generation."

"Aren't all men—skirt chasers, I mean?" Patty laughed. "Except you, of course."

As if his wife could see through cotton, Tim covered the pant pocket where he'd put Anna's number.

"Wasn't it a French painter your father fell in love with back in his army days?" Patty asked him.

Tim remembered why Anna had come back to Sherman. He found himself blushing. "She was a musician," he said quickly. "She played the flute."

"Daddy!" Isaac called from the living room. "Daddy!"

"Coming!" Tim shouted.

On his way out of his office, he patted his wife's shoulder. It was the kind of gesture—friendly but aloof—that had come to dominate their relationship. At the same time, he couldn't say he was tired of his wife or dissatisfied with her. In fact, he considered himself lucky to be married to her. Tim stopped in the entranceway of his office and turned back to her. He said, "Didn't my father fall in love with everyone?"

"Within a certain age range," she said, smiling. "Sixteen to sixty."

Tim's father married his mother two days after he turned eighteen; she was half a year younger. They'd been married for five days when he left to fight the Germans. Tim's brother, James, had been born a year after his father's return to the States. Tim had been born sixteen years later. His mother had had three miscarriages in between.

Tim's father had proposed to the French flautist. Tim wasn't sure Patty knew this part of the story. "I loved your mother and I loved Genevieve," his father said. "Asking Genevieve to marry me was the only way to show how deeply I felt about her."

"But marrying her would have been illegal," Tim said. "It's called bigamy, remember?"

"One wife in the States, one wife in France—who would know besides me?"

Tim had considered his father's behavior repellent and ridiculous. But now, remembering Anna in his arms, he thought: *I might be on my way to understanding him*. And his next thought: *I don't want to understand him*.

I like my life. I like my marriage.

Anna's eyes are the blue of a postcard sea.

Tim hoped playing Space Karate with Isaac would distract him from thinking about Anna. But the game wasn't demanding—most of it consisted of him watching Isaac move in slow motion—and he thought of his father's memorial service, which, appropriately, had been a paean to what was good about him: his work ethic, his sense of humor, his exquisite golf game. Tim's allusion to his father's affairs was, as he considered it now, oblique enough to be thought unintentional. "He was a man who loved to love and loved to be loved" could have referred to how his father felt about his family and vice versa.

The centerpiece of Tim's eulogy had nothing to do with his father's love life. Rather, it had been about their relationship, and it had culminated with the story of how his father had rescued him in a canoe during a thunderstorm on the Chesapeake Bay when Tim couldn't maneuver his Sunfish back to shore. "I owe my life to my father," Tim concluded. And, to laughter, he added, "I mean, I owe it to him twice."

Tim's mother knew about his father's affairs, and periodically she threatened to divorce him. James saw their father's affairs as the cause of his mother's depression—and even of her cervical cancer, although to Tim this connection seemed far-fetched. Their mother had died eleven years ago, at which point James ceased speaking to their father. He hadn't come to the memorial service.

After their mother's death, their father had gotten married again, to a woman he employed at one of his three car dealerships, but the woman had been less tolerant than Tim's mother of his affairs. They were divorced within eighteen months. No fewer than three women had come up to Tim at the memorial service and introduced themselves as his father's fiancée. Perhaps his father's death had been merely a dramatic way to avoid breaking two hearts.

Before Tim met Patty, he'd been in a total of four relationships, never, however, simultaneously. As long as he was unmarried, he had felt free to keep looking. But he always broke up one relationship before beginning another. After his wedding, he was certain he would never be with another woman.

Isaac threw a slow, sweeping kick into Tim's groin, planting his heel against Tim's testicles. Tim thought to scold his son, because even in Space Karate such a kick was prohibited. Instead, he gently grabbed his son's foot and returned it to the floor.

— During dinner, Tim watched his father's old army buddies drink. George preferred white wine. Arnold preferred red. Between them, they finished three and a half bottles. Tim knew he should be interested in their stories. At least a third of them concerned his father. But he'd stopped paying close attention after George and Arnold admitted to having also proposed to the French flautist. As the men told their stories of war and war's prelude and aftermath, Tim replayed his encounter with Anna. A hundred times she rushed into his arms with the grace of a phantom and embraced him with the force of a train.

Sometime after nine, Tim pleaded fatigue and said he was going to bed. He doubted this would inspire George and Arnold to head back to their hotel rooms, and he was right: They shook his hand, said how nice it had been to meet Don Kovitch's son, and turned their full attention to Patty, whose face bore a brief look of betrayal before flattening into resignation. "I owe you," he mouthed to her, although he wasn't sure she noticed.

Instead of heading upstairs, he turned into his office. He closed the door and placed the Oxford English Dictionary against it. Should his father's army buddies or his wife attempt to enter without knocking, they would be resisted by a million words. He fished Anna's number from his pocket, picked up the phone, and dialed. As he listened to the ringing, he thought she might have gone out. It was Saturday night, after all. She'd probably met up with a high school friend, one of the deadbeats who'd stayed in town instead of moving to Cleveland or Columbus or places more distant and exotic. Or maybe she was on a date with one of her new art professors.

"Hello?"

At the sound of her voice, he remembered the January of his senior year in high school, the beginning of swimming season. He'd been team captain. A sophomore, she came up to him in the school's third-floor hallway. They stood under skylights, and everything seemed dark in contrast to her. "I've just started the Tim Kovitch fan club," she said.

"Be prepared to be the only member," he said.

"Maybe one's enough," she said, smiling.

"Hello?" Anna said now.

They'd seen each other at swimming meets and other school events as well as around town. He'd had a girlfriend, although they broke up at the end of the school year. Three days after his graduation, Tim and Anna were at the same party, and they left the house together, as if by design, and stood under a buckeye tree, where the percussive beat from the second-floor stereo was muffled. He asked her about his fan club. "Still only me," she said. "Am I enough?"

He put his arm around her shoulder, and she leaned into him and tilted her face up for a kiss. The kiss, if it had happened, might have begun something serious, might have carried them into college. But a girl he didn't know came up to them drunk and distraught, and, after whispering in Anna's ear, cajoled her back into the house. Two days later, he was two hundred miles away, in a lifeguard's chair at the overnight summer camp he'd worked at since he was fifteen.

A third time, but without impatience, Anna said, "Hello?"

"Hello, Anna, it's me. It's—"

"Tim."

"It's Tim," he said.

"Tim."

"Yes, Tim."

"I think there's no doubt it's Tim. Tim who is whispering."

"Oh." He thought he should hang up now. If he lingered even a few seconds longer, he knew he would ask her to lunch.

She said, "I didn't think you would call."

With her insecurity exposed, he relaxed. As in high school, he had the upper hand.

She added, "So soon."

"Oh." He thought: *Tell her how nice it was to see her. Tell her you appreciated her coming to support you in your time of grief. Tell her you love her. No, tell her . . .* "I wanted to know if you'd like to have lunch."

"Great," she said.

"Terrific."

"Wonderful."

There was a silence. It was his turn to speak, but he'd never spoken with someone he at once wanted to seduce and never see again.

"Superb," she said. "Stupendous. Splendid."

"Excuse me?" he said.

"I thought you might be searching for another synonym." She said "synonym" as if it was a spice.

"Lunch," he said.

"Yes," she said. "I've agreed. A date?" she asked.

"Uh," he said. "Uh," he repeated. "Sure, let's call it a date."

She laughed. "A date," Anna said, "as in a day on the calendar. I could do it tomorrow, although I bet, it being Sunday and all, well, I bet you're tied up."

"Right," he said. He wanted to say, I'm not sure I should see you. My motives aren't gentlemanly.

He wondered which one of the thousands of novels he owned contained the phrase "My motives aren't gentlemanly." Whatever the book, it couldn't have been written in the last hundred years.

"Monday?" Anna asked.

"Great," Tim said. "But let me check my calendar." He picked up two file cards from his desk and rubbed them together. "Monday looks free."

"Where would you like to meet?"

The names of half a dozen hotels sprung to mind, but the only restaurant he could think of was one his father used to patronize. It was on the other side of town, miles from his house and the Book and Brew, miles from where a usual day would find Patty. "The Three O'Clock Café."

"I don't know it," Anna said.

"Neither do I."

— Tim didn't intend to arrive early, but every light he'd come to had been green, as if some higher power was easing his way. He parked near the restaurant's front entrance and waited, listening to a mixed cassette of pop songs he'd found in his attic. The music dated from his high school days, but the cassette wasn't his but his father's. His father had been indiscriminate in his musical tastes. Tim, by contrast, was a musical snob. If it wasn't Bach, it wasn't worth troubling his ears with. Tim listened to three songs on the mixed tape, all of which showcased their lead singers' desire to be someplace else, on a different emotional plane, and it was only an anonymous "you" who could lead them to this undiscovered country. When he found himself mouthing the words to the third song, as if in agreement, he hit the eject button.

He sat in silence and tried to recall even the faintest strain of the Goldberg Variations. But the only piece of classical music he could summon was "In the Hall of the Mountain King," whose climax, his father once told him, was the musical equivalent of an orgy.

After five more minutes in the car, Tim wondered if Anna might have come to the restaurant even earlier than he had. She might be sitting inside, fanning herself with a menu. He turned off the engine, pulled his keys from the ignition, and opened his door. He'd worn a white, linen-cotton blend shirt and sweat had gathered in his armpits. He flapped his arms, as if he might air dry himself this way, but he realized his exertions were only adding to the sweat problem. He slipped inside the Three O'Clock Café, whose walls were the blue of late afternoon.

Behind a podium in the middle of the reception area stood a dark-haired woman, who said, "Hello, Mr. Kovitch." In a lower voice, and with an impressive degree of gravity, she added, "I'm deeply sorry about the loss of your father."

In making the reservation, Tim had given only his first name. So how did the woman know him? She might have been a customer in his bookstore. But as he knew 98 percent of his customers, he decided this wasn't likely. Had she noticed a resemblance between him and his father? He had never thought he looked like his father, but perhaps today's rendezvous with Anna had given him the same adulterous glow.

"Would you like to sit at your father's favorite table?" the woman asked.

Turn around, he told himself. *It isn't too late to run.*

But he must have nodded because she led him to a booth in the back of the restaurant, near the kitchen. The cushions of the booth were black, the tabletops brown. The painting on the wall to his left was of a clown, with full makeup and red hair, on his knees, praying. "There will be someone else," he told the woman.

"I suspected," she replied, dropping two menus beside his trembling hands.

A minute later, Anna was sitting across from him. She looked no different than she had two days before. Tim acknowledged this. Or, rather, a small, rational part of him, preserved in an icehouse in his brain, did. The rest of him thought Anna looked twice as beautiful—and three times as desirable—as she'd looked on Saturday.

"You look . . ." he began.

She smiled, waiting.

"You look . . ."

"It's all right," Anna said. "I think I know what you mean. And I'm flattered."

"You do know what I mean?"

She smiled. A moment later, Tim leaned over the table and whispered, "They know."

Anna scrutinized him before also leaning across the table, her hair falling against the salt-and-pepper shakers. "Who are they and what do they know?" she asked.

"They know I'm my father's son."

Her lips were inches from his. "It doesn't take a genius to know," she said. "Your picture was on the front of the local section of the *SAP* today."

"I didn't look at the paper."

"There was a photo of you giving your eulogy. You're a dead-ringer for your old man."

"I never thought so."

"It's what happens when we get older. We all turn into our parents. Or we die fighting not to."

A waitress, who might have been nineteen or thirty-nine, with hair dyed the silver of knight's armor, stepped up to their table. "Your father had to die before you'd patronize his favorite restaurant?" she said.

"He never invited me here," Tim said. *I was the wrong gender.*

"Would you like his usual?" the waitress asked.

Tim glanced at Anna, who said, "He would. I'll take something green."

"It's amazing," Tim said when the waitress had left.

"What is?" Anna asked.

He was about to say, To know my father from the inside out. Instead, he said, "To see you again."

Her hair was still dangling in the salt-and-pepper shakers. He reached to hold the ends in his fingertips. His gesture felt as natural and instinctive as exposing his palms to catch raindrops, yet he looked at his hand as if it had declared independence from the rest of his body. She didn't flinch or pull back.

"You've been gone a long time," he said. The farthest from Sherman Tim had ever lived was Athens—Athens, Ohio, where he attended college—which was the traveler's equivalent of walking to the end of the block. "I'm envious of your adventures."

"Why didn't you ever leave?" she asked.

"I didn't think I should."

"Why?"

Tim was about to say, Someone had to keep my father in check. But far from keeping him in check, he'd been a mere witness to his father's recklessness and immaturity. "Maybe I thought I was happy where I was."

"Are you?"

His hand, the rogue element in his otherwise obedient body, moved from Anna's hair to her face. She leaned into his palm, and he felt her weight, her warmth. His lips—his body's second betrayer—moved to kiss hers, but presently he heard a shuffling of feet and a clanking of plates and their waitress was again beside them. She placed plates filled with pancakes, bacon, sausages, eggs, and baby back ribs on their table.

"No wonder my father had a heart attack," Tim said to Anna, although it was the waitress who replied: "He only sampled, never scarfed."

One man's modest indulgence, Tim thought, was another man's wretched excess. He looked past Anna to the front of the restaurant, to the heavy wooden doors, his escape route. He imagined Patty standing in the parking lot, waiting. He felt nothing less than love for her. But this didn't move him from his seat.

Tim and Anna had been served only water. This was rectified a minute later when a tall, dark-haired waiter in sunglasses came from the kitchen. The waiter put in front of them two tall glasses filled with an amber liquid. "Beer?" Tim asked.

"Your father's favorite," the waiter replied. "It's a microbrew called Tears of Fidelity."

Tim recognized a perfect exit cue, but he stayed, downing every drop.

— On his drive to Anna's apartment, Tim repeatedly glanced to his left and right, worried someone he knew would be in the lane next to him. He didn't doubt they'd be able to read his intentions on his face. A criminal is guilty, he knew now, from the crime's inception in thought. Yet Tim believed there was still a chance that, at the next light or the light after next, he would do a U-turn and head home, his reputation and marriage saved.

I'll turn around now, Tim thought. *No, now.*

He tried to call Patty to mind, tried to summon all her admirable qualities. He knew they were numerous. But all he could conjure was Anna under the buckeye tree at the party in high school. He saw her turn up her face. He saw her waiting lips.

His father used to be a map of the forbidden. Where the father ventured, the son knew to retreat.

Patty would leave him. She wasn't depressed and ill like his mother had been. If she found out about his affair by mid-afternoon, she would have his bags packed before dinner.

He drove on.

Anna's apartment complex was called The Heights even though the land it was on was at the lowest elevation in the county. In the parking lot, Tim pulled next to her decade-old Escort. It was red. He thought of traffic lights, stop signs. *My last warning*. He thought of how twenty years could feel like a day.

The Heights catered to medical students and young doctors. A couple of them might have been his customers, but he doubted he would know any of them by name. Besides, the parking lot was empty save his and Anna's cars and a Mustang old enough to have been the first car his father owned. "Welcome," Anna said, grabbing his hand.

He followed Anna into the building's front door and up two flights of stairs. When she opened her apartment door, he was struck by the smells, like spices from everywhere she'd been in person and spirit. "So you cook?" he asked.

"You wish," she said and laughed.

She closed the door with a resounding bang. She didn't go deeper into her apartment but leaned against the sliding closet door on her left. They stood the way they had under the buckeye tree. There was nothing to interrupt them except his conscience.

He thought it might have said, "Go home." But if it spoke at all, it spoke from a long distance and in a language he'd forgotten.

He kissed her. Her kisses were soft. Her kisses were slow. After a minute, Tim pulled back. "What's in this for you?" he asked.

"You mean, besides fulfillment of a groupie's fantasy?"

He looked at her askance.

"Remember, I'm the charter member of the Tim Kovitch Fan Club." Her tone was somewhere between derisive and devoted.

"And still the only member, I'm afraid."

"Didn't we decide one was enough?" she said.

He kissed her again. I have to go, he thought to say. Or had his father's ghost whispered the words in his ear to mock him? His hands moved inside her blouse, touching the flesh around her waist. Everything about her was soft and warm and inviting. "Do you think I'm mourning my father by acting like him?" Tim asked.

"I don't know," Anna said. "If I had to guess, I'd say you wanted to kiss me and never did."

He kissed her again. "I've kissed you. I should be done now."

"Are you ready to leave?" she asked him.

"Yes," he said. He kissed her again.

"You haven't left," she said. "Should I ask you to leave?"

"Yes," he said. In a softer voice, a pleading whimper: "Yes."

But when she opened her mouth, he covered it with his. "I'd rather you killed me," he said.

The problem with the way his father conducted his affairs, Tim had once told Patty, was that he tended to fall in love with the women he was having affairs with, and love made him reckless, made him oblivious to the consequences. I'll be careful, he told himself now, but he could hear his father laughing. No, it was Anna laughing as she grabbed his hand again and guided him deeper into her apartment.

To get to the bedroom, they passed Anna's walk-in kitchen and her living room. In time he would get to know every piece of art on the walls, all of it Anna's, wild splashes of color, like rainbows exploding from volcanoes. He would know everything else in her apartment: the art and photography magazines she stored in cardboard boxes against the far wall; the do-it-yourself bikini wax kits she kept below her bathroom sink; the Sherman High yearbook from her sophomore year (and his senior year) on her bookshelf beside the television. The only object in her apartment he noticed now, however, was the globe on the dresser in her bedroom. It was the size of a basketball, and he curled his palm around the North Pole.

"I've had it since high school," she said.

There, beneath his pinkie, was the Soviet Union, in lurid red. How easy it had been to have such a stark enemy, he thought. We congratulated ourselves on how much we weren't like them. Better dead than red. But what happened after red died? Tim gave the globe a spin.

Their clothes came off. Naked, she was what he feared: beautiful beyond his imagining.

He left the shore. The water was terrifying and tempting. *My God,* he thought, *I'll never find my way back*.

His father wasn't coming to rescue him.

Some time later, with Anna's sleepy head against his naked chest, he thought he could still see the globe spinning. He whispered, "I should go," but they both knew he wasn't going anywhere.

SECURITY

The day before Sonya was to leave for South Africa with her two-year-old son and sixteen-year-old stepdaughter, her husband said he had something important to discuss with her. It concerned Gia, who he knew wouldn't be content to go to bed at eight every night with her half-brother or hang around the house to talk politics until midnight with her great-grandfather.

"She'll want to go into Cape Town with her cousins," Marcus said. "Since I won't be on the trip, I've hired her a bodyguard—a security guard—an armed escort—whatever he's called. He'll come at eight every night and stay on duty until one, which is the latest curfew Poppy would consider. I'm using the best agency in the country—Poppy agrees, by the way—but I want you to have a look at the man they send. Make sure he looks suitable."

Sonya was surprised by Marcus's concern for his daughter, who, for as long as Sonya had known her, slipped in and out of their house like a cat and to whom Marcus paid only rare attention.

"What does suitable look like?" Sonya asked him.

"Make sure he looks like he'll protect her."

"Do you mean make sure he looks strong?"

"Listen," Marcus said, "I don't want this to come out the wrong way, but some agencies, even good agencies, are hiring blacks. Stop it. I know what you're going to say. But someone at the agency might remember Poppy's newspaper columns and his books and decide to punish him."

"By hurting Gia?"

"By sending someone who's unqualified, who won't feel the need to step in if a dangerous situation arises, who might even be a party to such a situation."

There was a pause, and Marcus looked her over. The first time he'd looked her over, his eyes had moved with the deliberateness of an elevator savoring every floor. "Never mind," he said, frowning, his gaze settling on something behind her. "Nothing will happen." He turned to her again and gave her a bright, reassuring smile. This was the familiar Marcus, confident the world would bless him. "Everything will be fine."

— Exactly three minutes after Sonya, Jared, and Gia arrived at Richard's house via car service from Cape Town International Airport, the bodyguard or security specialist (Sonya refused to think of him as an "armed escort" because it conjured an image of a gigolo with a revolver) showed up to introduce himself, a day in advance of the start of his official duties. Damon was, to Sonya's guilty relief, white. His broad chest and bulging arm muscles were a contrast to his diminutive stature. If he was more than two inches taller than Sonya, who was five-five, she would have been surprised. But Marcus hadn't mentioned short stature as a disqualifying trait. Damon, who was from Durban, wore a short-sleeved, button-down white shirt, khakis, and black sunglasses. He showed everyone the pistol strapped to his right shin. He said he'd never had to fire it.

"I hope that doesn't mean you aren't prepared to," said Richard, who, at eighty-four years old, was an imposing man—more than six feet tall, with widow's peeks in his snow white hair. His skin color seemed like a sunset, pink in places, red in others, white across his forehead.

"On the contrary, sir," Damon replied. He removed his sunglasses and to Gia, who, despite having slept during most of the three flights and twenty-two hours of their trip, seemed about to tumble over with fatigue, said, "You'll have the safest vacation possible."

After Damon departed in his red-and-white hatchback with the Armed Response eagles on the hood, Richard gave them a tour of his house, then invited them into the dining room. It had tan walls and three ink drawings of lions in gold frames above the buffet. A black man who looked even older than Richard shuffled from the kitchen to the dining room bearing plates with spaghetti and meat sauce. "His wife's the cook," Richard explained after the man departed, "so keep your criticism of the food to yourself." Sonya caught a glimpse in the kitchen of a freckled, brown-skinned woman in a red kerchief. She reminded Sonya of her high school art teacher, who'd been the first adult aside from her mother to admire her paintings.

"Do they live here?" she asked him.

"In the detached room behind the kitchen," Richard said.

The room hadn't been part of Richard's tour.

"I've forgotten why Marcus couldn't come with you," Richard said.

"Worker discontent," Sonya answered, using Marcus's phrase. "They want a new contract and are threatening to strike." Marcus managed the factory his father owned outside of Sherman, Ohio. The factory manufactured aftermarket crash parts—hoods and doors and fenders. It was one of only two American factories to do so. There were dozens in Taiwan. "He's also exhausted," Sonya added, explaining how he'd overworked himself in the past six months to ensure the factory's compliance with new industry standards. "And it's been hard for him to get a decent night's sleep with Jared waking up at four most mornings."

"I didn't know Marcus needed sleep," Richard said sincerely. "When he visits me, he's like a perpetual motion machine, one which accelerates after midnight." He gave Sonya a warm smile and, nodding toward his great-grandson, who was blond like Marcus, said, "I hope the little rooster doesn't make you an involuntary insomniac during your holiday here."

Although Richard ate with obvious pleasure, Sonya and her two charges were more tired than hungry. By nine thirty, they were asleep in the basement, Gia in one room and Sonya in another, with Jared in the portable crib at the end of her double bed.

Some time later, Sonya awoke in the dark. She thought to call Marcus's name but remembered her husband wasn't with her. She crawled to the end of the bed to check on Jared. In the glow from the blue nightlight, she saw he was sleeping on his back, his blanket wrapped around him like a wasp's nest. She left her bed and tiptoed past Gia's room to the carpeted stairwell. In the first-floor hallway, next to the front door, she stopped in front of a pad of numbers on the wall. If she moved another step, an alarm light would flash in the Cape Town offices of Armed Response and two of Damon's colleagues would be at the door within five minutes.

Richard had explained his security system even before he asked if Sonya or the children needed to use the bathroom. On the keypad, Sonya punched in four numbers. After a soft, mewing sound, she punched them in again. A green light flashed; she was free to walk around the house without a SWAT team being summoned.

There were four rooms on the main floor: the kitchen, the dining room, an office, and a large library whose east wall was a window. Marcus had said if she did nothing more than stand in front of this window, staring at the Twelve Apostles mountain range and the Atlantic Ocean, she would be glad she'd come. Now, however, she could see in the window only her own reflection: her straight black hair melting into her shoulders, her face so white it was as if she'd either seen a ghost or become one.

Sonya drifted from the window to the bookshelves on her left. There were books on British and South African history as well as volumes on South African wildlife, flowers, and trees. In the right corner were the books Richard had written, which, in addition to collections of newspaper columns and volumes on South African politics, included four novels and a slim book of poems.

Sonya reached for *Apartheid Today, Apartheid Tomorrow, Apartheid Forever*. On the back of the dust jacket was a black-and-white photograph, in profile, of Richard from thirty-five years ago. He stood at the apex of a mountain, an ocean below him. His jet-black hair blew in the breeze; a cigarette dangled from his mouth. He looked like an aging but still handsome Hollywood actor.

A voice interrupted her gazing: "You've come fifteen years too late. Even if you agreed with every word I wrote, what difference might you, or anyone, make? The great Mandela would still be smiling from his god's perch in history and South Africa would still be a country of murderers, rapists, thieves, refugees, corrupt incompetents, and, saddest of all, AIDS."

Sonya said, "You surprised me."

"I'm sorry," Richard said. "I should have expected jetlag would leave you restless."

She told him, again, how she'd slept no more than an hour or two on the flight from Atlanta to Cape Town. "I don't know why I'm awake."

"Marcus should have booked you first class. He and his father are captains of industry, for God's sake, even if they're making their money on imitations of the real thing. In the art world, we'd call them forgers." Richard smiled. "Of course, I don't need to lecture you on the art world."

Sonya was a painter—she had been, anyway, before Jared was born. She'd met Marcus at an art show his factory sponsored at the Sherman Art Museum. At the show, Marcus bought five of her paintings. He said he would buy a sixth if she agreed to have dinner with him. Although he was handsome—blue eyes and a child-like, crooked grin—whatever attraction she felt toward him was initially superseded by gratitude. By buying her paintings, he'd bought her the next three months.

"Sit down, please," Richard said, and he gestured toward the couch at the end of the room. She placed his book on the coffee table in front of the couch. Richard sat in an armchair across from her.

"I don't suppose you'd agree with more than 5 percent of what's in it," Richard said, nodding toward his book.

"I don't know," she said. Beginning to feel tired again, Sonya stifled a yawn. "I didn't have a chance to read it. Your novels look interesting."

"They share the concerns of *Apartheid Today,*" he said. "In other words, they're relics of a mind-set that has been, to put it gently, discredited."

Sonya nodded, although she was thinking of Marcus. She wondered if the labor situation at his factory might be resolved soon. (If this happened, Marcus promised he would join them in Cape Town, no matter how short his stay might be.) She wondered if Marcus had had a good night's sleep in their absence, with no wake-up call from the crib. At the same time, she asked herself, *Why isn't he here?*

"You probably think I'm a virulent racist," Richard said, "kin to the white-hood crowd down in Alabama and Mississippi."

"The Klan is everywhere," Sonya said. "I think there's a chapter, or whatever it's called, in Sheridan, which is thirty miles from Sherman." She felt angry, not at Richard, but first at Marcus, who'd convinced her that coming to South Africa with her toddler son and moody stepdaughter would be a rewarding adventure, and then at herself, for believing him.

"There's no disputing how much worse off this country is now than at any time under apartheid—for everyone," Richard said. "With refugees pouring in from all over Africa, and this ignorant government allowing them in, we have entire shantytown metropolises, where the chief industry is crime. And what has this government done about AIDS? Closed its eyes and said, 'If we can't see it, it doesn't exist.'"

Sonya wondered how she might excuse herself. Jared would be up soon; she found looking after him tiring enough when she was rested. "I don't know much about South Africa," she said. "But from what I've read and heard on TV, it's had a relatively smooth transition from white to black control."

"Oh, the transition was smooth all right. Saint Nelson had the world's eyes on him—and the developed world's wallet in his pocket. But with Saint Nelson off the stage, and the developed world's attention turned to terrorism and tsunamis, where is South Africa now? In an era of turmoil, destabilization, impending apocalypse. If you read my book closely"—he again nodded toward it—"you'll see I predicted it. In the tenth chapter, I speculate about what a black-run South African government would—and, especially, would fail to—do."

When Sonya yawned, she worried she might have offended Richard. And there was bite in his voice when he said: "You obviously need more sleep." In a softer tone, he added, "It's too early in the morning for a lecture." He gave her a quick smile, the wrinkles blooming on his face.

"I'd better sleep while I can," Sonya said. But then she heard Jared cry.

— Sonya woke up with a start, disoriented, dry-mouthed. She looked around, and ten seconds passed before she remembered where she was. She grabbed her wristwatch from the side table.

It was eleven fifteen, although she couldn't remember whether she'd set the watch to South African time. She crawled to the end of the bed and peered over the portable crib. Jared was gone.

As panic invaded her heart and riled up every nerve in her body, a memory came to calm her: Richard had volunteered to look after Jared while she caught up on her sleep. She'd imagined a catnap, half an hour, an hour at the most. She threw on a light summer dress and rushed upstairs.

Jared was sitting in the library on a couch next to Richard, who was showing him pictures in *Wild Animals of South Africa*. "Don't worry," Richard said, "I ignored his urgent request to have me read him one of my books. He remains innocent of his great-grandfather's barbaric ways."

What surprised Sonya was how comfortable Jared seemed on the couch, although after seeing her, he immediately rushed to her side.

"And your stepdaughter is in the garden," Richard said, as if Sonya might fail to ask. "Sunbathing." He looked at his watch. "She rose exactly sixteen minutes ago. Her breakfast consisted of a cup of coffee."

"Did Jared eat?" she asked, and Richard recited the menu.

After thanking him, Sonya stared out the window at the radiant January day. To her right, down the mountainside, the Atlantic Ocean was blue and inviting, although Sonya knew its waters were chilling. She turned her gaze to the bookshelf.

"You'll find my chapbook of poems the least detestable of anything I've written," Richard said. "They're mushy sonnets for Irene."

She was about to tell him she was sorry she'd never met his wife when the old black man shuffled in and announced, "Lunch is served."

Although she didn't say so, Sonya was disappointed in the meal, which consisted of chicken, boiled potatoes, peas, and lychees, a fruit Gia described, under her breath, as "frog brains."

In the home of a disgraced apartheid supporter, Sonya expected a sinful sumptuousness to the cuisine.

"Eat up, dear," Richard said, and Sonya, looking up from her plate, was about to reply when she saw he was speaking to Gia. Gia, whose height—she was four inches taller than Sonya—combined with her thinness and lime-sized breasts often gave her the waifish appearance of a twelve-year-old after a mammoth growth spurt, had eaten a bite or two of chicken and a few peas. Jared, meanwhile, had devoured most of what he'd been served.

When the old black man came to clear the table, Richard said, "Thank you, Jonah," and the old man mumbled a reply and disappeared into the kitchen.

"It's time for Jared's nap," Sonya said.

"And mine," Richard said.

Sonya led Jared to the basement bedroom. After she'd changed his diaper, read to him, and put him in his crib, she lay on her bed, thinking she'd rest for ten minutes. She woke an hour later.

Upstairs, Sonya found Richard sitting in an armchair in his library, reading one of his novels. He uncrossed his legs and stood, holding the book in front of him. "I wanted to see if anything I'd ever written might appeal to someone who never knew the old South Africa and whose opinion of it has been influenced by pusillanimous politicians and sanctimonious sissies in the media. But their echoing voices, I fear, would drown in bluster and broadside what they couldn't defeat with reason." He gave her a quick smile, the lines deepest around his eyes. "On a sadder note, I can't find a single paragraph I'm proud of for its fine turn of phrase."

Sonya asked about Gia. Richard gestured outside. "Sunbathing again," he said.

"Is it safe?"

"The courtyard is surrounded by brick walls with electric wire on top. She's safer in my courtyard than anywhere but a nuclear bunker."

"I mean, the sun. Isn't it fierce here?"

Richard paused, as if to assess this new and unexpected enemy. "There are creams. We'll have to buy her some."

It wasn't clear whether Richard had napped, but he seemed refreshed, and presently he proposed a trip to the playground at Mouille Point, a stretch of oceanfront land to the west of his house.

After Jared woke up, they climbed into Richard's 1975 BMW and wove down the mountain, passing house after house on whose gates were attached bold-colored metal signs: Guardian Security, Peaceforce Security, Cosmopolitan Security, Armed Response. There was no beach at Mouille Point, which disappointed Gia, who retired to a bench to look at her fingernails. There was, however, a swing set, a seesaw, a slide. Further down was a putt-putt golf course, a miniature version of the Johannesburg-to-Cape Town Blue Train, and what was billed as "The World's Third Largest Maze," made of tall shrubbery. Jared wanted to ride the Mini Blue Train, and Richard volunteered to go with him. Jared could fit into the tiny compartment easily, but Sonya thought Richard would break his back as he contorted his body to squeeze inside. He sat across from Jared, his head touching the roof of the train car.

The train jerked to a start and headed in the direction of the playground before looping toward the ocean. On its return, it passed through a twenty-foot tunnel. It completed the route a second time before stopping. "Again!" Jared shouted from his seat.

"I don't know if Poppy wants to go again," Sonya said, but Richard said, "I doubt I could get out now if I tried." So Sonya paid ten rand for two more tickets and they rode again.

"Where's Gia?" Richard asked at the completion of the second trip. Sonya gestured behind her.

"Please have her come near us. It's reckless of us to keep her at such a distance."

As Richard and Jared rode the Blue Train a third time, Sonya called Gia over to her. "Oh, please," Gia said after Sonya explained the possible danger. "Like anyone is going to kidnap *me*."

After they'd returned home and eaten dinner, Damon arrived, his casual outfit similar to what he'd worn the day before. Sonya scanned down his pant leg but failed to notice his gun. Gia, who'd sat sullen and uncommunicative at the dinner table before slipping off to her room, emerged from the basement in her evening attire. If Sonya had been her mother, she might have insisted she return to her wardrobe to find actual clothes. Richard said, "Half of a woman's beauty is the mystery of it. I'm afraid you're spoiling the game." If Gia understood or even heard her great-grandfather's words, she didn't acknowledge them.

To Damon, Richard said, "I spoke with her cousins, which is how we're defining their complicated familial relationship, and they said they'd be meeting in Camp's Bay, at the Ice Cream Emporium." Richard smiled. "I hope the meeting place wasn't chosen solely to appeal to my sense of nostalgia."

"They make excellent ice cream," Damon said agreeably.

"Midnight," Richard told Damon. "One in the morning at the absolute latest."

Damon appeared to give an abbreviated bow, like a butler, and Sonya found the gesture so comical she wondered if it was sincere. Damon turned and followed Gia out the door.

"He has a cell phone," Richard said. "I'll be calling it every half hour."

Sonya thought to laugh, but she stopped when she realized Richard was serious.

"Gia's cousins have an armed escort as well," he added.

Sonya excused herself to bathe Jared and put him to bed. When she returned upstairs, Richard was sitting in his armchair, a glass in his hand. "Would you like a drink?" he asked.

She'd given up drinking when she was pregnant. But she decided she could benefit from a buzz. "Thank you," she said. "I'll have what you're having."

Richard rose and poured her a gin and tonic. After only three sips, she could feel her mind begin to lift from her body like a hot air balloon from the earth.

"You've probably wondered why I can't admit I was wrong," Richard said from the armchair, "why I can't accept the verdict, the end of apartheid, the rise of a new South Africa. You probably wonder if I am holding on to my beliefs out of a stubborn and desperate effort to prove I do not deserve to be called one of history's fools."

Richard looked at her, although she wasn't sure he expected a reply. She leaned back on the couch before bending forward to pick up her drink from the coffee table. "Under apartheid," he resumed, "South Africa was clean. It was safe to walk the streets at night. Our facilities and infrastructure, from hospitals to highways, were top of the line. Now, as everything crumbles—literally, in some cases—I must live in a fortress and hire a $3000-a-week bodyguard so my great-granddaughter can spend a few evenings at a disco. Blacks who have any money and any sense also live in their own prisons. And whites and blacks too poor to afford to protect themselves soon enough recognize the price of this so-called liberty."

Sonya finished her drink, stunned by how fast it had disappeared. She wondered if Richard would offer her another. She wondered why Marcus hadn't called. She wondered what Gia was doing and tried to imagine her dancing. But Sonya could only picture her seated, twirling the straw in her Sprite, staring without interest or affection at people on the dance floor or at the gaudy artwork on the walls.

Richard reached for her glass. "Another?"

"Please," she said, hearing the eagerness in her voice.

Richard didn't stand immediately. "Is it a condemnable offense to say that apartheid offered a better life for the majority of

South Africans, black and white—especially if the AIDS epidemic is considered—when the facts clearly demonstrate this? Is it equally condemnable to suggest that a return to such a life, even a modified return to such a life, would be preferable to this march toward chaos and extinction?

"No matter what the country, no matter what the government, there will always be people with power and people without power, people who decide and people who must abide by the decisions, people in a position to be benevolent and people who are dependent on their benevolence. The former group will always be a minority. In South Africa, we merely formalized this essential truth. We gave it a name, we defined its rules, and our honesty of nomenclature, even more than the shortcomings of our system—and I'll admit there were regrettable incidents—inspired the world's outrage."

Sonya remembered how her high school art teacher had once required her to draw a still life, of pears and pomegranates, with her left hand. "It will be like learning another language," her teacher said. "It will teach you to value your own." Sonya didn't know what she meant until the next week, when she painted the same pears and pomegranates, this time with her right hand. How much more precise, detailed, and vibrant this painting was than anything she'd painted before.

What if she'd been forced to live her life left-handed?

"It's unfair to give all the power to a single race," Sonya said.

"But this is precisely the situation we have now!" Richard exclaimed.

"It's a democracy," Sonya countered—weakly, she suspected.

"It's despotism masquerading as democracy. Enlightenment and benevolence have been overthrown in favor of greed, incompetence, and outright criminality. South Africa used to be the jewel of the continent. Now it's only another overpopulated, disease-ridden, crime-infested backwater—poverty's final African conquest."

Sonya thought about the apartment in East Cleveland where she, her mother, and her brother lived after her father died, how several neighboring apartments had been broken into, how in the bedroom she and her mother shared she could hear the high-pitched celebratory squeal of rats as they investigated the garbage left on the curb for pick up the next morning. She thought about the money she didn't have when it came time to pay her junior-year tuition at Ohio Eastern University and the student loans she hadn't applied for because she couldn't imagine ever being able to repay them. She thought about the six years she worked as a waitress before she met Marcus.

In retrospect, her life before Marcus seemed like a perpetual tightrope walk above catastrophe, although she'd managed to keep painting. In light of her recent inactivity, she wondered if she'd painted because of, rather than in spite of, her circumstances.

After a pause, Richard stood, refreshed his drink, and made her another. "Well," he said, handing her her glass. "I think it's time we checked up on Gia."

He stepped out of the room to make the call. When he returned, he said, "They're at a club, something with shark in the name. Our friend Damon is keeping a close eye on her."

Remembering Gia's outfit, Sonya thought, *I bet*.

A few minutes later, after she'd finished her drink and before Richard could settle on another topic, she said goodnight. Richard said he planned to stay up until Gia's return.

— The next afternoon, Marcus called as Sonya was napping. Richard said he hadn't wanted to wake her. Marcus, he said, would call back. When by ten o'clock, he hadn't, she phoned him at home. It was Sunday, three in the afternoon in Sherman, and she was hoping to catch him watching football or strumming his electric guitar. When she heard his cheerful, inviting voice say, "Leave a message at the beep," she remembered him saying a man's voice should always be on the answering machine in order to deter would-be rapists and thieves.

She tried his cell phone, although he often turned it off on weekends, and reached only his voice mail. She left the same skeptical message: "Hello, sweetheart, are you there? Marcus? Marcus, are you there?"

— Their subsequent days in Cape Town followed the pattern of their first full day, at least for Sonya, Jared, and Richard. Jared never tired of the playground or the Blue Train. They'd traveled halfway around the world, yet Jared was most interested in doing what they could have done, with slight variation, at the Sky Lake Mall in Sherman.

For her part, Gia rarely rose before noon, and after lunch, she liked to sunbathe in the courtyard. From a distance, with her height and thinness, Gia was striking, but up close, her face was too narrow (and four unflattering freckles surrounded her nose like corners of a picture frame) and her short black hair seemed too flat, as if it was painted on her scalp.

At meals, Gia answered questions about her previous night's activities with "It was cool," which is about all Sonya had ever heard her say of anything related to her life. She never mentioned her mother, who lived with a boyfriend in Mexico. As far as Sonya knew, Gia never saw or heard from her.

— Over lunch one day, Richard suggested they all go to Duiker Island, on the Indian Ocean side of the Cape, the following morning to see the seals. Gia, however, balked at rising before noon, no matter what they might see. Richard grudgingly agreed to let her stay behind, but insisted she remain in the house until they returned. He also had her memorize the Armed Response phone number.

The next morning, Sonya, Richard, and Jared left the house at eight and were on a ferry in Hout Bay Harbour by nine thirty.

They had good seats, on the port side, and when the ferry neared Duiker Island, which was no more than a collection of rocks, it slowed to allow the fifty or so passengers a view of the seals. There were hundreds of them, some in the water, most lolling on the rocks. Their habitat reeked of feces.

"Who made the stink?" Jared asked, holding his nose.

The ferry moved on, passing a wrecked ship, the U.S. flag painted on the hull, before turning around and giving the ferry's passengers another look at the seals. Sonya wasn't prone to seasickness, but the terrible smell from Duiker Island, combined with the ferry's slow rocking, made her nauseous. At last, the ferry broke free of the island, and Sonya pulled in a few deep, clean breaths to ease her stomach.

A minute later, Richard pointed to something in the water. Sonya saw the shark only as a fin and a dark shadow beneath the surface.

"It's lunchtime," Richard said, "and the seals of Duiker Island are today's special."

"They'd better call Armed Response," Sonya said.

"Who had better?"

"The seals," she said.

There was a silence. "Oh, I see," he said. "You're having a joke."

She was surprised to find him so humorless.

In the middle of the boat was a large map of South Africa, which highlighted the country's beaches and wineries as well as the island prison where Nelson Mandela had lived for more than two decades.

"I assume you think I'm unduly frightened," Richard said, "someone who sees danger everywhere."

Sonya did think Richard was terrified of blacks coming to kill him because of what he'd written. But she couldn't say whether his fear was unrealistic.

"A seal!" Jared said, and he stood on his seat and leaned over the rail. "Look! Look!" he shouted, and Sonya saw it all in a flash: Jared toppling over the rail, the ferry motoring on, her diving into the warm water but too late to save him.

She grabbed him and pulled him on her lap. "Sit down, Jared! You scared me."

"But a seal, mommy. A seal!" he exclaimed, as if he hadn't seen a hundred seals five minutes ago.

Even after the ferry docked, Sonya's heart was thundering against her chest.

On their drive back to Richard's house, Jared played with the straps of his car seat, and Richard talked about other wildlife on the Cape. Sonya looked out the window, at the beautiful houses and their iron gates and barbed wire. She wondered if their owners were like Richard, at once nostalgic and apocalyptic.

Sonya remembered when, having dated Marcus for a year, she'd become convinced he wasn't serious about her. He was eight years older than she was, but despite his important job and the factory he stood to inherit, he seemed as carefree and ungrounded as the boys she'd dated in college.

One night, she left her diaphragm in her medicine cabinet because she was afraid she might be sixty years old and still waiting tables at the Three O'Clock Café, still hoping to have a show of her art in a gallery in Cleveland or Columbus. When she discovered she was pregnant, she was furious at herself, at how she'd allowed her insecurity and fear to make her stupid and rash. She was sure Marcus would insist on an abortion.

But when she told him she was pregnant, his enthusiasm was like fireworks: "We'll get married before the day's over." And as if once having conceived the thought he had to act on it lest it drown in the sweet waters of other distractions and delights, they did marry the same day, at the Sherman Courthouse, with Gia, looking suspicious and bored, standing with them.

Half a mile from Richard's house, an Armed Response car passed them in the oncoming lane. Sonya was about to ask Richard if he'd had a look at the driver, but he was on to another subject and she decided she had imagined Damon behind the wheel.

When they returned to Richard's house, Gia was awake, but she'd obviously risen only recently because she was showering in the basement bathroom. Presently, Richard's two black servants arrived from their room behind the kitchen and noiselessly began to prepare lunch.

When Gia came upstairs to eat, Richard clapped his hands and said, "Good. We all survived the morning."

After lunch, Sonya put Jared in his crib to nap. She fell onto her bed and closed her eyes. She saw seals lounging on their island and lolling in the water around it. She saw the shark swimming out to rupture their world.

Jared woke her with his babbling. After she changed him and brought him upstairs, Richard told her Marcus had called again. "I offered to wake you, but he said he was in a rush. He keeps forgetting about the time change, he said, and so most times when he lifts the phone to call, it's three in the morning here."

"I don't believe him," she muttered. She had a vision of her and Jared on a rowboat, in the middle of a vast sea. For the moment it remained in her mind, the image was so clear she could have painted it.

— The next day, Sonya coaxed Jared out of a visit to the Blue Train with a promise of ice cream. At the Ice Cream Emporium, Jared ate twice what his mother managed and ten times what his half-sister deigned to nibble. Only Richard had a comparable appetite. Afterwards, they walked to the beach at Camp's Bay. Gia lounged on a beach towel, reading Glamour and Elle, while Sonya held Jared's hands as he ran in and out of the cold, crashing waves. Richard watched them all from under a palm tree in a fold-up chair. He looked too elegant to be a Secret Service agent, but he wore the sunglasses—and the tense look—of one.

Back at Richard's house, Sonya called Marcus, first at home, then on his cell phone, then at work, where she reached his assistant, who said she'd leave him a message. "I've left messages," Sonya snapped and hung up.

"I'll get a hold of him for you," Richard said with irritation. "I'll call his father if I have to."

"He'll call back," Sonya replied doubtfully.

Half an hour later, however, Marcus did call. He fired questions at her with his usual enthusiastic impatience: "How's Jared? How's Gia? How's Poppy? How are you holding up? Did you have a look out Poppy's library window? Isn't it beautiful? Have you been in the ocean? It's damn cold, isn't it? Is Gia having fun? Does the bodyguard Poppy hired look rough and tough enough?"

This was his conversational style, the rush of his words an exhilarating ride. When she handed the phone to Richard, she was smiling.

Richard, however, didn't appear as easily thrilled. He spoke to Marcus in a monotone and without anything resembling humor. Only at the end of the conversation did Richard seem to lighten: "Yes, we are having adventurous adventures and seeing wonderful wonders. And, yes, doubtless they would be even more adventurous and wonderful if you were here."

— During the next several days, they ate ice cream and played on the beach. But on the afternoon of their last full day in the country, at Jared's insistence, they returned to Mouille Point. Instead of heading toward the Blue Train, however, Jared veered toward the World's Third Largest Maze. "Ride this ride!" he announced.

The man behind the counter at the maze's entrance looked like he'd made a living playing mad scientists in movies. Sonya was worried his wild white hair, cataract-infected blue eyes, and prison-camp-like gauntness would frighten Jared, but Jared seemed determined to go forward. When the man turned to Richard, he said, "I see an emissary from the old regime."

"May I assume I'm not alone in mourning it?" asked Richard, who didn't wait for the man's reply before questioning him about whether there was more than a single entrance and exit to the maze.

"The only way in is the only way out and vice versa," the man declared.

Richard declined to go in. "I'll stand guard with Gia." But Gia stepped past her great-grandfather. "What the hell," she said, the loudest words she'd spoken during the entire trip.

The maze's ten-foot hedges were haphazardly trimmed, as if by a blind person, and its grass was shin high in places, absent in others. A dozen feet into the maze, the path forked. When Jared and Sonya committed to a direction, Gia chose the other route. From the outside, the maze didn't look large, and Sonya thought its wild-haired proprietor had been exaggerating when he said it would take twenty minutes to navigate. But inside, she had a different view of its complexity.

Sonya followed Jared around the maze's outer edge. At one point, she peered into the hedges and saw, between a screen of leaves, the ocean, crashing relentlessly against the rocks. A moment later, her view of ocean and rocks was obstructed by a muscular white man dressed in a white shirt and khakis. Leaves blocked her view of his face. Damon? she was about to ask, but the man stepped out of her sight. She was glad she hadn't spoken. She was beginning to see Damon, the roving protector, everywhere. She wondered what this said about her.

Because Jared was intent on returning to the same dead ends and the same overgrown garden and splinter-filled bench in the middle of the maze, it took them twenty-five minutes to find their way to the exit. Even so, they beat Gia. Five minutes passed, then ten.

"I think it's time we called her," Richard said. At first, their voices were barely louder than their speaking voices. But soon, they were shouting.

"Maybe she met up with the prince of the labyrinth and they're walking down the wedding aisle as we speak," the maze's proprietor said.

"Were you telling the truth about there being only one exit?" Richard asked, anger and worry in his voice.

"If you follow the paths, there is only one exit," he said. "If you fly like a bird or dig like a worm—or if you crash through the hedges like an animal in heat—there are other exits."

When Richard stepped toward the man, Sonya thought he might hit him. Instead, he said, "Your little jokes are insulting."

"My apologies, my dear man," said the proprietor, fluttering his eyelashes.

Presently, Gia strolled out of the maze like someone being paid to walk with lazy deliberation. Yet Sonya noticed the flush in Gia's cheeks; she noticed two scratches on her neck. She thought Gia might have found herself lost and frustrated; in her growing panic to find the exit, she might have crashed through hedges.

"I couldn't find the way out," Gia said. There was nothing sincere in her tone, and Sonya, contradicting her first impression, now thought Gia had purposely taken so long in order to scare them.

"Well, that was a cruel trick, leaving us worried like that," Richard said. "But the joke's over and no one had a heart attack."

"Yet," added the maze's proprietor.

Richard ignored him, and they walked to the playground to make use of the remaining daylight.

— Because of their early flight the next day, Gia had had to say goodbye to her cousins and her bodyguard the previous night. On their return to Richard's house, however, Gia lobbied her great-grandfather for one more night on the town. With more feeling than Sonya had ever seen her display, she said, "Damon told me he'd be available to work tonight. He said he'd hold open his spot until I talked to you. Please, Poppy. Please?"

"I told Damon and his agency that I would be requiring their services only through last night," Richard said, "and I have absolutely no intention of changing my mind."

After eating a few bites of her dinner, Gia walked down to her bedroom in an angry retreat and didn't return upstairs until morning.

Anxious about the return trip, Sonya didn't eat much more than Gia. After putting Jared down for the night, she walked upstairs to the library, where Richard handed her a gin and tonic. As they sat down, he said, "During your stay with me, I see I haven't persuaded you even a step toward my way of thinking."

Sonya sighed. She was tired, a tiredness different in quality than the exhaustion she'd arrived with. It was a tiredness flamed by worry, an uneasiness whose cause she couldn't pinpoint. "I'm not very political," she told Richard. "If I had been living here during apartheid, I wouldn't have been marching in the streets or getting arrested. I would have been painting seascapes and gardens. So I don't stand on high moral ground. But someone who defends apartheid now, with whatever statistics and stories . . . well, it's insulting to the people who suffered so much."

"Someone will always suffer—it's the human way."

"I agree with you, Richard. But no one should choose to make another person suffer. There's suffering enough without your help."

Richard frowned, almost invisibly. "As you might expect, I have arguments to make in my defense," he said. "But I think it would be best to allow my guest the last word." He smiled, lifted his glass, and drank.

Although Sonya was prepared to go on, she was relieved she wouldn't have to. Beneath her relief she rediscovered her weariness. "I'm sorry, Richard, but I think I need to call it a night. I have a long day ahead of me tomorrow, and it'll seem twice as long if Jared is awake again during the entire trip."

"I understand," he said, rising.

There was an awkward moment in which Sonya didn't know how to leave him. Their custom, a simple "Goodnight," didn't seem sufficient. While she detested his politics, she admired his honesty; he doubtless knew she would never be sympathetic to his views, but he hadn't tried to protect her from them. In this, she found being with him reassuring, like walking a well-known, well-lighted path.

She stepped over to him, hugged him, and gave him a swift kiss on the cheek. It seemed he wanted to say something else, but for the first time since her arrival, he fumbled over words. In the end, he offered her a wave, his right hand trembling.

— Marcus didn't pick Sonya, Gia, and Jared up at the Sherman Airport as he'd promised; Shelly, his assistant, met them instead. Nor was Marcus home when they arrived. It was Friday, six o'clock in the evening, and after putting Jared down for a nap—he'd slept a total of four hours and seventeen minutes on their return trip—Sonya walked around the house, noting, in what struck her as a premonition realized, the missing furniture: the couch from their basement den, the bed from their guestroom. She tried to temper her anxiety and anger by imagining Marcus in the midst of a refurnishing project, but she found herself periodically falling to her knees and crying. Marcus didn't answer his cell phone. Gia, meanwhile, had left the house minutes after their return.

By the time Marcus arrived five hours later, Sonya had had a nap, and although she felt far from rested, she didn't feel like crying anymore. Sonya's first impression of Marcus was how, in his below-average stature as well as in his careful choice of casual clothes, he resembled not his grandfather but Damon.

"What the hell is going on?" she asked.

"I want a divorce," he replied with the good humor of someone ordering an appetizer.

Although she had anticipated these exact words, and even his casual tone, they had the force of a punch. She gathered in a breath. "So there's another woman?"

"She's older than you," he said, as if this might help her understand the situation or assuage her jealousy. "She runs her family's Nissan dealership on Airport Avenue. She's my peer, you could say, someone who knows my business. I think I've finally grown up." He added, "I'm sorry. I'm a terrific asshole."

He agreed with every insult she screamed at him.

When she'd run out of words, her anger giving way to a wave of exhaustion and vertigo, he asked her if Gia could remain at the house. "I'd hate to have to uproot her in the middle of her junior year, when she needs to get serious about college," he said. "It'll be only until the end of the school year, in June." After a pause, and as if in response to a question she hadn't asked but had meant to, he said, "Springtime."

— On the advice of one of her former art professors, whom she called because she didn't know whom else to call, Sonya hired a lawyer, but the lawyer produced bad news: Marcus owned no share in his father's factory. He had only his general manager's salary, which was $45,000 a year, and a one-tenth ownership in a racehorse in New Jersey. It was George and Melinda, Sonya remembered, who had paid for their Caribbean honeymoon and everything else of note.

"You'll receive child support and alimony, of course," the lawyer said. "And since he has vacated the house, I would hope he'll concede all interest in it to you. The mortgage is obviously steep, but . . ."

Sonya's mother, who lived in Arizona, didn't have a job; sometimes Sonya's stepfather didn't either. Her brother lived in Montana and was sporadically employed in the timber industry.

"I will, of course, do all I can to get you every penny the bastard owes you," the lawyer said.

"His father knew he couldn't be trusted," Sonya said as if she'd made this revelation long ago. "If he'd put even a third of the factory in Marcus's name, he knew it would be gone in a paternity suit or divorce."

She thought she would have to leave Sherman. If she didn't, she would find herself waiting tables at the Three O'Clock Café or standing behind the counter at one of the novelty stores downtown. Inevitably, she'd have to serve Marcus or Marcus's lover or both.

She called George because he'd always been nice to her, more so than Melinda, anyway, but even before she'd spoken a dozen words, he cut her off: "At this point, Sonya, it's best to let the lawyers handle the situation."

— In the house, Gia was as reclusive as always. She never ate meals at the same time as Sonya. Instead, she picked at the leftovers in the refrigerator like a mouse.

On occasion, Sonya would hear, pounding from within Gia's room, music that sounded like a scream. Inside her bedroom, Gia could have been shooting heroin or fucking a boy's brains out. But Sonya thought that if she opened the door, she would find Gia doing nothing more than gazing out a window at the troubled world.

Some days, Sonya didn't see or hear Gia at all.

— Three and a half months after Sonya returned from South Africa, she awoke at three in the morning because Jared had cried out from his crib. Although Jared fell back to sleep, Sonya knew she wouldn't be able to. She put a bathrobe on over her nightgown and walked down the stairs to the kitchen, where she poured herself a glass of milk. She looked at the green numbers on the clock on the microwave and added seven hours.

Sonya had thought from time to time of calling Richard, although she didn't know what she hoped to gain by it. Even if he sympathized with her, even if he acknowledged the wrongs Marcus had done her, she doubted he could convince his grandson he was making a mistake, though because Richard had been forthright with her, she would confess to him her willingness to take Marcus back. What she wouldn't admit: She wanted to hold on to her marriage at least long enough for Marcus, or his parents, to pay for her to finish college. She would change her major to something practical, like nursing.

She dialed the strange prefix and the number. The phone rang twice before a voice unfamiliar to her, a deep, African voice, said, "Who is this, please?"

"This is Sonya, Sonya Gordon—Richard's granddaughter, his granddaughter-in-law. I was hoping to speak to him."

"I'm sorry. He died two weeks ago Monday."

"I don't understand," she said.

A pause. "My grandmother said he didn't have the same appetites lately. She said he became like a spider's web, poised to catch whatever sickness might fly toward him. He died of pneumonia."

It was difficult to imagine Richard, who ate and drank with such pleasure, lacking an appetite. But she pictured him as he'd been on her last night in Cape Town, pictured his quivering wave. *What did he want from our talks?* she wondered. *Only to justify his past? Or to repel me so that when we left, he wouldn't feel he was losing anything he hadn't already lost?*

"Did Richard's family—his son and his grandson, my husband, I mean—come to the funeral?"

Sonya knew her question must have seemed strange to the man on the phone, but he answered it politely: "His two nieces came from Cape Town and other relatives came from Johannesburg. But his son didn't come. No one came from the States."

Why? she wanted to ask, although she thought she knew the answer: *Because when Richard learned what Marcus had done to me, he told them—*

Well, she thought, *it isn't impossible.*

Intending to be polite, she asked, "Have you been hired to look after the house until it's sold?"

There was a pause before he said, "I am Jonah and Beauty's grandson. Richard left his house to them, and I am helping them make it theirs."

Jonah and Beauty. The names were, at first, unfamiliar to her. But she recalled an old black man shuffling into Richard's dining room and an old black woman with freckles and a red kerchief lowering dirty plates into water frothing with soapsuds. Jonah and Beauty. In her week and a half in South Africa, she hadn't said more than "Thank you" to either of them.

Did he leave the house to them out of guilt? Or were they the last friends he had?

She asked, "Did you work in Richard's house too?"

The man laughed. "I'm a lawyer in Cape Town. But growing up, I spent many afternoons with my grandparents. I liked Richard very much—until I was old enough to read. And even then, I never hated him."

As if they were sitting across the table from each other, she nodded. She said goodbye, hung up, and burst into tears.

— In the middle of June, a day or two after Gia's school year finished, Sonya pulled open the door of her second-floor bathroom and found Gia standing naked in front of the full-length mirror beside the sink; one of the billowy cotton dresses she'd taken to wearing since the weather had turned warm lay in a pile beside her. Gia glanced at Sonya before turning her gaze back to her reflection. She was cradling, with both hands, her rounded belly, the protrusion incongruous with Gia's small breasts and Popsicle-stick-thin legs. Her face was contorted, as if from disbelief or shame.

Sonya pictured Damon behind the wheel of his Armed Response car, behind the leaves of the World's Third Largest Maze. She knew how far along Gia was—too far to stop it.

"I know who he is," Sonya said, her eyes fixed on Gia's swollen belly. "Have you contacted him?"

"I talked to him once," Gia said, collapsing onto the tile floor. She began to cry, her body shaking, her emotion, in someone usually so withdrawn, shocking to see. "But the next time I called, the agency said he'd quit and had gone back to Durban. He knows my phone number. I keep waiting."

She turned to Sonya, her face damp, red, and full of anguish. "What will happen to me?"

Sonya kneeled beside Gia and placed Gia's hands between her own. Gia dropped her head onto Sonya's shoulder; her body trembled against Sonya's body.

I'll take care of you, Sonya thought to say. She listened to Gia's crying diminish. She listened to the silence. And still, she couldn't say anything. She couldn't lie.

IF LAUGHTER WERE BLOOD, THEY WOULD BE BROTHERS

Paul shows up at Harlem Tropic at ten, his first visit since he was last in Ryeville, in August. Stephanie isn't here. There's a wedding party in the club, which is wood-paneled and smells of oranges, and the bride and groom are dancing in a corner. They're in their late forties, Paul guesses, their dances like the ghosts of more enthusiastic dances. Before long, the band finishes its set with a drum-dominated version of a James Taylor song. The lead singer screeches the words like someone in distress.

Paul finds a booth across the dance floor from the club's main entrance and orders a Heineken. The wall to his left holds a framed print of Van Gogh's "Sunflowers" and a painting, probably by a local artist, of a pair of naked lovers sitting side by side in bed, their lower bodies covered by silver-white sheets, their hair dissolving into different visions of twilight. Paul is thirty-six, but he'll be thirty-seven before the dorm at Georgia Southern College is painted, its rooms scraped like the inside of a pumpkin, then covered with the same gray primer and paint he's been using since he first came to Ryeville twelve summers ago with a crew of two, which included Shelly, his then fiancée. Shelly owns a seafood restaurant in Monroe, Louisiana, now. She's married. Two children. Three?

Although Paul has regular, if small-time, painting work back home in Sherman, Ohio, his main employment during the school year is as an adjunct communications instructor at Ohio Eastern University. He's grown tired of this job, too. After ten years' worth of excuses to postpone his next move, he's been fantasizing about living far from Sherman. He's conjuring West Coast cities—Los Angeles, Portland, Seattle—when Stephanie walks in.

Despite the four years he's known her, he has never become entirely accustomed to her handicap. He watches her as she moves, her real leg, her right one, supporting her prosthesis by alternately bending and straightening, and her waist moving in abrupt contortions. He has never seen her fall; still, even now, he often half holds his breath in anticipation. Stephanie doesn't seem to see him, and she stops to talk to a couple at a table beside the stage. They offer her a seat, and she sits with her profile toward Paul. Her face is thin, with freckles like miniature pennies. Her shoulder-length hair is the same copper color as her freckles. Paul thinks he should approach her, ask her to dance, as he did the first time, four years ago. (He saw her dancing with Tim, the nightclub's septuagenarian owner, so he knew what she was capable of.) In recent years, however, he has always allowed her to spot him across the club, to come over to his table to resume the relationship they always suspend when he returns to Ohio after the painting is done. He waits, but for the longest time, she doesn't see him, doesn't come over.

— Alex shoots foul shots underhanded, too tired to shoot them the regular way. He has worked ten hours, rolling oil primer, and his arms ache. His cheeks still bear the impressions of the mask he's worn, and his chin, where its rubbery bottom has rubbed all day, is dotted with pimples. He's twenty years old, but his face makes him look fifteen. He's sure girls would find him repellent now. Of course, he doesn't see many girls here, except at meals. He eats at the back of the cafeteria, at the "painters' table," in his paint-flecked white shirt and pants. The summer students living in the dorm eat at one long table at the front of the cafeteria. He's had his eye on one girl; she has long black hair and tan skin that glistens like it's oiled. He held the door open for her once as she left the dorm. When she said thank you, he noticed her accent. He imagines she's from a tropical island where people speak Spanish, have midday siestas, and eat dinner at midnight.

The basketball court is directly outside the dorm room where he'll be living for the next six weeks. For the rest of the summer, he's lined up his regular summer job at the playground near his house in Sherman; he won't do much more than sit in a shed and hand out volleyballs and basketballs and, for the little kids, plastic shovels and rakes for the sandbox. The job doesn't pay much, barely half the nine-dollars-an-hour he's making painting, but when work ends at six, he'll be free to do whatever he wants. Watch TV. Play his guitar. Go downtown or to the Sky Lake Mall, where he might run into Ashley. He hasn't spoken to her in a year, since the summer they graduated from high school. He wants to know what she thinks of him. He wants to know if, maybe, she still loves him.

— Paul might have invited his crew, composed of five Ohio Eastern students, to join him tonight, but after four days on the job, he has decided he likes only one of them, Alex, who is staying in the room next to his. Last night after the two of them played basketball and returned to their rooms, Alex strummed his guitar softly and sang the kind of melancholy songs Paul sings when no one is listening.

Five minutes pass, and Stephanie doesn't notice him. Or is she ignoring him?

Paul feels stiff—this is his excuse—so he stands and stretches. Although he is of average height, if he reached up, he could touch the ceiling, where the ends of several blue and green streamers, remainders of a party, are taped. Now Stephanie waves, and he waves back, aware, before long, of how large his smile is. She leaves her table and approaches him, her body rocking as if in the face of a strong wind. She stumbles once, her good leg kicking out to balance her prosthesis, and he opens his arms to catch her. But, as always, she doesn't need his help. "Hello there," she says, her tone at once casual and distant. "I thought you'd be here last week."

"No," he says. "We're right on time." Their first conversation of the summer is always awkward. "I'm glad to see you. Sit down."

He pulls out a chair for her before motioning to the waitress. She is young and black, with too much lipstick and too bubbly a personality for a club like Harlem Tropic—or the sophisticated and cool club Paul imagines it wants to be. He orders Stephanie a mineral water and himself another Heineken. "How's your job?" he asks. She works at her parents' flower shop in downtown Ryeville.

"The same. How's your painting?"

"So far, so gray."

The band has returned from its break, and the lead singer, the annoying, long-haired boy who butchered the James Taylor song, is speaking, his voice rasping off the walls. The waitress returns with their drinks before rushing off. Stephanie spins her Perrier bottle on the table.

"Are you still living in the same apartment?" Paul asks as the music explodes.

She nods. Her apartment, a two-bedroom above the flower shop, features Guatemalan wall hangings, a ceiling fan, and an air-conditioning unit jammed like dentures into the mouth of the street-side window. Like Paul, Stephanie likes gourmet coffee, and each year she has a new favorite. In the mornings, her apartment awakes with coffee smells. "Still painting?" he asks.

"Some," she says.

"Good," Paul says. "I could use you."

It's an old joke between them. This time, a quick smile is all she gives him.

If she has stayed on schedule, Stephanie is nearly done with her M.F.A. in visual arts at Georgia Southern. She likes to paint scenes of what she calls Main Street of the Mind, average settings—the outside of a post office, the inside of a diner—with a single strange or unsettling detail. On one of the tables in her diner scene, for instance, there is, between a mustard bottle and a saltshaker, a severed finger.

Paul doesn't like talking above the music, whose volume strips his words of nuance. He'll save intimate talk for later, after they've gone to her apartment and had a glass of wine; he'll save it for after they've made love. "Dance?" he asks.

She hesitates. He wonders what could be wrong. Her leg? "All right," she says.

He takes her hand, and she leans into him, by accident or with intention, he isn't sure. It doesn't matter. He is here again, with her.

— Alex shoots a foul shot. It clangs off the rim. He's been playing for an hour, and his arms feel as loose and rubbery as octopus arms.

"You were doing better underhanded," someone says. Startled, Alex turns to find William, the dorm's security guard, behind him.

"You were watching me?" asks Alex, embarrassed.

William, wearing his canary yellow uniform, steps into the light of the basketball court. "I have my eye on everything," he says. "That's what they pay me to do around here. You made six of eight at one point, then you missed three in a row."

William is several inches shorter than Alex and significantly wider. With his oval, hairless face, he looks like a baby. Two nights ago, William bragged of his job duties to Alex and Paul, and after he waddled off, Paul whispered, "He thinks he's the head of the fucking FBI. I'd like to see someone stick a gun his face and time how fast the shit hits his underwear." Paul was Alex's communications instructor in the fall, and he had seemed removed, aloof. So Alex was surprised and amused by his sardonic comment. He hopes he and Paul will have more moments like this.

Alex shoots again, the ball nicking the back of the rim before settling into the net.

"Better," William says.

At his house—his mother's house—Alex has a basketball hoop in the driveway, and when Ashley came to see him, they would sometimes play H-O-R-S-E. Most of the time, she sat on the wooden steps leading to his back door, and they would talk as he shot baskets past dusk. Now he moves around the court, shooting from various angles before stepping beyond the three-point stripe and making three in a row. He played on an intramural team his freshman year at Ohio Eastern, and his teammates frequently urged him to try out for the JV squad.

Alex retrieves the ball and dribbles out to the top of the key, spins, and jumps. His shot drops into the bottom of the net. William gives him a long, appreciative whistle. *JV team hell,* Alex thinks. *I'm good enough to play varsity.*

— Paul holds Stephanie around the waist. She doesn't dance as close to him as she did by the end of last summer, when he could feel her hard nipples against his chest. He's disappointed, although he knows he shouldn't be. Even an old relationship like theirs needs warming after dormant months. He's had no lover in the ten-and-a-half months since he last saw her, a span that included an embarrassing attempt at seducing one of his ex-students. Twice, he ran into her at the Book and Brew. After the second time, as they walked outside into a windblown evening, he asked her if she'd like a "night cap" at his apartment. She laughed nervously and veered down a side street, her breath shooting above her like smoke from a locomotive going somewhere fast.

Paul set the rules with Stephanie after their first summer together. They wouldn't call or write each other because after spending five nights a week together during the summer, their communication would seem insufficient. If they hadn't found other lovers by the beginning of the following summer, they could resume where they'd left off. Paul expected Stephanie to break the rules and was disappointed when she never did. Several times this past winter, he was tempted to call her. But he didn't want her to think he felt lonely.

The song finishes. Stephanie nods toward their table, and he follows her. After the waitress comes with more beer and mineral water, Paul proposes a toast to the renewal of their friendship, and they click bottles. But if she smiles, it happens too fast for him to see.

Paul wants to ask her if he looks older. The way his hair is receding in his temples, he fears, makes it seem like a pair of double-lane roads are being paved to his crown. "Did you come here a lot over the winter?" he asks.

Stephanie shakes her head. "I was in England until about a month ago."

"Yeah? Doing what?"

"Studying photography with C. P. Reeves. Have you heard of him?"

Paul admits his ignorance.

"I guess you could say he's famous in the photography world. Anyway, I'd hit a plateau with my painting, and I'd always been interested in photography, so I thought I'd try something different."

"Sounds great."

Stephanie says nothing, so Paul says, "I haven't been to England since my junior year abroad. I'd like to go back. Maybe . . ." He is about to say, "Maybe with you," but instead he says, "someday."

He *would* like to go places with Stephanie, he decides, although not England, where he'd been homesick and just plain sick during most of his six-month stay. But he would like to go to Spain with her. Or Boulder. Or Los Angeles. He recalls thinking something similar at the end of his stay in Ryeville last summer. Maybe this year he'll invite her to travel with him somewhere.

— Alex's dorm room at Georgia Southern is the last on the hallway, and tonight, as he lies in bed, he doesn't like the tall, slim dresser in the corner, which seems like a sentinel, watching him, or the broad windows in front of the bed whose Venetian blinds don't close completely. Alex doesn't think it's healthy to live in a dorm room at the same time he's painting dorm rooms; everything reminds him of work. Today he painted the small, narrow closets in what seemed like a hundred rooms, his mask pressing up into his face, making his temples throb. He felt trapped, confined. Unlike his fellow painters, he didn't bring a tape player or radio, so there was nothing to listen to but his thoughts, which, as the hours dragged, became increasingly dark and unpleasant. He should have anticipated this; there had been precedent. In the weeks after his thirteenth birthday, when his father lost his job as assistant sports editor of the downsizing *Sherman Advocate and Post* and his parents began a loud, angry prelude to divorce, he spent afternoons and evenings after school in his tiny bedroom, staring for hours at his pimples in a handheld mirror, plucking them, pinching them. He suspected he was making himself look even more hideous, but he couldn't stop. Seeing what he had made of his face, his mother talked about having him speak with the young minister at the church she recently had joined, but when he made the basketball team at school, he didn't spend so much time in his room or in front of a mirror.

Today, stuck in closets, cramped and exhausted and lonely, he found he couldn't think about anything but Ashley. Each of the closets was a womb, and once he conceived of this metaphor, he couldn't shake it. The closets reminded him of his guilt and cruelty.

Last summer, he was working his playground job when Ashley came up to him, pale and agitated. She'd been crying, he could tell. She'd cried in his presence only once before, when she was worried he liked Heather Chimes. She insisted he walk with her to a part of the playground where there were no children, and as if they could hear her anyway, she whispered. He had to ask her to repeat herself—a boy was screaming in the sandbox.

"How do you know?" he said after he'd understood her.

"I bought one of those kits today. It was positive."

"I don't think those kits are very reliable." He had no idea if this was true.

"I haven't, you know, had my period in two months."

With this he couldn't argue.

"What are we going to do?" she asked.

It bothered him, the way she said "we."

She started to cry, although she was fighting it. He reached to hold her—he knew this was the right thing to do—but he saw how pitiful she was, and began to despise her.

"What are we going to do?" she asked again.

"It's all right," he said, patting her on the back the way a parent would. He wanted her to stop crying and tell him it was no big deal.

After a while, she said, "We could get married."

"Yeah," he said, and he realized he sounded sarcastic. In a softer voice, he said, "Except we're going to different colleges. I mean, we'll still see each other, like I said we would, but we're going to be a few hours apart."

"What are you saying?" she asked.

They both knew what he was saying.

Alex sits up in bed. It is almost one. He won't get nearly the eight hours of sleep he needs. He spreads two flaps of the Venetian blinds and stares out at the basketball court. The light is on, but the court is empty. He thinks about playing his guitar, but he doesn't know if Paul has returned. Last night, Alex played for an hour, and in the morning he remembered how thin the walls were. At breakfast he waited for Paul to make a joke about his guitar-playing, but Paul only asked him, with apparent sincerity, if he played in a band.

Ashley loved his guitar-playing; he thought all girls would. But Heather Chimes listened to only one song he played before turning on the radio next to his bed and moving the dial from the university's alternative station to 100.5, "The Bliss."

Alex falls back onto his bed and closes his eyes again. What he sees now is what awaits him in the morning: an endless series of closets, which he'll inhabit like someone imprisoned, rolling his slim jim on their ceilings and sides, his eyes aching from the potent sting of the primer, his thoughts always returning to Ashley.

Forget about her, he tells himself, opening his eyes. *Forget about her, don't worry about her, it's all right.*

He drove Ashley to Cleveland so she could have the abortion. Afterwards, he drove her home. Before she stepped out of his car and walked to the door of the townhouse she shared with her mother and stepfather, he said, "It'll be the same as it was. You'll see." He kissed her on the cheek.

He isn't sure now whether he waited for her to reach the door before he drove off.

For three days, he didn't return her phone calls. When Ashley came to see him at the playground on the fourth day, he greeted her with the exaggerated friendliness he displayed toward his mother's dates. She said she hated him.

He told himself that what had happened between them wasn't his fault. But it was he, seeking the greater pleasure, who had lied about not having a condom, though one was in his pocket. It was he who had promised Ashley he would pull out. And even if he doesn't believe that abortion is the equivalent of murder, that he isn't, as the young minister at his mother's church put it in the only sermon Alex had heard him preach, "an accomplice to the slaughter of the innocent," he sometimes feels queasy and guilty when he sees a baby. Now he is sure his worst sin was the way he treated Ashley, someone he loved but had pushed aside expecting to find someone sexier, funnier, cooler.

He conjures Heather Chimes, her large breasts and fat lips, and for the purpose of his self-pleasure, whose release he hopes will help him sleep, her image suffices. But, afterwards, he thinks about how little he and Heather had to say to each other, how, as if they had made an agreement, he stopped calling her and she stopped calling him. He thinks about how often over the last year he expected—hoped—to pick up the ringing phone and hear Ashley's quiet voice.

— Paul and Stephanie stand beside her Mercedes, a hand-me-down from her parents, in Harlem Tropic's parking lot. The band has finished, and there are only a few stragglers inside. He thinks of her in bed. He isn't turned on, as some men might be, by her missing leg. Their first night together, she whispered, "You can touch me wherever you like. And if you don't want to touch me someplace, I understand." Her lines felt rehearsed, and later he thought she must have practiced them for him. He has never asked her about her past lovers. Sometimes he thinks he might be the only lover she's ever had.

"Well," Paul says. He kicks a rock and listens to a car's roar from the nearby road. "You know, I've been thinking. I've had really good times with you in the summers, and, I don't know, I figured if we could have a good summer again, maybe, well, maybe we could do something more at the end of it."

He forces a smile. She smiles back, although carefully. Something slips into his heart, a knife-blade of fear.

She takes his hand. Her gesture makes him feel both soothed and suspicious. "You know I've wanted something more with you ever since the first summer, four years ago," she says.

"I know," Paul says. He stares past her, looks at her again. "I remember how hard it was to say goodbye that first summer."

"It wasn't hard for you," Stephanie says. "It was never hard for you."

Yes, it was, he wants to say. I just didn't know it. "I was wrong," he says instead, and he squeezes her hand. "I was wrong to think it could be only a summer relationship."

"You *insisted* it couldn't be anything else."

"I was wrong," he repeats. "All right?" He tries to smile. Her face gives him no confidence. He wonders if he should apologize. But for what? For keeping his options open while employing her as the fallback plan, renewable every summer? He wants to move quickly past their awkwardness and into the usual place where they're laughing with each other, where he's stroking her copper-colored hair. "Do you think we could maybe, you know, start again, have a new summer, and . . . and . . . I'll promise a little more at the end?"

Stephanie looks away. "When I was in England this winter, I met someone. He's C. P. Reeves's assistant. He's a wonderful photographer."

"All right," Paul replies flatly.

"I'm engaged to him."

Paul spreads her fingers on his palm and gazes at them in the streetlight seeping through the leaves of the live oak. "You don't have a ring."

"I didn't wear it tonight." Her voice has gone matter-of-fact, almost stern.

"On my account?"

She doesn't answer.

"You're joking, right?" he says.

Quickly, she pulls her hand from his. The coolness she has shown him all night appears again in her face.

"Well, congratulations," Paul says. His tone is off. Aiming for indifference, he reveals surprise, hurt, alarm. He tries to recover with sarcasm: "I'm very happy for you." He finds himself backpedaling, as if having been pushed.

"Paul?" she says.

"Congratulations," he says again. He wonders if he's drunk. He stops moving. He closes his eyes and opens them, prepared to feel dizzy. But the world defies him; it holds steady.

"I was going to tell you right off," she says. "I should have."

"But instead you decided to preface your remarks with false hope—drinks, dances."

"False hope?" she asks.

I didn't know, he wants to say. *I didn't know I wanted this so much*. "Goodnight," he says instead, and he waves at her with the manufactured enthusiasm of someone sitting atop a parade float. He knows there is something cowardly, infantile even, in his retreat, but he can't help himself. He walks swiftly toward his Subaru, which in each of its twelve years has sunk closer to the ground. He opens the door, drops into his seat, and turns the ignition. When he pulls out of the space, Stephanie is already in her car. He has miscalculated, as usual, how quickly she can move.

— It's almost three in the morning, and Alex can't sleep. Goddamn, he can't sleep. Four more hours and he'll have to be up for breakfast, eating soggy dorm pancakes and drinking diluted orange juice. And then he'll be in those closets, cramped and dark with hot fumes. He'll suffocate.

Jacking off to memories of Heather Chimes distracted him for a few minutes. But afterwards, he could think only about Ashley and the abortion and the awful way he spoke to her—like a game-show host to a contestant—and the hot, small closets he will have to paint in a few hours.

A few days before he headed off to Ryeville, he saw Ashley in the Sky Lake Mall, looking into the window of Victoria's Secret. She was evidently back in Sherman for the summer. She was as slim and pretty as always, her black hair cut pageboy style. She was with a guy so tall he must have been a basketball player. Alex followed them at a distance of twenty feet past Gap Kids and Dollar General until they reached the Sky Lake Cineplex, where they held hands in the ticket line. He was desperate to know what movie they were going to see, as if this might explain something. But they slipped inside the theater complex and he turned away.

Alex throws off his sheet and climbs out of bed. He puts on his shorts and T-shirt and walks out of his room and down the hall. He flings open the front door of the dorm and steps outside. The night is cool, thank God.

He isn't alone. Standing to his left, leaning against the building, his yellow uniform aglow in the floodlights, is William.

"Howdy," William says.

"Hey."

"It's a sweet night," William says. He holds up his hands and seems to fondle the air. "Too bad we're not sharing it with a couple of babes."

The way William pronounces "babes" makes them seem theoretical, like undiscovered planets.

"Life without women," William says. He takes a step toward Alex and grins. "In a life without women, a man's forced to be his own everything."

Alex knows what William is referring to: William saw him through the blinds of his dorm-room window, saw what he did to sleep, to forget Ashley. He wants to punch him, punish the smirk on his round, fat face. "What do you know?" Alex says.

"Sorry?"

Alex steps toward him. "What the hell do you know about women?"

William frowns and steps back outside the glow of the lights. He suddenly looks older, much older than Alex thought. "Nothing," William says. He shrugs and looks away. "I was married once. For six months." He tries to laugh.

Alex's anger is gone. "What happened?"

He shrugs again. "She didn't like me working nights, I guess." He gives another false laugh. "Hell, I don't know what happened. She ran off with another guy."

There is a squeal of tires, and Paul's Subaru pulls into the dorm's parking lot. Paul steps out, shuts the door absently behind him, and walks toward them. His hair stands on end in an unintentional Mohawk.

"You didn't close the door tight," William says. "The light's on."

Paul turns around, steps back to his car and karate-kicks the door closed.

"You've had a few drinks," William says.

Paul pats William on the shoulder and winks at Alex. "You can't get anything past this guy."

"That's what they pay me for," William says.

"You earn every damn cent. Hell yes, I've been drinking. I went to Harlem Tropic and met up with my old friend Stephanie. She told me her good news: She's engaged! So I decided to celebrate at A.J.'s. And now I'm feeling better. Is that all right with the Gestapo?"

"Sure," William says. Alex isn't convinced William knows what the Gestapo is.

"I'm feeling so good that I've decided to take the day off tomorrow," Paul says. "The whole crew gets the day off. What do you think, Alex?"

Alex wonders if it is the beer speaking now, and if tomorrow morning Paul will be rapping at his door, telling him he better get up before he misses breakfast. He says, "I think we could probably use it."

"You bet," Paul says. "We could all use it."

— At ten the next morning, Paul and his crew drive to Tupelo Springs, an hour outside of Ryeville in the Florida panhandle. Paul says he'll pay admission and buy lunch—he'll even buy them souvenirs, but only if they're tacky enough. Alex wonders if Paul slept at all the previous night. After he returned to his room, Alex fell asleep immediately, exhaustion trumping his desperate thoughts.

Now his four fellow painters are sunbathing on the sand, but Alex has seen the dark-haired girl from the dormitory, reading under a palm tree on the lawn above the beach area. Her two friends are asleep on towels beside her. He stands above the girl until she looks up from her book. "Hey," he says.

She shields her eyes, even though his shadow is cast over her. "Hi."

"You're from Matthews Hall at Georgia Southern."

"Yeah. How do you . . . oh. Are you one of the . . ."

"Painters, yeah."

"I didn't recognize you."

"I'm not in uniform. It's our day off."

"Oh."

"We've worked only four days, but I'm beat. I never work this hard in college."

"You go to college?"

When Alex nods, she smiles, her teeth a spectacular white. "I thought you were, you know . . ."

"A professional painter?"

"Yeah."

He laughs. "I'm a biology major. I'm hoping to get into med school." It's a line he has used before, with some success. He hasn't decided on a major. He would like to be a doctor but wonders if he has the stomach for it.

Alex notices the Frisbee resting against the tree behind her. He points to it. "Do you play?"

"Sometimes."

"Wanna toss it around a little?"

She puts her book on her towel. "All right."

She grabs the Frisbee, and they walk up the lawn toward the large, white manor house. Tupelo Springs used to be a private residence before it was opened to the public two decades before. The beach area is crowded, but the lawn is nearly empty. It feels good to walk without shoes in the cut grass. They stop a dozen yards below the manor house, and Alex breathes the warm air.

— The far side of the lake is more than a hundred yards away. Live oaks line the distant shore. In the water beneath them, alligators lurk. This, anyway, is what the warnings posted on the beach say, although Paul can't see a single alligator from where he's standing, at the back of the high-dive platform. But thinking of Stephanie, he looks again.

When she was fifteen, Stephanie came here after dark with a group of her high school friends. The park was closed, and they cut the lights on their cars and drove in. They left their cars under cover of bushes and tiptoed to the water. There were eight of them, five girls and three boys. After half an hour, everyone quit swimming, and the couples sneaked off. Stephanie knew she'd be stuck talking with Dolly, the other girl without a boyfriend, so she went back into the water. She saw a spot of moonlight beyond the buoys; she wanted to lie on her back in the middle of it.

Stephanie was a few strokes from the moonlight when she felt the alligator's mouth close over her leg. She heard the crack of her thighbone, like lightning splitting a tree. She swam frantically toward shore, but she wasn't moving fast, and soon she lost consciousness. If it hadn't been for Dolly, who was a strong swimmer and as brave as a Green Beret, she would have drowned.

This was fifteen years ago, and a lot of alligators have been shot here since. The public area is supposedly safe, yet swimmers are still prohibited from going beyond the buoys, and people diving off the platform are supposed to swim straight for the ladder.

Paul moves toward the front of the platform. At the edge stand half a dozen boys, none older than twelve, daring each other to jump. On seeing him, the boys spread. One whispers, "He'll do it." Paul walks like a zombie to the edge of the concrete platform, curls his toes against it, and hurls his body toward the water.

— "Sweet!" Alex says, catching the girl's throw after a short run.

She stands twenty yards from him, her hands raised to catch his return throw. "Don't make me run a mile this time," she says with a smile.

He holds the Frisbee against his thigh. "I bet I can guess your accent," he says.

She drops her hands to her side. "You're an expert? Go ahead."

"Puerto Rican," he says.

She shakes her head.

"Cuban?"

She again shakes her head.

He has exhausted his list of islands with Spanish-speaking inhabitants.

"Jamaican?" he ventures hopelessly.

She laughs. "Close. I'm from Patterson, New Jersey."

Later, he will think he should have said, "That was my fourth guess." But he is troubled by how wrong he was about her, his tropical island replaced by a turnpike.

He hears a shout from the beach area. Dozens of people are standing on the shoreline, pointing at the water. Alex sees a figure swimming across the lake. "What idiot would do that?" says the girl, now standing at his side. "There are alligators over there."

It is impossible to see the swimmer's face, but Alex thinks he recognizes the red swimsuit, visible in the clear water. "Jesus. I think I know him." He jogs toward the beach; the girl follows. When they reach the place where lawn gives way to sand, the swimmer is more than halfway across the water, stroking steadily toward the trees on the opposite shore.

"There are alligators over there," the girl repeats.

"I know him!" Alex exclaims. "He's my boss!"

"He's crazy," the girl says.

Paul is nearing the far shore, and Alex and the girl stare in silence until he reaches it. "Made it," Alex says as Paul climbs out of the water, his pale skin a contrast to the deep shadows of the trees. Paul raises his fists in triumph, a gesture some of the men on shore imitate.

"Crazy," the girl says.

"Yeah," Alex says, tapping the Frisbee against his knuckles. A breeze blows off the water and he smells the girl's lotion, like coconut. Ashley wore similar suntan lotion, he recalls. Or maybe she didn't. But he remembers her at Sky Lake the summer after their junior year in high school. They used to sail to Murderers' Cove, where in the twenties and thirties gangsters supposedly did their dirty work, and they would find a dry place on shore to throw down their beach towels. They would lie down, and she would remove her bikini top to sunbathe, and they would talk until dinnertime. Anytime he wanted, he could kiss her.

He pictures her holding hands in front of the Cineplex with the basketball player. *JV team hell. I'm good enough to play varsity.* Another of his delusions.

If he could only start again. He drops the Frisbee.

"Where are you going?" the girl asks him.

— Paul squats behind a live oak, his feet sinking so far into the mud that he's worried he won't be able to pull them free before the police or some other authority arrive, as they inevitably will. He holds his head in his hands. At the same time, he is laughing, laughing the way a person laughs at something unpleasant, laughs during wakes and funerals.

He hears a sound, something rising out of the water, and he stops laughing. Have the alligators come to devour him after all? He hears his name called by a familiar voice short of breath. It's Alex, who must be on the near shore, in front of the live oak.

Alex is laughing in the mad way Paul has just laughed. If laughter were blood, they would be brothers.

Paul doesn't call Alex's name immediately, although he will soon enough so they can assess their options, plot their escape or surrender. First, however, he'll upbraid Alex for his impulsiveness, the folly of following him across the water without the excuse of wanting to assuage one loss by risking another. He thinks of Stephanie, thinks, again, of her missing leg. He thought it would always keep her where she was, waiting for him at the beginning of every summer, happy at his return.

At the end of last summer, he even told her he loved her missing leg. He'd never told her he loved her.

AFTERWARDS

— 1 —

After Ray Perkins made his statement, Peter Marcello asked two of the three officers in the room to leave. The remaining officer—six months from retirement, with bad hearing—sat in the corner, shaking dandruff onto his blue-uniformed shoulders. Marcello gestured toward Perkins's handcuffs. "I'd take them off if I could."

"I know."

Perkins was pale, slim, about five-foot, ten. He had reddish-brown hair. The three-day growth on his face was more red than brown. Marcello was the same height as Perkins, although he was heavier by forty pounds—maybe fifty, the way Perkins looked now, like a Dust Bowl farmer.

"Ray . . . Ray."

Marcello could have repeated his friend's name the entire afternoon. It was the only word he could articulate in response to what Perkins had done. But if he could have spoken other words—in condemnation, in sad wonder—he knew they wouldn't change what had happened. "Your visions, Ray. You said you interpret your visions as prophecy."

"The way an ordinary man can see across a room, I can see across years."

"How long have you had this ability?"

"It started two months ago."

"And two weeks ago," Marcello said, "you had a nightmare vision of your family."

"I'd had visions of my family before. But my visions were never as clear as what I saw two weeks ago."

Marcello had heard all of this. He wanted to see if Perkins, whom he'd known since elementary school but hadn't seen or spoken to in the last six months, would say something different now, with no one writing anything down. Marcello lifted the dark blue coffee cup from his desk. There was nothing inside. "Let's take each member of your family," he said. "Jason first."

"You know Jason's situation," Perkins said, his voice a monotone, his eyes expressionless. "Life was hard enough for him under ideal circumstances."

"I know what a struggle it's been for you and Lucille."

"It wasn't our struggle as much as his."

"If it was too much to bear, Ray, there are public facilities in Columbus for kids like Jason. The government pays for it—or at least for some of it."

"It was never too much."

Marcello knew he shouldn't be proposing solutions to extinct problems. If he talked Perkins out of his madness, it wouldn't bring Perkins's family back to life. Perkins looked like he hadn't slept in months. The blue half moons under his eyes were as deep as reservoirs. "And Lucille?" Marcello asked. "And little Beatrice? They didn't have cerebral palsy. You don't think they might have survived, and maybe been happy sometimes, in this apocalyptic world you see coming?"

Perkins shook his head slowly. "You weren't listening to what I told you, Sheriff."

"You don't have to call me Sheriff. No one's taking notes anymore, Ray. I guess I'm having trouble believing this happened. Shit, Ray, I didn't even know you owned a gun. I would have bet you'd be the last man in the world to do what you did."

"But you don't see what I see."

"Let me be sure I understand. What you see is the world oil supply slowing to a trickle in a few years. The United States and China sending their armies into the Middle East and eviscerating each other over what's left. Washington, New York, Chicago, and most of the West Coast obliterated in a nuclear exchange with the Chinese. Mass starvation. What have I missed?"

"The devastating effects of global warming. The brutal competition over diminishing food supplies. Winter floods and summer droughts. A five-fold increase in tornadoes and hurricanes. Heat like we've never experienced."

If Marcello turned around and opened the blinds in his office, he could watch the traffic on Main Street. Gasoline prices were the highest they'd ever been, but traffic was as robust as ever. Marcello had never thought about the end of oil. And until recently, he'd dismissed global warming as a myth invented by solar-energy entrepreneurs and tree-hugging fanatics. His doomsday scenarios involved Consuela, his wife. He feared she would discover one of his marital indiscretions and, as he was sleeping, castrate him.

"There will be one landowner in Sherman," Perkins continued, "and he'll have a three-hundred man militia to oversee his slaves, made up of Sherman's surviving population."

"And Lucille?"

"A slave—raped repeatedly. But with her diabetes, she wouldn't live long. There won't be any insulin."

"And little Beatrice?"

"There will be no inhalers. With her asthma, she would have suffocated, and I could only have watched her choke on air."

What had seemed implausible, a fantastic lie, to Marcello only three hours ago when he'd heard the news about what his friend had done now felt like an old story, something he'd known for years. "When is this all supposed to happen?" Marcello asked.

"Slowly, then quickly. But as a species, we're past the tipping point. There's no going back to innocence."

Depending on the jury, Marcello thought Perkins might be found not guilty by reason of insanity. But after today, he doubted Perkins would ever be sane again. "Why did you do it now, Ray? Why not next year? Why not after the first nuclear exchange between us and the Chinese?" Marcello knew the answer, and he knew to hear it again would break his heart a second time, but he waited, listening.

"Because their suffering hadn't started yet. Because they could at least die happy."

— Marcello could have left his office anytime after Perkins had been escorted from it on his way to the Central Jail, but hoping to find an antidote to the horrors of the day, he lingered in front of his computer, playing chess against an Internet program called Deep Indigo. After two draws and a loss, he trolled the back alleys of the Internet until he found a Brazilian porn site, where he lingered without pleasure.

By the time Marcello left his office, it was ten after eight. Although he thought about stopping at Don's Underground for a beer, he didn't feel like hearing hell from Consuela later. Besides, he might drink too much, and if he drank too much, he was likely to do or say something to Consuela he'd regret. She, in turn, would threaten to leave him and take Nicholas with her.

At the end of such an abysmal day, he wanted no arguments with his wife. After he'd eaten, after Nicholas had gone to bed, he and Consuela could sit in the living room, the lights low, the TV off, and he could tell her about Ray Perkins. *I thought I knew Ray better than I knew myself. Now I don't know either of us.*

He tried to remember the last time he'd seen Perkins before today. For the past six months, he'd been spending whatever time he could find outside of work with Patty Kovitch, whose husband owned the Book and Brew. But Patty had ended their affair a week ago.

Pulling into his driveway, Marcello noticed no light on in his house. When he stepped inside, he called Consuela. There was no answer, and although he knew there would be no answer, he called again and a third time. He turned on the living room lights, the kitchen lights. He grabbed a Corona from the refrigerator and returned to the living room and sat in his police-blue easy chair. He clicked on the television. He told himself they'd be home any minute. They'd gone to Food World. They'd gone to Silver's Gym, where Nicholas was sitting on the floor with a pile of Lego pieces as Consuela rode a stationary bike. They'd gone to the Arctic Emporium for ice cream.

As Marcello finished his beer, he had another idea: Thinking he was being merciful, thinking he was saving them from the hell to come, Perkins had come to his house and killed them. Marcello stood with a start and flew around his house, clicking on lights, shouting Consuela's name, Nicholas's name. He finished in Nicholas's room. He didn't recognize it. Everything save the bed and dresser, it seemed, was gone. Even the sheets were gone. Out of habit, Marcello turned to look at himself in the mirror above his son's dresser. Expecting to see his olive skin, his shaved head, he saw only a blank blue wall.

Marcello heard a knock on his front door. *She's back,* he thought. *She couldn't leave me, no matter what she thinks I've done to her*. He felt a grin cover his face. At the same time, he felt a familiar surge of anger. *How dare she screw with my emotions*. He clenched his fists.

By the time he opened the door, however, he knew not to expect Consuela and Nicholas. The door was unlocked. Consuela would have walked right in.

"Is it true about Ray?" asked Billy Lyons, who'd gone to high school with Marcello and Perkins. Billy, whose adolescent chunkiness had evolved into obesity, lived across the street. He worked under his father at the Ohio Eastern University Parking Authority.

Marcello said, "Uh-huh."

"Jesus," Billy said, shaking his head. "Did I ever tell you I slept with Lucille once, after her freshman year at Ohio Eastern?"

A few seconds passed before Marcello understood to whom Billy was referring.

"It was after she and Ray broke up and before they got back together." Billy spoke breathlessly, as if he'd waited all evening to tell the story. "I saw her at the Book and Brew and we had a good, long talk, a heart-to-heart sort of talk. It was late when we left, and on the sidewalk outside, she turned to me and said, 'I know you've always wanted to fuck me, and tonight I'm lonely enough to give you the chance.' I was still living with my parents, so I sneaked her into our basement, and—"

"She's dead, Billy. For Christ's sake, have some respect."

Billy held up his hand, as if to deflect Marcello's criticism. "What I was leading up to is whether Lucille might have been, you know, shopping her services elsewhere. Maybe Ray walked in on her with someone."

"You mean if Lucille screwed you she'd screw anyone?"

Marcello waited for Billy to grimace, to draw back, to call him an asshole. But Marcello's insult hadn't altered Billy's expression. "It's a theory," Billy said.

"I'll see what I can uncover," Marcello said. And without saying goodnight, he closed the door on him.

Marcello knew his wife and son had gone to Ecuador. A month ago, Consuela had bought them tickets to travel to Quito in December; she must have changed the dates. *Clever fucking bitch*. He looked at his watch. They were probably somewhere over the Caribbean now.

The only time he'd been to Consuela's native country was six months after Nicholas was born. He hadn't wanted to go. He couldn't stand airplane flights of more than two hours; his nerves threatened to overwhelm him. But resigning himself to the trip and comforting himself with his plan to drink himself to near oblivion before stepping on the plane, he bought *The Rough Guide to Ecuador* and underlined all the places he wanted to go.

He spent all ten days of the trip at his in-laws' house, a one-story, wooden structure with four bedrooms and a kitchen with a dirt floor. He didn't remember how to get to his in-laws' house from the Quito airport, but he knew their address, so any cab could take him. He felt certain—almost certain, anyway—that he could woo Consuela back. He'd done it before.

But how long after she returned to Sherman would he, during one of their arguments, slap her face or pin her against a wall? How long after would he start up with another woman? In Perkins's madness he saw his own.

He knew Nicholas would be fine in Ecuador, where the weather was better and the food was fresher. Even if Consuela's parents were poor, they could offer Nicholas everything a boy of five needed.

His in-laws had no phone, so to communicate with Consuela and Nicholas he would need to write. He sat down at his desk and held a pen against a sheet of paper. When half an hour passed and he'd written nothing, he grabbed a blue marker from the drawer. He drew a house with a lone stick figure at the window. "Mr. Lonely" he titled it before throwing it away.

— In the Central Jail, Ray Perkins didn't sleep for more than an hour or two a night, if he slept at all, but this had been true for months. His prophetic visions, however, had deserted him.

The lawyer assigned to him, Nick Papadakis, had done his undergraduate work at Yale. But wanting a legal career in his hometown, he'd attended law school at Ohio Eastern. After Papadakis had met with Perkins twice, he introduced him to Dr. Eileen Maples, the head of the psychiatry department at Ohio Eastern's medical school. She asked him the same questions the police, Marcello, and Papadakis had asked him. She asked him a question they hadn't asked: "Why didn't you also kill yourself?"

"Because I wanted to be prepared to save everyone else."

"How would you have saved them?"

"The same way I saved my family."

— 2 —

Perkins's trial was held in front of a three-judge panel at the Sherman County Common Pleas Court. Months had passed, but Perkins appeared no closer to sanity. His face looked ashen, and gray had invaded his hair. He seemed capable of only a single expression: a slack, lifeless stare.

In front of the three judges, Papadakis set out to prove that Perkins had been insane when he'd murdered his family. His first witness, Randolph Hicks, the manager of Perkins's car washes, said his boss, in the couple of months before "the incident," would do nothing more at work than sit at his desk, his head in his hands. Once, Hicks testified, he caught Perkins lying on his office floor, which wasn't carpeted. "When I asked if something was wrong, he said he was only tired and could I help him up. I lifted him to his feet, but ten minutes later, he was back on the floor." Two weeks before the murders, Hicks testified, his boss stopped coming in to work at all.

Wendy Messersmith, a friend of both Perkins and his wife, also described his deteriorating state of mind. "I think we all thought he would snap out of it," she said. "I think we all thought he would soon go back to being the kind, loving family man he was."

Dr. Maples testified about Perkins's mental health. So did Jason Fuller, a psychiatrist from the Central Ohio Psychiatric Institute. Both gave Perkins the same diagnosis: major depression with psychosis. "Ray Perkins didn't kill his family," Dr. Fuller testified, "his illness did."

The prosecutor, Bradley Oswald Jr., contended that Perkins was tired of his home life and wanted to be free of his family. "With his business about to go bankrupt, he knew he wouldn't be able to afford a divorce, alimony, and child support, so he murdered them all," said Oswald, whose black pin-striped suit gave him the look of an undertaker. "Now he's hiding behind a shield of apocalyptic nonsense. The defense calls it depression. I call it evil."

Oswald called to the stand a single witness, Rudolph "Mack" Macon, the seventy-eight-year-old man who lived across the street from Perkins. He had snow-white hair and liver spots like little islands on his cheeks. In the weeks before the murders, Macon testified, Perkins would often stand on his front porch, staring into the distance "as if he was planning to travel a long, long way from the tired old place he was living."

On cross-examination, Macon acknowledged that Perkins could have been daydreaming. "But after what happened," he said, "you have to figure he was planning some kind of escape."

Papadakis told the judges that Perkins's business—his four Ray of Light car washes—had lost money in each of the past three years. "Given the number of his employees, given his large payroll and the benefits he offered, he couldn't have made money without downsizing or, as other car washes in town have done, automating," Papadakis said. "But Ray Perkins refused to cast off the hard-working men and women he employed. In the end, he was fairer to his employees than he was to himself. Ray Perkins and his family were living off savings he'd squirreled away for his daughter's college education and for whatever care his son might require as an adult.

"There is no evidence—zero—that Ray Perkins wanted to be rid of his family because he had a lover he wanted to be with or because he was attracted to a different, more appealing life," he said. "There is no evidence—zero—that he wanted to cash in on life insurance policies he may have taken out on his wife and children. There were no such policies. There is, finally, no evidence that Ray Perkins ever felt anything but deep love for his wife and children.

"There is only evidence that Ray Perkins was, and is, deeply, deeply disturbed. As his mind slipped into the abyss, he became haunted by waking dreams and visions—dreams and visions more real than anything in his life, more real than his children's smiles and his wife's laughter. This is the truth and the tragedy."

Marcello attended as much of the four-day trial as he could. He made no effort to disguise the outcome he favored. Before the trial began every morning, he walked to the defense table and whispered words of encouragement to his friend, even as Perkins sat stone-faced and silent.

Perkins's mother, who lived in North Dakota with her second husband, sat behind her son. She was sixty-eight years old and, as her deceased daughter-in-law had, suffered from diabetes, a disease to which she'd lost two toes and most of the sight in her left eye. Every so often during the trial, she shook her head vigorously, although in response to what, Marcello wasn't always sure.

Perkins's mother-in-law, who was as short and thin, and doubtless as quiet and withdrawn, as her daughter, sat behind the prosecutor's table, knitting a blue scarf. Each day, she seemed to sink lower in her seat until, from where he was sitting, Marcello couldn't see her at all.

When the judges announced their decision, Marcello pumped his fists and hurried to the defense's table. But if he had been anticipating even a glimpse of the Ray Perkins he used to have towel fights with in the locker room after high-school wrestling practice, he was disappointed. Perkins looked like he'd been condemned to die. Perhaps, Marcello thought, he would have preferred this.

— Before she left Sherman, Perkins's mother asked Marcello if he could look into selling or declaring bankruptcy on her son's business. She had hired a realtor to sell his house. "I've known you for a long time, Peter," she said, holding his right elbow with both of her hands. "And of course I trust you'll do what's best."

Marcello supposed he was an ideal candidate to oversee the liquidation of Ray of Light. If polls conducted by the *Sherman Advocate and Post* could be trusted, he would soon be unemployed. He was running third in the race for sheriff, an elected position since the late 1960s, which is also when the job title was changed from the authoritarian-sounding Chief of Police. The story accompanying the poll blamed Marcello's low poll numbers on his "rabid" support of Perkins, although it also mentioned "irregularities" in his personal life.

In order to understand Perkins's financial situation, Marcello needed contracts, bills, and other documents in Perkins's house. Two days after a Civil Commitment hearing ruled that Perkins should be committed to the Central Ohio Psychiatric Institute, Marcello drove to 1202 Cinnamon Street. If Perkins's house had been in Los Angeles or New York City, and the story of what he'd done to his family was half as well-publicized as it had been in Sherman, it would have been ransacked five times over. Marcello thought it might have been better if it had been. There was something disturbing about how undisturbed the house was.

After he had found what he needed in Perkins's first-floor office, he walked up the worn carpeted stairs and stood outside the master bedroom. He remembered what he'd seen inside it on the day of the murders. He also remembered what Perkins had told him about that day. At dawn, Perkins had carried his two sleeping children into the master bedroom, where he and Lucille had a king-sized bed.

"They were all asleep," Perkins said, closing his eyes. He held them closed for a long time. "No," said Perkins, his impassive face, for the briefest moment, contorted into something recognizable as grief or horror, "I can't be sure."

—3—

Perkins's room at the Central Ohio Psychiatric Institute (old name: Center State Hospital for the Criminally Insane) was as wide as his single bed was long. In length, it extended only a few feet past the end of his bed. A toilet was in the far left corner.

He was a threat to kill himself. But there was nothing to kill himself with. He wore paper gowns without strings. His pillow had no pillowcase. His window was made of shatter-proof glass. All the same, he wasn't left unwatched for more than five minutes, even when he was on the toilet.

He ate his meals in a square room with schizophrenics who spoke to Jesus and depressives who had chopped off their fingers and had carried revolvers into post offices. There were four large tables in the room, and he always tried to find a seat at the end of one. He never spoke unless spoken to.

"The visions, the waking dreams—whatever we're calling them—were a product of your brain chemistry," Dr. Fuller said at the beginning of all their private sessions, held twice a week in a narrow room with a single window, its glass stained pink. "The chemical disturbances in your brain forced you into a state of psychosis. You had no control. It was as if they'd enslaved you."

The first few times, Perkins said, "But I could see what was to come as clearly as I can see you in front of me now." Thereafter, he said, "You're the doctor" and "You're the expert."

Dr. Fuller had a full head of white hair, and his blue eyes had a radiance Perkins would first think of as sinister, later as serene. At each session, Dr. Fuller asked him, "Do you want to kill yourself?"

Sometimes Perkins said, "Yes." Sometimes Perkins said, "I don't care." Sometimes Perkins said, "Nothing matters."

Perkins dutifully swallowed every antidepressant and antipsychotic he was given. There were occasions when his hands began to shake uncontrollably and his arms flapped like wings. At these times, he couldn't keep still, and he paced back and forth between the door and window in his room like a wild animal. One night he woke up thinking he was having a heart attack. He hoped it was true. But ten minutes later, his heart returned to its normal, dull beat.

The drugs were causing his restlessness, Dr. Fuller told him. He implemented another drug regimen.

One morning, two and a half months after Perkins had entered the institute, Dr. Fuller said, "I recommend you have electro-convulsive therapy." Dr. Fuller explained how ECT differed from old-time electroshock treatment. "What do you think?" he asked Perkins.

"I don't care."

"I think it might help."

Perkins stared at him blankly. "All right."

— In the fifty-eight steps between the back door to his office and the front door to Don's Underground, Marcello's stomach began to ache like it had been punched. Inside Don's Underground, he bypassed his usual seat at the bar and headed straight to the bathroom, where he commandeered a stall. He was still in the stall five minutes later when two men entered the bathroom and stood side by side at the pair of urinals. From a crack in the stall door, Marcello could see the backs of their black shoes.

"Hopplemeister will beat his sorry ass," one of the men said.

"Hopplemeister's a criminal. If people don't know it now, they'll know it soon."

"So you think the English professor will win?"

"Lewis? It looks like it. There's no doubt Marcello's finished. No one can stand him. His wife obviously couldn't—his first wife, too, for that matter. And the way he came to Ray Perkins's trial every day—he's supposed to be the chief law enforcement officer in town and he's working behind the scenes to let a murdering sicko go free? So who's looking after the interests of Ray Perkins's dead wife and kids?"

"Prick."

To be defamed is one thing. To be defamed by two men in the act of relieving themselves is another. This, anyway, is how Marcello would begin the story in the months and years afterwards, always with a smile. In memory, he didn't even pull up his underwear and pants before he jumped from his stall, teeth clenched, fists raised. When his right fist connected with the jaw of the man at the nearest urinal, a man he thought he knew or should know, he concluded, *I've killed my chances at reelection.* And knowing this, he felt freer to throw the second punch and even freer to throw the third.

Meanwhile, the other man raced out of the bathroom and returned a minute later with the bearded bartender and a busboy who looked all of fifteen years old. By this point, Marcello was straddling his adversary, his penis—or so he would tell the story—less than a foot from the man's face. Had the men intervened even two seconds later, Marcello would recount, they would have caught him pissing up the nose of Steven Erickson, who, as the coach of the Ohio Eastern University football team, was one of the most well-known men in Sherman.

In the anger management class he would take as part of his plea-bargain, Marcello was required to record, in chronological order, all the violent acts he had committed from his boyhood forward. He doubted they would fill half a page. But his hand cramped after five-and-a-half pages, and he'd reached only his twenty-first year.

— Ten minutes after he'd woken up from a nap following his first electro-convulsive treatment, Perkins stumbled into the dining hall at lunch and, over a hamburger the size of a Frisbee, said to the fifteen people at the table, "I want to see my wife and children again." He sobbed.

One of the nurses, a man named Jack, whose long, black hair parted like raven's wings down his back, said Perkins must be feeling the effects of the anesthetic. "After my hernia operation," Jack said, "I cried like the world had disappeared."

"Mine has," Perkins said. He dropped his head into his hands. He cried until Jack led him out of the dining room and into a narrow room with a table and two soft-cushioned chairs.

"Let's talk," Jack said.

"I miss them," Perkins said. "I miss them, and I'm their murderer."

He cried himself into exhaustion, and Jack led him to his room. He didn't wake up until dinnertime, the longest sleep he'd had in months. He wasn't awake more than a minute before he remembered where he was and what he'd done. He fell onto the floor and sobbed. He didn't know the nurse on duty had come into his room until he felt her hand on his back.

Unlike Perkins's bedroom, the dining hall had ample windows, with a view, across a single-lane road, of an apple orchard. After his third ECT treatment, the windows revealed a spectacular late fall day; the leaves of the apple trees seemed ablaze with orange light. But because of the shatter-proof windows, there was no sound accompanying the view. He wanted the unbreakable windows broken. He wanted to let in the birds' music and the smell of apples, although he knew he didn't deserve them.

After his seventh ECT treatment, he wanted to bring flowers to the graves of his wife and children. He wanted to whisper to them, his lips against the grass: "I'm sorry. I miss you. I love you. Will you ever forgive me?" Again, he cried, and again Jack led him to the private room to talk.

Perkins had five more ECT treatments, although they felt superfluous. He literally had been shocked back to who he'd once been.

In addition to keeping Perkins on an antidepressant, Dr. Fuller prescribed him lithium, which he hoped would keep Perkins's mood stable. Somberly, Dr. Fuller told him, "It's likely you'll be on one form of drug therapy or another for the rest of your life."

Perkins said, "I wouldn't have expected otherwise."

In his improved condition, Perkins was allowed visitation privileges. Visits occurred in the eight-foot-by-ten-foot family room, which had a mud-colored carpet and a black-and-white TV with rabbit ears. Marcello came twice a week, bringing upbeat news about Ray of Light, which he'd renamed Day of Light. Under his management, the business was again solvent.

Marcello also told Perkins about his election defeat. Hoplemeister had been caught growing two acres of marijuana on land he owned in southern Ohio, and Lewis, the retired Ohio Eastern professor, had won. Marcello finished second, six percentage points behind Lewis. The *Advocate and Post* had called Marcello's showing a moral victory. "To have the word 'moral' used in conjunction with anything I do," Marcello said, "is the real moral victory."

— Leaving the family room with Perkins one afternoon, Marcello bumped into a tall, attractive woman whose red hair corkscrewed around her cheeks and neck. She was being led down the hallway by Jack, whose hair had grown longer and more lustrous. They looked like a fairytale couple on their way to a happy ending. "You'll have to introduce me to her," Marcello whispered to Perkins.

"My pleasure," Perkins said. "But first a little background: She threw her two-year-old twins out of a window on the twelfth floor of a building in Columbus. God told her to do it."

"Everybody has a bad day."

"For some of us, our bad day is hell itself."

The same night, Marcello wrote to Consuela, "I am sure I made your life hell sometimes. I am sure there are times you thought I might even kill you. I am sick now to think how scared you must have been."

— Even though he saw Marcello often, Perkins wrote him long letters. He needed to write to someone about what he was feeling, what he was remembering. He described scenes he remembered from his life with Lucille, Jason, and Beatrice. He wrote about how, as he slid deeper into madness, his inability to protect them against his business's failure and impending bankruptcy had mutated into an inability to protect them against the coming apocalypse. He wrote him about how deeply he hated his weakness in the face of what he'd believed was coming, and how, beneath what he was conscious of, he must have hated Lucille and the children for how, with their tattered clothes and illnesses and hunger, they would have exposed his impotence. He had bought the pistol after he was robbed at gunpoint at a gas station he'd managed in his mid-twenties. On several occasions, he'd thought of getting rid of it. But he'd always stopped himself, thinking he might need it one day.

For every three letters Perkins wrote, Marcello wrote one in return, which Perkins thought was more than a fair exchange given the free time each had in his day. In one of his letters, Marcello wrote, "Write to me about your life before Lucille and the kids, before you even knew Lucille. Write to me about high school. Tell me what I missed because I was drunk or stoned or too busy chasing ass to notice."

At first, it felt like a betrayal to write about his life before Lucille. Perkins wrote about it modestly, as if it had meant nothing to him, as if his true life started when he met Lucille during his freshman year at Ohio Eastern. Before long, however, he found himself writing with feeling about who he'd been, what he'd done, the hopes he'd had.

This was before he knew about the end of oil, before he knew about global warming and melting polar ice caps. This was before he owned Ray of Light and before Ray of Light began to fail. This was before anything of consequence was at stake. If he rediscovered his foolishness and self-centeredness, he also found again, in himself at seventeen and eighteen and nineteen, a willingness to trust his adaptability, to welcome surprise and uncertainty.

— 4 —

After two years and a month in the Central Ohio Psychiatric Institute, Perkins was allowed to visit his hometown under the supervision of two hospital employees, young men with crew cuts who sat in the backseat of Marcello's Accord and scanned the passing trees, flush with new leaves, like Secret Service agents. Marcello had warned Perkins about the changes he had made to the business; he had replaced the employees at three of the four car washes with automated equipment and had bought an additional pair of car washes on Route 40.

"We'll have a grand tour of our empire," Marcello said now.

"Could we limit ourselves to only one of the car washes?" Perkins asked softly. "I feel like I've been living on the moon. I need a gradual reentry to our atmosphere."

Marcello came into town by the most direct route, barreling over what townies called Heartbreak Hill and racing across the Main Street Bridge. A right turn and two blocks later, they pulled into the downtown Day of Light, the lone car wash to have retained its employees. Marcello parked in one of the self-wash stalls. The other four self-wash stalls, plus three of the four full-service stalls, were occupied. Marcello and Perkins stepped out of the car, the two men from the hospital following. Perkins glanced at his wrist, but he wasn't wearing a watch. "I don't think I've ever seen it so crowded here," he said.

"Let alone at ten o'clock on a Wednesday morning," Marcello added.

Perkins followed Marcello up the wooden steps of the car wash's main building. Marcello had removed the gray carpeting and had stained the wood chestnut brown. The second floor, which was above the full-service stalls, had four rooms, the first of which was Perkins's office. Aside from removing pictures of Perkins's wife and children, Marcello had left the office as it was the day Perkins last saw it.

Standing in front of his old desk, Perkins looked uncomfortable and anxious, as if he was trespassing and might soon be discovered. "Let's move on," Marcello said.

The other rooms used to house replacement parts for the car washes, but Marcello had returned most of these to the manufacturers. Inside the second room was a ministore, stocked with various automobile products such as windshield wiper fluid and car deodorizers. The next room was what Marcello had dubbed the "Nostalgia Arcade"; it featured games from the early 1980s, including Pac-Man, Centipede, Defender, and a pair of pinball machines, one with a *Star Wars* theme, the other with *E.T.* The arcade figured prominently in all of Marcello's advertising and was turning twice the profit he'd anticipated.

"So now we're in the entertainment business?" Perkins asked, and even if what his friend had said came unaccompanied by a smile, Marcello detected lightness in his voice.

In the last room were four heat lamps and a single massage table. The room smelled of eucalyptus. In a chair in the corner sat Debbie Patterson, slim and red-haired, her face like a face Picasso might have drawn as he moved toward the cubist. It was her irregular face, more than anything else about her, that made her desirable in Marcello's eyes, although his single overture to her had been quietly but firmly rebuffed.

Perkins looked at him, this time with what, if Marcello were to interpret it generously, might be called a minuscule grin. "You're kidding, right?"

"Our massage room is the most productive component of our business," Marcello said. "By the time they've finished their fifteen-minute massages, our clients don't care what their cars look like. They'd be happy to drive away on tricycles."

In a whisper, Perkins asked, "Do I still own any of this?"

"All of it," Marcello said.

Perkins smiled, something brilliant and brief. But as if in condemnation of his pleasure, he was soon wearing a look of abject despair. Marcello looked behind him at the two men from the hospital. He was worried they would cut Perkins's outing short. "Come on," Marcello said, leading Perkins to the massage table. "Take off your shirt." Marcello helped Perkins up onto the table.

"I don't deserve this," Perkins said as Debbie put a CD in the player. The music sounded like someone sweeping snow with a harp.

"No one deserves this," Marcello said. "But we're here, and what are we supposed to do?"

— In the Central Ohio Psychiatric Institute, Perkins had begun reading again, something he hadn't done regularly since he dropped out of college. He read paperbacks he pulled from the bookshelf in the lounge area and religious and philosophical texts given to him by Father Ryan Hannah, a regular visitor to the institute.

One morning, strolling on the caged-in patch of grass connected to the hospital's east wing, Perkins waved to Father Hannah as the priest, whose curly brown hair made him seem younger than fifty-five, walked toward the institute's main entrance. Father Hannah came up to Perkins, and they talked through the iron fence. They talked about the weather. They talked about the books Perkins had read. Eventually, as usual, their talk turned to Perkins's family.

Father Hannah didn't pretend to have a balm to heal Perkins's conscience. "But I know this to be true," he said, his hands on the bars as close to Perkins's hands as they could be without touching them. "They would not want their deaths avenged;

they would know there is no one upon whom to enact vengeance. They lost their lives because of madness, not malice. Your true self, suppressed by the disease, loved them as much on the day they died as on any other day. To give up on your life, or to condemn yourself to solitude and suffering, does not honor them. It does the opposite."

—5—

"Buckle up," Marcello told Perkins as he eased his new car, a white Prius, down the Central Ohio Psychiatric Institute's long, black driveway. "I don't want to hit a deer and have you flying out the windshield into eternity—at least not before you've had a beer."

"I thought you didn't drink anymore." Perkins spoke softly, his body pressed against the passenger door, his hand tight around the grab handle. He had been anticipating this day with both dread and longing, but dread was prevailing now.

"I don't," Marcello said. "I'll have my customary apple juice and seltzer mix. We'll toast your return."

Perkins's brow was damp; his hands were wet. It was early spring, and the air coming into the car from the open windows felt like it had first passed over a fire. Perkins thought of global warming, of the earth cooking in a greenhouse its human inhabitants had built out of car exhaust and coal-fired power plants. But three years after he'd foreseen doomsday, the apocalypse no longer seemed so imminent or awesome. "It's generous of you to let me stay in your house," he told Marcello. "You've been so kind."

"Christ, Ray, you sound like you're talking to a stranger," Marcello said. "If we're taking measure here, well, I'm sure I'm the one who's in debt to you. Remember: You turned a small-town politician whose career had hit a donkey's rear end into your business partner, a veritable captain of industry. And now I have my reputation back. I didn't tell you, but last week the *Advocate and Post* named me one of Sherman's twenty notable citizens thanks to the money I—*we*—donated to good old Sherman High."

Five minutes later, they saw the first sign to Sherman. "I've been meaning to ask you something," Marcello said.

"Okay."

"If you don't want to answer it, I understand and we'll forget about it. But when you had your visions of the future . . . well . . . where did I fit in?"

"You?"

"You probably didn't even think of me."

"No, I did." Perkins looked out the window. The oak and maple trees, the grass and the weeds—they were all a rich green. But it was easy enough, even now, to picture them brown and wilted. The sky was blue but he could picture it the coal-gray of nuclear winter. "You were the security chief for Sherman's only landowner."

"I see," Marcello said. "And who was Sherman's only landowner?"

"Steven Erickson."

"Coach Erickson?" Marcello asked. "Coach Erickson who . . ."

"One and the same."

Marcello laughed—briefly. "I'm sorry," he said.

"For what?"

"For laughing."

"Don't apologize. The ancient Greek playwrights expected the audience to laugh during their tragedies. Father Hannah said the playwrights knew it wasn't out of disrespect but sometimes out of relief—relief their own lives weren't so awful—and sometimes because it was the only fitting way to respond to the absurd ways we suffer."

There was a pause, and Marcello said, "Listen: You might want to start thinking of yourself as something besides a Greek tragic hero."

"Like what?" Perkins said.

"I don't know," Marcello said. "Like a French waiter or an Italian barber. Or—I've got it—an American car wash impresario."

—6—

Marcello checks his friend's pill bottles to make sure he's taking his medications. If Marcello is around at ten at night, which he usually is, he listens to Perkins's nighttime ablutions from outside the second-floor bathroom, listens to him fill his plastic cup with water, pop the pills into his mouth, drink.

Having Perkins in his son's old room reminds Marcello of Nicholas's absence. Some weeks, he calls Nicholas every evening—Nicholas's grandparents have, at last, had a phone installed in their house. They talk a lot about soccer—Nicholas plays on his elementary-school team—and whatever festival is coming up. Sometimes Marcello calls Nicholas just to say goodnight. When he's lucky, which is the case more frequently lately, Consuela will come onto the line after their son goes off to bed.

— Even after only a month of working by Perkins's side, Marcello knows why his friend was going broke. It wasn't because of bad luck. It wasn't because his competition outworked him. It wasn't even because of his depression, the severest manifestation of which followed, rather than preceded, his financial woes. Ray Perkins was going broke because he was and is a dreadful businessman.

Perkins, Marcello has discovered, is reluctant to make even small changes to the business. His idea of radical innovation is replacing conventional light bulbs with fluorescents. In Perkins's utopia, the world would be a museum.

Fortunately, Perkins now recognizes his deficiencies, and when, four months after his release from the Central Ohio Psychiatric Institute, Perkins and Marcello open a Cello diner on the southern end of the Ohio Eastern campus, he quickly installs himself as a breakfast cook. Most of the restaurant's customers are students, transients who know nothing about Perkins's past.

— Marcello's conversations with Consuela grow warmer, eventually inhabiting a zone of intimacy he hasn't experienced with any woman. During one call, he apologizes again for all the times he hurt her. "I wish I could undo everything hurtful I've done to you and Nicholas," he says.

"You can't," she says. "But it is in your power never to hurt us again."

"I know," he says. "And I won't. I promise. And I promise my promise means something this time." They both laugh at this, but he senses she believes him, and this brings him such relief he begins to cry. She comforts him with endearments in Spanish, sweet words he hasn't heard in years.

One night, he tells Consuela, "I think I'm ready to come see Nicholas. If you approve." There is a pause before he adds, "And I think—I know—I'm ready to see you."

Despite their newfound intimacy, he expects her to refuse—he has been absent too long and there is too much pain in their past. Even so, he hopes.

"Come during Christmas," she says. "Nicholas will be glad to see you." She pauses a moment before saying, "So will I."

— At six-thirty one morning, an octogenarian couple, their faces as tight and severe as hawks', have Perkins called from the kitchen of the diner. When he stands in front of them, they point their fingers at him and damn him to hell.

"You should have charged them an extra ten bucks for stupidity," Marcello tells Perkins when he finds him two hours later, buried under blankets in his bed.

Perkins lifts the blankets off his face. "Maybe I should leave town," he says, something he has said before.

"Because a couple of geezers want to spend their golden years casting stones?"

"I think I'll take the day off."

"The hell you will." Marcello pulls Perkins to his feet, wraps his arm around Perkins's back, and leads him to his Prius. "You're too good a man to let narrow-minded fools fuck with your conscience," he says.

As they're driving to the diner, Perkins says, "I know I should be deeply grateful to you, Peter. And sometimes I am, when my mood holds a little light. I hope you know that."

"And I'll say what I always say in response," Marcello replies, but he stops himself before he can repeat his blather about how, thanks to Perkins, he is now a captain of industry. He thinks: *I lost my family the same day Ray lost his. But I might get mine back. And the two aren't unrelated.*

"We grew up together, Ray."

— Perkins sees a psychologist once a week and Dr. Fuller once every eight weeks. He has seen Father Hannah several times since leaving the Central Ohio Psychiatric Institute. Yet suicide is never far from Perkins's mind. Perkins has never said as much, but Marcello, with a vigilance he is ashamed of, read his friend's diary one morning. *I want to honor my family, but I cannot help feeling grief, shame, and guilt. Sometimes I wonder when relief will come. Sometimes I think it will come only when I'm dead. And so death becomes, again, desirable.*

Marcello cannot say he doesn't imagine a life free of Perkins. In this vision, his wife and son would return, and Consuela would be the one putting dinner on the table instead of Perkins, whose cooking talents don't extend beyond diner food.

One evening, as Marcello walks down the hallway of his house, he imagines detouring into his bedroom, imagines Consuela waiting in the red lingerie she wears when she wants him, imagines the two of them, after love, entwined around each other like a knot they've invented. His fantasy dissolves when he stops in front of Perkins's bedroom door. *Oh, hell,* he thinks, knocking twice.

"Come in."

Perkins is sitting cross-legged on his double bed. In all the time he has lived in the room, he hasn't altered it at all. It's as if a ghost has been living here. Perkins's diary and a black pen are next to him. Classical music plays from the stereo on the windowsill. Perkins's hair is neatly combed. Marcello stands for a moment at the foot of the bed, struck, as he often is, by how removed his life is from any he'd expected to live. "What are your plans for Christmas?" he asks.

Perkins has a soft look, a look of dreamy meditation, in his eyes. It is a look not quite of this world. Perkins's body is here, but Marcello wonders if his spirit will ever return. "Nothing," Perkins replies, his smile faint and faraway. Marcello supposes he'll always be trying to drag his friend back to the present, back to life.

"Great. You'll come with me to Ecuador." And then Marcello blushes, but whether because he has revealed he can't trust his friend not to kill himself in his absence or because he's made it obvious he can't bear to be without him even for a couple of weeks, he doesn't know. He adds, with finality, "I've already bought the tickets."

THE BOY BEHIND THE TREE

My father and I were on the third tee at Wildwood when a boy in a red golf shirt stepped from behind an oak tree next to the ball washer. "Mind if I join you?" he asked.

He was about my age, fifteen, although there was a toughness about him—the squint in his eyes, the wiry muscles in his neck and forearms—I associated with older boys. He no doubt drove his older brother's motorcycle even if he was too young to have a license. I was sure he had access to drugs—reason enough to attract friends of both sexes. I was jealous of him immediately.

After waving him onto the tee, my father told the boy, "I had a birdie on number two. Tell me you beat it, and you're either lying or you've got a tour card in your pocket."

The boy smiled, not in the smug way I did in response to my father's attempts at humor, but with genuine amusement. His teeth were crooked enough so they gave him a rough, authentic appearance but not so crooked as to make him look like a hillbilly. (I had been wearing braces for two years.)

"I had a par," the boy said. "I was putting for birdie but a leaf blew in the way. Stopped my ball an inch short."

"You sure it wasn't Big Foot who did it?" my father asked.

The boy's laugh sounded like backfiring engines. I could tell he and my father were going to be friends. And I was right: Over the next sixteen holes, my father told golf jokes he'd told me at least twice, but this time they were received enthusiastically. And the boy—his name, we learned on the fifth fairway, was Jack—had his own jokes, more graphic than my father's. My father laughed at all of them.

Wildwood was one of only two courses in our hometown of Sherman, Ohio, that didn't require golfers to use carts, which is why my father preferred it. He needed the exercise, he said, because of his blood pressure, his cholesterol level, and his indulgence in an occasional cigarette. After we played a round, my father and I would stop for a Coke and a hotdog in the clubhouse—far from a heart-friendly snack, it's true, but we'd earned it, my father always said—and I would catch him up on my life.

My parents were divorced, and I saw my father only once every month. His construction company had grown so large he had to devote most of his daylight hours to it. But he'd once had time to assist the football and baseball coaches at the high school where I was now a sophomore. In his fantasies, he had a son who played quarterback in the fall and shortstop in the spring, with scholarship offers in both sports pouring in from colleges across the country.

I believe these fantasies started when I was in the womb. The year I turned five, he signed me up for every sports camp open to boys my age. But while I didn't mind throwing or kicking a football, I dreaded being tackled. Wherever the action was on the field, I stayed as far from it as I could, as if I might catch a disease. I liked baseball even less. I lived in constant fear of the pitcher beaning me or a fly ball landing on my head.

Coaches were happy to let me sit on the bench, and I was happy to be safe from harm and humiliation. Even so, my father came to every game, and sometimes he was rewarded when I made an appearance in the fourth quarter or the ninth inning of a lopsided matchup.

When I was in the eighth grade and my sister a senior in high school, my father and mother announced they were divorcing. Even so, they lived with each other during the next eleven-and-a-half months. During the Year of Acrimony, as my sister came to call it, our parents seemed to forget about us. Seizing her opportunity, my sister applied only to colleges in the West, eventually deciding on the University of Arizona. I, meanwhile, severed all my connections to athletics, even though I knew I risked widening the divide between my father and me. Turning in my last uniform was like handing over a prison outfit. In the fall, I joined the chess club and the drama club and was appointed secretary of the English club—an unprecedented honor for a ninth grader.

My father, who was forty-four years old, set up bachelor's quarters in an apartment complex on the edge of Partytown, the student-dominated section of Sherman, and attached himself to a red-haired hardware store employee named Sierra. But he hadn't given up on making his son an athlete. He had a new plan for me: golf.

"In golf, you don't have to be afraid of the ball," he assured me. "In fact, the ball should be afraid of you."

A week later, I had my first lesson, at Wildwood, with the course's golf pro, Sherwood Anderson, who shared a name with an Ohio fiction writer I'd lately been reading. Mr. Anderson was wrinkled and tan, so wrinkled and tan he looked like he'd been stewed in a pot of boiling wood refinisher. He could no longer hit the ball far, but he always hit it straight, and sometimes as he was instructing me, he'd hit a dozen or more shots in succession, ostensibly to teach me but mostly, I suspected, because he felt like it.

I enjoyed golf no more than I did any of the sports I'd tried—nor was I any better at it than I'd been at the others—and I looked forward to the end of a round as if it were the end of a school day. So when my father allowed Jack, whom I already despised, to play with us in our first round of the year, it gave me one more reason to hate the game. Although Jack's golf bag looked like the sack of a homeless Santa Claus and his clubs appeared to be made from bamboo, he proved himself a good golfer—no, an excellent golfer. No matter that Jack's English was to language what a truck stop café is to fine dining, he hit shots my father whistled at the way certain men whistle at women.

Jack inspired my father to play his best. I'd never seen my father so focused, so intense—or so joyful. By the twelfth hole, a par four with a creek curling in front of the green, my father and Jack had begun to bet: twenty-five cents a hole. Both of them cleared the creek with their second shots. I put both my third and fourth shots in the muddy middle of it. "You're scaring the fish," my father said with a smile, and Jack laughed his rat-a-tat-tat laugh.

In appearance, my father wasn't unlike Jack. He had dramatic features: deep-set eyes, a long nose, and muscles he'd toned as a boy on his family's farm outside of Sherman. His hair was black like Jack's, although the one time he grew a beard, it came in gray.

For the rest of the round, my father said perhaps a dozen words to me. It was as if I weren't playing the same hole as he and Jack. They'd boom their tee shots, and I'd dribble mine. As I hacked in the rough, they stood together in the fairway, conferring in whispers. Jack was nearly as tall as my father, who was at least three inches taller than I was, and he immediately picked up one of my father's favorite expressions: "Sing hallelujah to the Lord of the Links," shouted after an especially good shot.

The only time Jack acknowledged me was when, on the sixteenth hole, I took a vicious swing—born of a growing anger with how the day was going—and missed the ball entirely. "Strike one," he said. Although he'd spoken softly, I'm sure my father heard him because he chuckled before pretending to cough.

At the end of the round, Jack owed my father a quarter. After pausing, perhaps to contemplate the penny-sized hole in the right sleeve of Jack's ragged golf shirt, my father said, "We'll keep a running tab. I'm sure we'll see each other again. I hope so, anyway."

As Jack turned to go—headed away from the parking lot, which meant he had come to the course without a motorized vehicle—my father said, "Why don't you join us for a hotdog and Coke?"

I'm sure my face revealed exactly how I felt about the prospect of Jack joining us. But Jack didn't look at me. "I appreciate it, Mr. Graver," he said. "Maybe next time."

"Definitely next time," my father insisted.

Giving a short wave, almost a salute, Jack turned and walked off into the April afternoon.

"He probably has work he needs to get to," my father said, "like I did at his age."

After picking up hotdogs and Cokes at the clubhouse café, we sat on the veranda overlooking the eighteenth green. My father said if Jack didn't play golf for his high school team, it was a shame. "He could probably play college golf right now. I wouldn't be surprised if he's being recruited." My father wondered whether Jack played other sports. "He looks like a second baseman," he said. "Or a scrappy third baseman. If he plays football, I bet he's a cornerback."

We were done eating by the time my father turned his deepset eyes to me. "So what's new in your life?" he asked.

Ordinarily, I would have unburdened myself of whatever was on my mind: girls, classes, the week's news, girls. But I felt a wild resentment of all the time he'd spent playing with, and talking about, Jack, so I shook my head. "Nothing much," I said. "We should go."

— My father and I played again in May, and Jack met us on the course, in his usual spot. I accused my father of arranging the meeting, but he denied he had. When, during our round, my father asked Jack if he bothered to pay greens fees or simply started his round at the third hole, Jack blushed and apologized profusely, as if he had somehow injured my father with his transgression. My father laughed and said he used to sneak onto courses all the time when he was Jack's age. "Besides," my father said, "good golfers barely disturb the course. It's the duffers who tear it to shreds and keep the greenskeepers sweating."

Jack laughed his backfiring engine laugh and shot me a glance, perhaps to see if I, unquestionably a duffer, had taken offense. I fired back a grin. Two days earlier, I'd kissed Jessica Sanders, the treasurer of the English Club. We'd been discussing a D. H. Lawrence novel when it happened. Golf seemed inconsequential compared to Jessica's red lips and braces-free teeth.

As before, my father and Jack ribbed one another and applauded each other's shots while I trailed them, hacking away as if my clubs were farm tools. I could have planted several gardens. I tried to think about Jessica Sanders—about how her lips had felt, about when I would kiss her next—but my father's and Jack's conversation intruded like an alarm clock into a dream.

On the eighteenth tee, I hit my ball deep into the woods. While I was in no rush to find it, I was furious when, a few minutes later, I saw my father and Jack on the green, three hundred yards distant, finishing their rounds with tap-in putts. They slapped each other high fives, then walked off the course as if they'd forgotten all about me. Perhaps they had.

I didn't bother finishing my round, but marched straight toward the parking lot, where I stood beside my father's Ford Taurus, my arms crossed, until he came along, pulling his golf bag. "No Coke and hotdog?" he asked, but he had already unlocked the doors. "I didn't think you were ever coming out of the woods," he said.

"I was considering becoming the next Thoreau," I replied.

"One of golf's pioneers," he said, smiling, although I put the odds at no better than 50-50 that he knew who Thoreau was.

— In June, my father and Sierra spent ten days in Toronto, where her family lived, while my mother and I met my sister in Phoenix and drove to the Grand Canyon.

When I was younger, the times I felt closest to my father were on long car rides. My mother and sister would fall asleep, their heads against windows, and my father would tell me about his uncles, Hank and Sam, who, as they grew up, were in constant competition with each other. They'd compete to be the first in the bathroom in the morning, the first to step on the school bus, the first to kiss a girl. They played football, of course, in the days before players wore helmets, or so my father claimed. His best Hank-and-Sam stories were of their most dangerous competitions—swims up raging rivers, hikes down mountains at dusk without flashlights. Although their feats in these tales seemed suspiciously superhuman—certainly far beyond what I could imagine myself doing—I found the stories riveting, and my father's voice overcame its Midwestern flatness and gained an inexorable rhythm as he told them.

When the four of us stopped going on family vacations, my mother tried to make up for my father's absence with books-on-tape. But even when the books were read well, they couldn't duplicate the small thrill of having my father pause at a critical point in the story, like a magician holding off revealing what is in his hat, until I exhorted him to continue.

Despite his storytelling skill, my father didn't read much beyond the sports page, books of silly quotes, and collections of columns by Dave Barry. He did like movies, however. So when, in mid-July, he called and suggested we see a movie, I should have said, "Great." Instead, I said, "What, no golf?"

"I get the feeling you don't like golf."

If I admitted I didn't like golf, I feared I would be invalidating all the times we'd played, and I was concerned he would withdraw from me even more. I said, "I do like it . . . sometimes."

This was all the endorsement he needed. We arranged to play the following Friday. My father warned me that the weather might be scorching, but it was like an early autumn day, with temperatures in the 70s.

The knowledge that I'd passed on a chance to see a movie with my father—there was a film based on Tolstoy's last novel currently playing as part of Ohio Eastern University's Russian film series—made me feel masochistic. I felt worse when, on the first tee, I sliced my ball into the opposite fairway, coming within a foot or two of hitting Father George, the ancient priest who had married my parents when both still considered themselves Catholics. "Tell him the Devil made you do it," my father said as I walked with bowed head toward my ball.

I felt even worse when, on the third tee, Jack stepped from behind his hiding place and asked if he could join us. I was sure my father had let him know we would be playing today. I also suspected that he and my father had played on several occasions since August because they fell into an easy rapport, the kind of everyday conversation, full of gentle quips and genuine interest, that tended to elude me and my father, even at our most communicative.

After my father and Jack teed off, I stepped up to my ball, desperate to outdo them. They'd both hit impressive drives, 250 yards down the right side of the fairway. If I had given the situation any thought, I would have realized I had never hit a ball so far in my life, and any attempt to do so was certain to lead to disaster. I brought back my driver until the head dangled past my knees. After a brief pause—during which I should have realized the futility of my ambition—I swept the club around my body and smashed the head into the ball, which flew, waist-high in a perfect diagonal, into an oak tree five yards from the tee box and rocketed straight back into my chest. I toppled over.

My father rushed over to me. Jack was more casual about it, but before long, he, too, stood over me, asking if I was all right, a faint grin on his face. The pain where the ball had struck me, to the right of my heart, was considerable, but it paled in comparison to the pain of my humiliation. Tears dribbled out of my eyes.

By the time I stood up, Jack had lost interest in me and was practicing his swing. My father, too, seemed eager to proceed, although he asked, "Do you need to put some ice on it?"

What I most wanted to do was fling my golf clubs into the woods and declare my golfing days over. "Yeah," I told my father, "I think I'll go find some ice in the clubhouse. I'll catch up with you."

Later, when my father and Jack made the turn, they found me in the clubhouse, reading a Steinbeck novel I'd discovered in the locker room. I told them I wasn't feeling 100 percent, which could have described any day of my life, and encouraged them to finish their rounds without me. By the time they reached the eighteenth fairway, I'd taken my novel out to the veranda. I saw them hit their second shots. As they walked toward the green, where both of their balls had landed, I heard them talking. Although I couldn't make out the words, I understood them to be part of a friendly ribbing. There was music in their voices, and contentment.

I could have found the scene disturbing, could have worried I was losing my father to my more talented and congenial rival. But I recognized that I had lost him long ago in a procession of dropped fly balls and tackles I'd avoided by running out of bounds (and, in one memorable instance, in the wrong direction) and in glory I'd never achieved because I was sitting at the end of the bench. Or perhaps it was I who had abandoned him by not toughening up and working to overcome my fear of fastballs and bone-breaking linebackers. I'd given up sports for books, whose authors had become like substitute parents to me, offering me insights about what was worth caring about and what might await me as I moved into adult life. If my father had brought Jack into our relationship, I had brought Tolstoy and Camus and James Baldwin. And although Jack might have hit 250-yard drives, Tolstoy and company were the real big hitters, their power extending beyond the body's graces.

My revelation—my epiphany, as it were (although I would begin to read Joyce only the following year)—gave me such a feeling of lightheartedness that after my father and Jack putted out, I applauded as if I were an immense gallery. Jack looked up at me suspiciously, but my father smiled and waved his putter at me.

Over the next few years, I heard my father mention Jack on several occasions, and I began to think of him as a kind of stepbrother. (Although my father eventually married Sierra, they never had children.) I didn't stop being jealous of Jack, and once I said something sarcastic when my father mentioned him, something like, "How the hell is old Jack the Ripper?" But I had my own life—before long, college; after this, graduate school; after this, a tenure-track position at Oberlin, a wife, a baby girl.

Two weeks before my father died of a heart attack, he came to the opening of a play I'd written. It was set in the Soviet Union in the year preceding the fall of the Berlin Wall, its subject matter far removed from the concerns of small-town Ohio. His praise was hesitant, mostly, I suspected, because he was worried he might sound ignorant. His only criticism was of the way I'd portrayed the relationship between a boy and his father: Even fathers who had little in common with their sons, he seemed to say, can feel more than bewilderment and disappointment, although what left his mouth was fumbling and uncertain, the equivalent of my typical golf shot. I thanked him twice for coming.

Aside from money, he didn't leave me much in his will—Sierra inherited the majority of what he'd owned. The most notable item he bequeathed me was his bag of golf clubs. If I had still been cynical—if I had still been a teenager—I might have read something mean in this gift, my father emphasizing my inadequacy as a golfer, as a son. But I figured he was making one last effort to reach me on his terms.

My father had told Sierra, only partly in jest, that he wanted his ashes spread on a golf course. But even if his remains had been buried near his parents in a cemetery outside of Sherman, I thought his spirit might decide to reside at Wildwood. So the day after his funeral, I threw my father's clubs in the trunk of my car and drove to the course, which I hadn't stepped on since being struck in the chest by my errant tee-shot.

As usual, the course wasn't crowded, and so I set off on my own. My father used to say that taking time off from golf was healthy because you could forget your bad habits. If anything, however, I was worse. By the time I stepped on the third tee, I was ready to quit. I hesitated, though, half-expecting Jack to step from behind the oak tree and ask to join me.

Minutes passed, and I began to wonder if Jack had ever existed. When I tried to picture him, I saw only a younger version of my father. Perhaps my father had conjured him in order to keep company with someone who understood and appreciated him, as I had found myself in the company of characters from novels and plays. What we couldn't get from each other, my father and I, we might have evoked for ourselves.

Or perhaps I had been the one to conjure Jack, someone to please my father and free me to be myself.

Before I retired from the course, I left my father's clubs behind the oak tree and called Jack's name, in my loudest voice, into the woods.

THE INCURABLES

When Adam "Drew" Drewshevsky, a.k.a. Dickie De-Long, returned to his hometown of Sherman, Ohio, his old friend Barry Borkowski took him out for a beer at Don's Underground and raised a glass to the Prince of Porn. There was truth to the title: In the past decade, Drew had made more than three hundred erotic films of varying length and quality. But his career, he told Barry, was over.

"I need a new life," Drew said.

"Can I have your current one?" Barry asked.

Drew didn't tell Barry he had herpes, which no medicine he'd taken and no diet he'd tried had prevented from erupting every couple of weeks like chicken pox of the penis. And he didn't confess to Barry his more troubling problem. Even after near-overdoses of Viagra and every one of its pharmaceutical competitors, even after sucking back blenders full of supposed cock-hardening concoctions—*green bananas,* the woman in the Oriental scarf and red eye-patch had told him; *sperm whale eyes,* said the man with three gold rings on his lower lip—even after six trips to a specialist in erectile dysfunction (which one of his former costars and former girlfriends, Misty Moans, called erectile dishonor), even after praying to all the gods and all the false gods he knew, his penis remained paralyzed.

Drew hoped to find something in his hometown that would return him to the man—the boy, really—he'd once been. But three minutes into their conversation, Barry reminded him about how, when they were twelve years old, they'd stolen *Playboy* magazines from Reeves' Drugstore and had simulated intercourse with the centerfolds on the floor of Barry's basement.

"You were born a porn star," Barry said.

— Drew's father had died of a heart attack when Drew was ten years old. His mother found Jesus soon after Drew told her what he was doing in California. She'd moved to Georgia five years ago in order to live closer to the television preacher whose show, she believed, had changed her life. Drew's paternal aunt, his only living relative left in Sherman, set him up with a job at the Sherman Public Library. He was in charge of stacking books, cleaning the bathrooms, vacuuming the rugs, and rebooting the four computers in the children's section whenever their screens froze.

In his first week on the job, no fewer than three library patrons asked him if they'd seen him before. "I grew up here," he told each of them, but two were recent arrivals to Sherman and the third said he was positive he had seen Drew on TV. Drew's blindingly blond hair was hard to forget. It made him look Danish, thus his casting as Hamlet in *Ophelia, Nymph in Thy Orgasms*.

In his second week, a woman who recognized him—and obviously knew why—grabbed her red-hatted toddler and fled the library as if he'd exposed himself, herpes and all. During his third week, he wore sunglasses. The head librarian, who, per the cliché, was bespectacled but had a body most of his former costars would have taken out a second mortgage on their souls to acquire, chided him for looking like a Secret Service agent and scaring the children. "Besides," she said, "you shouldn't hide such a pretty face." Two days later, she invited him to dinner.

Before he'd finished his salad, she smiled at him and, as her feet crawled up his legs, said, "I know what I want for dessert."

He told her he was considering joining the priesthood.

"But you're Jewish," she said.

"I'm hoping they're desperate," he said.

During his lunch break the next day, Drew did go talk with the priest at Our Lady of Perpetual Tears. Like the librarian, the priest pointed out the problem of Drew's religious affiliation. "And I'm not sure I understand your reasons for wanting to join the priesthood," he said. "Could you restate them plainly?"

All Drew could think to say was: I'm in a pit and I'm reaching toward whatever light I see above me. Instead, he said, "I've forgotten."

"Well, if you remember, come back," the priest said. "And why do I have this feeling I've seen you before?"

— On a Wednesday of his sixth week back in his hometown, Drew was supposed to meet Barry for drinks at Don's Underground. He was going to tell him everything. But Barry had left a message with the bartender saying he wouldn't be able to make it. After Drew finished his fourth beer, the bartender asked him if he was planning to drive home.

"I'm on foot," Drew assured him, although he felt obliged to look down to make sure his feet hadn't deserted him.

As he drank his fifth beer, Drew recalled, for perhaps the two hundredth time, a conversation he'd had with one of his former costars. In *The Good, the Bed, and the Naughty,* she had played Mabel Syrup. She was what all the cowboys had with their breakfasts.

Her screen name was Amber Waves. Before performing the climactic scene, a shootout followed by an orgy in Betty's Bordello, they'd sat half-clothed on a red velvet couch. The smile she'd worn every time he saw her, on camera and off, vanished. She stuck out her hand and said, "My name is Erin." After he'd introduced himself, she said, "You remind me of my stepfather. He had hair like yours—like he'd stuck a paintbrush into the moon and swirled the color all over his head."

Her voice, high and childlike—like a cartoon duck's—made everything she said seem frivolous and inconsequential. "Well, let's not say the moon," Erin amended. "I love the moon, and I didn't love him."

Erin gazed into his eyes. He was shocked by the intimacy of the gesture, and he bowed his head to look at his bare feet. "When I was twelve," she said, "my stepfather raped me. It wasn't the last time. I've never told anyone."

When Drew looked up at her, she was staring at him with the same fierce, shocking intimacy, and although neither of them moved, he felt the distance between them disappear. "What do you want me to do about it?" he said, although this wasn't what he'd wanted to say.

She didn't reply. A moment later, it was time to shoot the scene.

One morning soon thereafter, Drew woke up to find his penis inert and covered with raging, red blisters.

"I'm on foot," he assured the bartender when, after finishing his sixth beer, he stumbled to the door of Don's Underground. He turned and waved. The bar had recently banned smoking but nevertheless seemed suffused with a gray-green haze, the color of a Los Angeles rush hour. Drew decided he wouldn't miss any of it.

A minute later, he was standing in the middle of the pedestrian walkway on the Main Street Bridge, staring over the edge, wondering how far the fall was.

Far enough, he decided.

With both hands, Drew grabbed the topmost bar of the railing, which was a little higher than his chest. Slowly, he lifted his right leg and positioned his foot parallel to his hands. He looked like he was either preparing to kill himself or was warming up for a role in *The Nutcracker*—or *The Nutlicker* (he'd played the Mouse King).

"Good night," he said to the night.

A hand clasped him on the shoulder. "Hello," said a man's voice. "I can't let you do what you're about to do."

Drew, who hadn't noticed a police car pull to a stop in the middle of the bridge, returned his foot to the ground.

"I think you could use some help—don't you agree?" said the man, who introduced himself as John Lewis, Sherman's sheriff.

"You'll hear no argument from me," Drew said.

The sheriff looked like Santa Claus without the beard. "Do I have your permission to take you to the hospital?"

"Permission granted," Drew said. "But I'm incurable."

In the Matthew A. Dunkirk Psychiatric Ward of the Ohio Eastern University Hospital—known, the nurse who registered him said without irony or apology, as the MAD—Drew would be identified only by his first name and his photograph, which the nurse snapped in a red-curtained booth behind her desk. Despite his months of misery and tonight's drunkenness (a condition Sheriff Lewis said he would ignore because of rules prohibiting the inebriated from being admitted to the psych ward), his snapshot showed him looking raffish, even, given the Valentine-colored backdrop, romantic.

The nurse who did Drew's intake survey was named Herman. "As in Herman's Hermits," Herman said. "But I don't suppose you know who I'm talking about."

Drew did—one of his first film roles was the drummer of The Kinky in *The British Invasion (Our Music Wasn't All That Made 'Em Scream)*.

"So what in your mind or spirit brought you tonight to the brink of welcoming eternity?" Herman asked.

Drew named the reasons, although as he did so, they seemed insubstantial. They didn't, anyway, appear sufficient to warrant a dive from the Main Street Bridge. But Herman nodded and nodded again. "Loss," he said. "Of virility. Of career. And your herpes is a recurring reminder of both."

Herman had gray streaks in his hair and wrinkles at the edges of his eyes. He might have been old enough to be Herman Hermit himself, if there was such a person. "You have work to do," Herman said, "and drugs to take."

Herman handed Drew a ham sandwich, which Drew ate in the ward's dayroom. The dayroom looked more suited to a child-care center. The wallpaper featured a circus motif, with pink elephants and baby-blue lions. In the front of the room were a table with six chairs and a bookshelf with two dozen Bibles, a deck of jumbo playing cards, and five board games, three of which were Chutes and Ladders. At the far end of the room, below a window with a view of the hospital's parking lot and, beyond it, Ohio Eastern University's football stadium, was a wide-screen television. Sitting cross-legged in front of the TV was a woman about Drew's age, in pink pajamas, watching *Winnie the Pooh*. He focused on her hair, a color between blond and brown. It had hundreds of corkscrews and was as short as a man's.

When Eeyore, the donkey, appeared on the screen, the woman turned to Drew with exasperation and said, "You know what he needs, don't you?"

Drew shook his head.

"Electroshock," said the woman. "ECT. Like me." She laughed. "I have my sixth treatment tomorrow." Her voice was a whisper: "Don't tell them, but number five put me in a mania. I'm feeling good right now. Are you single?"

Drew knew he should be attracted to the woman, who was pale and slim and had small, strawberry-colored lips. Any heterosexual man in his right mind, and with functioning and unsullied equipment, he decided, would be. "Yes, I'm single."

"Well, I'm not," she said, shrugging. She turned again to the TV.

She diagnosed all the characters: Piglet needed anti-anxiety meds, Tigger had ADHD. "And Pooh's a honey junkie," she said. "Sugared up but always thinking about his next fix."

A nurse popped into the room to tell them it was ten o'clock, time for lights out.

"I'll see you tomorrow," Drew said to the curly-haired woman.

"Only if I haven't escaped."

"So this place is locked?" he asked.

"Where do you think you are," replied the woman, smiling, "the Four Seasons?"

Drew discovered he was sharing a room with Rusty, a dark-bearded man of uncertain age and enormous girth. Drew imagined that Rusty owned a loud motorcycle and a pit bull. Rusty apologized in advance for his snoring.

"My last girlfriend said it was like a Bach fugue," he confided with a grin. His face clouded over. "I didn't know what the fuck a Bach fugue was, so I beat her again."

At midnight, Drew woke up. From the bed next to his issued a sound not unlike what might play outside a haunted house at Halloween.

— After a breakfast of eggs, toast, and orange juice the next morning, the patients had an hour to themselves. Most of them opted to return to their rooms and sleep, although at least two signs posted on the walls of the ward discouraged napping. Drew remained in the dayroom, anticipating a conversation with the Pooh woman. But as she reminded him, she was scheduled to have her sixth electroshock today. She returned to her room and emerged wearing a blue hospital gown. Her feet were bare.

"You'd think I was about to give birth or have my appendix removed," she said. "My name's Erica, by the way."

Drew introduced himself, and they shook hands.

"You have cold hands," she said. "You know the saying about cold hands."

"Cold hands, warm heart?" he said.

"Oh," she said, "is that it? I thought it had something to do with vampires."

Presently, a nurse came for her. "When I come back," Erica told Drew, "I may not remember we had this conversation. So I hope you don't mind if we have it again."

Erica walked beside the nurse toward the double doors to the left of the nurses' station. Before departing the ward, she turned and blew Drew a kiss.

— "Are you Adam?" a woman's voice asked.

He opened his eyes. "I go by Drew," he said.

"Follow me, Drew," the nurse said, and she led him out of the dayroom to a small conference room at the back of the ward. Inside was a man whose peach-fuzz hair made him look like a cancer patient or the singer of a punk band. His skin was as white as his doctor's coat, and a scar ran diagonally from the far corner of his left eye to the left corner of his lips. He introduced himself as Dr. Ramshide.

"And please call me Dr. Ramshide rather than by my first name, which is Sebastian, or any of my nicknames, one of which is Rambo," he said.

"Will do," Drew said.

"You forgot to add something."

"I did?" Drew said.

"Yes, you forgot to add my title and my last name."

When Drew said nothing in response, the doctor said, "Dr. Ramshide, remember?"

"I haven't forgotten," Drew said, sitting in a chair across from Dr. Ramshide's oversized desk.

Dr. Ramshide asked him the same questions Herman had, and Drew answered the same way. After a pause, Dr. Ramshide said, "I want to start you today on ProPax. It's an excellent antidepressant. Unfortunately, we won't be able to gauge its effectiveness for six weeks. And there's one major potential side effect."

"What's that?" Drew asked.

"Impotence," Dr. Ramshide said.

Drew opened his mouth, but couldn't find the words to convey his incredulity. At last, he managed, "Haven't you read my . . ." But there was a knock on the door. It was the nurse with another patient.

— Lunch was followed by dead time. As Drew sat slumped in one of the dayroom's chairs, he saw Erica return, a nurse escorting her. Erica moved slowly, her shoulders sagging. She looked like she was about to collapse. When she saw him, she stopped but gave no sign of recognition. He lifted his hand, a tentative wave.

"All right," said the nurse, who was as dark as Erica was fair, "enough of the *One Flew over the Cuckoo's Nest* routine."

Erica laughed and stood straight. "They're no fun here," she said, winking at Drew.

Despite her apparent cheerfulness, she returned to her room to sleep and didn't reappear until after lunch, during Art Therapy class. She found a spot next to Drew on the floor.

"How was your treatment?" he asked her.

"Shocking," she said.

The art therapist, a short, round-faced woman from India, asked the patients to paint their worst nightmare on one half of a sheet of paper and their happiest dream on the other half. For Drew, the nightmare was easy, a collision of reds: engorged body parts, blood, herpes. The happiest dream was harder to conjure.

During his first year in California, he'd dated a woman named Barbara, from Santa Barbara. He'd teased her about this, as if he'd been the first person to make this joke. Her gaze was appealingly asymmetrical (her right eye was larger than her left) and she enjoyed fiddling with words. They would play late-night games of Scrabble or, as they drank a bottle of wine on her couch, rewrite the lyrics of pop songs so they'd all mention dandelions or flatulence. He never worked up the courage to tell her how he really made a living, although she must have discovered the truth. She stopped returning his calls.

He held his paintbrush over the blank right side of his paper, wondering.

"How does it feel to be back in kindergarten?" Erica whispered to him.

"I was thinking preschool," Drew said.

"Five more minutes," the art therapist said.

Drew began painting without intention. He ended up with a dark landscape. The art therapist said she was certain she saw a serene moon emerging from behind black clouds.

Erica had painted a picture of the Devil sword-fighting with the Easter Bunny. "It's always war with me," she said, sighing.

In bed that night, Drew wondered if he should try to masturbate. But he imagined there were sores on his penis, sores as prominent as moguls on a black diamond ski slope. Besides, on the rare occasions he'd tried to pleasure himself, the nude women he summoned from memory and imagination inevitably dissolved, distressingly, into their prepubescent selves. They even spoke to him in age-appropriate voices. One blond-haired girl—six years old maybe, her pubis as hairless as glass—said, "I want to be a veterinarian when I grow up, but I'll probably end up sucking cocks." Another girl, even younger and with curly black hair and rose-red lips, said, "For me, self-empowerment will mean allowing anonymous men to fuck me four ways to Friday so other anonymous men can watch my DVDs and videos and pretend they're fucking me six ways to Saturday. I also like ponies and rainbows."

— In the next morning's Re-Entry into Society group, in which patients were expected to share their fears and hopes about returning to their lives on the outside, no one said anything.

"Would anyone like to speculate about why we're so silent today?" asked the group's leader, a social worker named Bradley, whose six gold earrings—three in each ear—shone like circles of fire against his ebony skin.

After another few minutes of silence, a new admit, a woman in her late forties who constantly chewed on her lower lip, said, "Were you on the Ohio Eastern basketball team about five years ago?"

Bradley sighed. "Yes," he admitted.

"I knew it!" she squealed. "I knew it was you!" She turned to her fellow patients, as if hoping to find similar enthusiasm. No one said a word.

The silence continued until the same woman turned to Drew and said, "And you look familiar too."

Eyes turned to him. He swore he heard a growing murmur of recognition. But the silence returned and prevailed.

"Why isn't anyone talking?" Bradley asked.

Five minutes later, he asked the same question.

When the session ended, Drew idled in the dayroom with the rest of the patients until his appointment with Dr. Ramshide. He made certain to call him Dr. Ramshide three times within the first minute, figuring if he could appease the doctor's need to be addressed formally he could question him about his treatment plan. But the doctor was more interested in hearing details of Drew's film career. Dr. Ramshide mentioned the names of porn actors with the casual expertise of a baseball fan reciting the starting lineup of his hometown team.

Drew tried without success to change the subject.

— In the afternoon, the patients had an hour of Recreation Therapy, in the first-floor gymnasium. They were led in calisthenics by another former Ohio Eastern basketball star, who, given his enormous height, must have played center.

During sit-ups, Drew held Erica's feet. "Let me warn you, I'm still in a big-time mania, so take everything I say with a tablet of lithium," Erica huffed as he softly counted the number of her sit-ups. "But I think you're cute."

"My dick doesn't work," he whispered back.

She didn't break her sit-up rhythm. "For how long?"

"Eight months."

"Winters in Siberia are longer."

"And I have herpes."

"So did my grandma," Erica said. "And when she died, of a heart attack, she was with a UPS driver who certainly knew how to deliver a package."

Erica laughed in a huffing way.

"I used to be a porn actor," Drew said.

"There are worse ways to make a living," she said. "If I could have a hundred dollars for all the loveless sex I've had, well, I'd be right where I am today—only richer."

He tried to smile and half succeeded.

"I still think you're cute," Erica said. "Have I done fifty yet?"

— The next morning, Drew was promoted to Level Orange, which gave him the right, twice a day, to follow one of the nurses into the hallway, down two flights of stairs, and into a fenced-in courtyard. At the end of it, in the middle, was a locked gate. It was made of the same black iron as the rest of the fence except its lock was red. It seemed, Drew thought, like a fairy tale door, like something you'd walk through to enter a new world.

On his most recent outing to the "Cage," as even the nurses referred to the enclosure, Drew wore only a T-shirt and blue jeans, but he could see his breath pour out of his mouth. It was about nine in the morning, but what month was it? he wondered.

When Drew returned to the dayroom, Erica was sitting cross-legged in front of the TV, which was off. "Good show?" he joked, but she didn't reply. Erica was only at Level Red, which meant she couldn't go outside. The risk of her escape, or her suicide, was too great, even under supervision.

Level Red also meant she couldn't have any visitors. Drew was allowed this privilege, but when Barry called Drew before lunch and asked if he could come see him, Drew said he would prefer to recover in anonymity. "It's just as well," Barry said. "If I showed up, they'd probably want to keep me."

After lunch, Erica again sat in front of the blank TV. Her eyes were closed and she was whispering something.

"Meditation?" Drew asked.

Erica opened her eyes. "No, something more ambitious," she said. "I'm trying to communicate with aliens. I'm begging them to take me away from this sad, sad world."

A moment later, Drew was called in to see Dr. Ramshide. But Dr. Ramshide had been replaced by Dr. Salvador Hernandez, a man in his sixties with a lean, freckled face, a silver mustache, and a gap-toothed smile. The desk, too, had changed—from gigantic to medium-sized.

"What happened to Dr. Ramshide?" Drew asked.

"Rambo?" Dr. Hernandez said, shaking his head. "He's been transferred to Food Services."

Drew couldn't tell if he was joking.

"With your permission, I'll be changing your meds," said Dr. Hernandez. "The idea of throwing ProPax on top of erectile dysfunction is like treating heat rash by sending the patient to a tanning salon."

After they had talked for a while, Dr. Hernandez said, "I think your herpes is both a real affliction and a form of self-punishment."

"Self-punishment?" Drew asked.

"Even if you wanted to resume your sex life—and your impotence, I'm convinced, is a problem of desire, or lack thereof, rather than anything physical—your herpes, by its near-continuous presence, would keep you celibate. It's your superego. It is saying, 'Never again.'"

They talked more, and Dr. Hernandez suggested Drew might write to a few of the women with whom he'd had intercourse on film and now thought of with regret and guilt. Specifically, he could write to Erin.

"What would I say?" Drew asked him.

"You could tell her you remember her," Dr. Hernandez said. "You could tell her you hope she's all right."

"That's it?"

"I don't know," Dr. Hernandez said, smiling. "Throw in a marriage proposal. See what comes back."

— "Why don't you try acting in regular movies," Erica said. "You know, the Hollywood kind."

They'd finished their twenty-eighth game of Crazy Eights. The dayroom was empty except for Rusty, who was snoring in front of a football game on TV. It was late. The nurse would soon tell them to go to their bedrooms.

"I'm not convinced I can act," Drew said.

"I can," Erica said. "Watch."

Erica dropped her head onto the table and began to cry.

"That's good," he said.

She lifted her face. Her cheeks were red and damp.

"Very good," he said.

Drew waited for her to stop crying, to wink. When she didn't, he felt a rush of anxiety, and he turned to look for the nurse. But instead of going to find her, he put his hand on Erica's shoulder. Still crying, she leaned her head against it.

"You get the part," he said.

She didn't smile, but she stopped crying.

— In his next meeting with Dr. Hernandez, Drew talked about all the women he'd been involved with romantically and how he'd given up dating anyone but the women he worked with.

"Why?" Dr. Hernandez asked.

"I was lazy, I guess," Drew said. "I knew them already."

"Did you? Did you really know them?"

"I thought I did. Or maybe I told myself I did so I didn't have to know them."

— For Drew, evenings now had the feel of a slumber party in which he left the boys in order to sit with the host's sister in the den and play cards and talk. If there was anything good about the MAD, it was this, even when, as now, Erica stared up at him from her cards with a look so drained of emotion, so stripped of life, he doubted he could reach her with even the most outrageous declaration.

He wanted to say something to her, though, something kind, but every phrase he conceived seemed as stilted and unimaginative as a line from one of his movies. So they played cards without saying anything at all.

— In their next meeting, Dr. Hernandez said, "Are you aware that the Ohio Eastern University Hospital has one of the most well-respected sex addiction clinics in the country?"

"Are you suggesting I'm a sex addict?" Drew asked incredulously.

"Not at all," said Dr. Hernandez. "But after your discharge, you'll walk past the sex-addiction waiting room. There's a chance you'll be recognized."

"It won't be the first time," Drew said, smiling.

Dr. Hernandez touched his silver mustache. "I think you're ready to go home."

"But the antidepressants haven't had a chance to kick in," Drew said.

"We'll have a thorough outpatient treatment plan in place for you, but you've done much of the important work already. And you're telling the truth when you say you don't feel like jumping off the Main Street Bridge now, correct?"

"I don't think I'd even stop to look over the side."

— "I've seen only one porn film in my life," Erica told Drew.

It was night, and they were playing their fourth game of Chutes and Ladders. Erica had won the first three, and when Drew said she must be cheating, she said, "No, it's because I've had hours of practice. Every stay-at-home mom learns to become a Chutes and Ladders all-star."

Drew had asked her about her children and husband once, but she'd told him she didn't like to talk about them—it made her too sad, she said—so he hadn't asked again.

"My brother and a friend of his found or rented or stole a porn video," Erica said. "They were watching it late at night in the basement of our house. My parents were sleeping—or maybe they were out of town; my brother might have been old enough to look after both of us. When I walked in on them, they pretended they didn't notice me."

Rusty, sitting on the couch, was snoring, the noises he produced at once comical and funereal. In the lone window, the lights of the hospital parking lot looked like fluorescent heads on thin black stakes.

"Were they watching hard-core?" Drew asked. He didn't think he would have been old enough to have appeared in the movie, although he braced himself to discover he had.

"Hard enough," Erica said, "although, to the movie's credit, there was a plot, which had to do with a knight, a princess, and a sex-crazed stepmother of a queen."

Drew relaxed: He hadn't appeared in the film. He hadn't even heard of it, although he could guess its title: *A Knight in Shining Ardor*. No, he thought, too soft, too sweet.

"They didn't try very hard with the setting," Erica continued. "It was supposed to be a medieval castle, but I could see a washer and dryer in one scene. I guess we weren't supposed to notice much besides the screwing, which I did find interesting. At first. But not even halfway through the film, I saw how mechanical it all was. It reminded me of a cuckoo bird in a cuckoo clock—in and out, in and out—with plenty of nonsense cuckoo noise." She paused. "I'm sure your movies were better."

"I never watch them," Drew said. This had been true, anyway, for the past couple of years.

"I guess I'm a romantic when it comes to movies," Erica said. "I want there to be courtship, kisses—poetry, even—before the clothes come off."

Drew glanced out the window and saw that the stadium's lights had been turned on. There could be no game at this hour, so the stadium crew was probably testing the lights. But Drew preferred to think the lights had come on by themselves, fulfilling a spontaneous desire to shine.

He turned to share the scene with Erica, but she'd buried her head in the crook of her right arm and was softly sobbing.

A nurse announced it was ten o'clock and time for bed.

— In their last meeting, Dr. Hernandez told Drew, "There's one more piece of advice you need to accept."

"All right," Drew said.

"It comes in three parts."

Drew nodded.

"First, forgive yourself. Second, forgive yourself. And third— "

"Forgive myself," Drew cut in.

"Third," said Dr. Hernandez, "look at your case of herpes as an occasional annoyance, a permanent but manageable affliction acquired in a job and a life you have outgrown. Do not see it as a sign from God or fate of your complicity in the continued suffering of human beings—unclothed women in particular. Meanwhile, look at your impotence as temporary, a holding pattern you've put yourself in as you establish a new balance in your life between sex and love and trust.

"And also," he added, "forgive yourself."

— At midnight Drew was awoken by a soft whisper: "Let's get out of here for a while." It was Erica, her face moon-bright in the dark of the room. In the bed next to Drew's, Rusty's snores sounded like a clarinet concerto played in a garbage can.

Erica, who was wearing blue jeans and a brown T-shirt, watched him dress. In his old life, he would have felt at ease with this; he wouldn't even have noticed her presence. But as he stood in his underwear and a short-sleeved, button-down blue shirt with yellow pinstripes, he felt self-conscious. He caught her eyes, and she smiled before turning her head. He finished dressing.

"Where are we going?" he whispered.

"To breathe," Erica said.

The nurses' station was empty. But to the left of the station, sitting slumped against a wall, was Herman. He appeared to be talking to himself.

"We'll get caught," Drew said resignedly.

But Erica kept walking. From up close, Herman looked like a koala bear in the wake of a eucalyptus binge. He lifted his right hand and formed a peace sign.

"What's wrong with him?" Drew whispered.

"Ecstasy," Erica replied. "Not the drug, but the state of mind." A few more feet down the hallway, they reached the locked door. *Here's where the adventure ends,* Drew thought, but Erica produced a ring full of keys.

"Did you steal them off Herman?" Drew asked. He knew he probably shouldn't be so interested in the nuts and bolts of their breakout; he might be called on to testify to his part in it.

"Herman and I agreed on an exchange," Erica said. Before Drew could inquire, she added, "Desperate times call for blow jobs."

Drew thought he'd heard the line before, in *The Postman Always Comes Twice*.

As Erica pushed the key into the lock, he caught a glimpse of the keychain. It was a miniature of Freud smoking a cigar. Erica saw him looking at it. "This is what passes for humor around here," she said. "Now show me a keychain of Freud with a cigar up his ass and smoke blowing out his ears, then I'm laughing."

Drew wondered what would happen to him if they were caught. Would he still be allowed to return home tomorrow? Or would his return be postponed indefinitely and his unit status reduced to Level Red?

They walked down two flights of steps, pushed open another door, and found themselves in the Cage. Drew thought their journey was finished, but Erica marched to the iron door at the far end. After several keys didn't fit the red lock, she held up a gold key. It looked as ancient as a key to a treasure chest. She inserted it and the door sprung open.

A few hundred yards in front of them, the football stadium looked like a diaphragm for a giantess.

"Wow," Erica said, breathing in the cool air, "we could do anything now. We could even kill ourselves." She turned to him. "Do you want to?"

Walking at even a leisurely pace, they could be at the Main Street Bridge in an hour. Or they could climb onto the stadium's roof or to one of its high corners, with their easy-to-scale guardrails, and jump. But death held only a faint appeal to Drew now.

"I didn't think you did," Erica said. "Too bad. I guess we'll have to go to the fifty-yard line and fuck like high school kids on prom night."

Drew sighed. He was about to speak when Erica said, "Herpes isn't an obstacle." From her pocket, she removed a batch of condoms, in silver, red, and baby blue packaging. A couple of them trickled out of her palm and fell to the asphalt. She didn't bother to pick them up.

They headed across the empty hospital parking lot toward the stadium. The parking-lot lights were enormous, white-yellow balls.

"You're married," Drew said.

"And my husband is a beautiful, kind man," Erica said sincerely. "He's the vice principal of an elementary school over in Sheridan. We have two beautiful children, a boy and a girl. They're 99 percent perfect, which is about 49 percent more than a parent has a right to expect. All three of them write me every day. I used to have visiting privileges, but the last time my husband came to see me I tried to hang myself with his belt.

"You're luckier than I am," she continued. "At least you have something to pin your condition on. You have the whole porn career, your venereal disease, and your abusive father."

"How do you know about my father?" Drew asked, not with anger but out of startled curiosity.

"I guessed. Find me a white coat, and I'll be part of your treatment team."

They left the parking lot and stood at the locked gates of the stadium. Again, Erica produced her ring of keys. On her first try, she opened the gate.

"I don't understand," Drew said.

"You mean why Herman would have keys to the football stadium? He's sixty-five years old—he's held every job in this town twice. I think he was even mayor once, back in the mid-seventies."

There was something awe-inspiring, Drew thought, about football stadiums, latter-day Coliseums. The near goalpost, shrouded in mist, looked like a redesigned crucifix. And Drew swore he could hear echoes of voices swirling around the concrete stands and aluminum seats.

Drew felt Erica's hand in his. "Don't worry," she said, "we won't do anything you don't want to do. I know you're concerned about my marital status. I'm sure that plenty of the ladies you worked with were married and you probably didn't care, but I respect that you're in a new stage of your life."

They stopped at the fifty-yard line and Erica let go of his hand. He immediately missed her touch. She began to undress, lining up her jeans, T-shirt, and shoes on the grass as if outfitting a reclining mannequin. He hesitated before doing the same with his clothes.

"That's right," she said. "Let it go." She unsnapped her bra, releasing breasts larger and less firm than he would have thought. She covered both of her nipples with her index fingers. "A year and two months," she said. "I nursed my oldest—the boy—for a year and two months. But my daughter, I barely nursed at all. After she was born, I had postpartum depression so bad it was like the Devil shoved his pitchfork in my head. I haven't been the same since." She lowered her underwear to her knees. "I had the perfect life and what did I do with it? I huffed and I puffed and I blew myself right out of it."

"It's waiting for you," Drew said.

"It won't be the same."

"It doesn't have to be. What's there is more than enough."

"All right, doctor."

He wanted to say more, to jolt her in a way her electroshock treatment couldn't. He wanted her to be happy, wanted to make her happy. When had he last felt this impulse?

"You're still wearing your underwear," Erica said.

"Right," he said, and he lowered it solemnly. His penis was flaccid, but in the darkness his herpes sores, if he had them, were disguised. If the night was cold, he didn't feel it.

Erica took his hand again. "Onto our beach blankets," she said, gesturing to their clothes, and they lowered themselves onto them. Above them, blue-gray clouds dominated the black sky. Here and there, like cats' eyes peering from a closet, were stars.

"I've always thought the Big Bang really was a big bang," Erica says.

"What do you mean?"

Erica laughed softly. "God's beautiful orgasm."

They were still holding hands.

"I think I'm getting better," he ventured.

"I know you are," she said. "And you're leaving tomorrow. Were you going to tell me or just leave me heartbroken?"

"I have mixed feelings about it," he said.

"It's normal to feel ambivalent about leaving a secure place. Even prisoners are ambivalent about going home when their sentences are up," she said. "But I wish you had told me."

"I'm sorry."

"You're forgiven." She squeezed his hand and sighed. "I wish I was getting better. But the chemistry experiment in my head went wrong and all these drugs and electroshock treatments are doing is confirming my hopelessness. I'm incurable."

"I thought I was too," Drew said. He breathed in. The air was moist and fragrant. The grass smelled like flowers. Or perhaps the smell was Erica. He breathed out. "But the problems I told you about are still problems," he said.

"I think you need a new fantasy," she told him.

He waited for her to explain.

"After you hit puberty, I bet you became fixated on the standard heterosexual male fantasy—probably involving two or more women, right?"

"That was fantasy number one," Drew admitted.

"But you've actually lived out fantasy number one as well as fantasies two and three and three hundred," she said. "And turning these fantasies into reality depended on the participation of certain kinds of women, most of them with histories you wouldn't wish even on a girl who'd broken your heart a hundred times. So now your fantasies make you sick."

"True," Drew conceded.

"Anyway," Erica said, "it's time for you to fantasize outside the box." She giggled. "I meant that metaphorically, but I guess it applies literally as well."

"All right. What should I fantasize about?"

"Anything besides a ménage-à-trois or an orgy or anal sex," she said. "Anything besides legs glistening with baby oil and boobs as big as volleyballs. Anything besides women—or men, for that matter. Fantasize about the sky, the clouds, the moon."

"You're kidding."

"There's nothing sexier than a moonlit night. I've had some of my best orgasms looking up at the stars, thinking about nothing but how gorgeous they are." She paused. "Look, you can see a little edge of the moon, like her pale foot. But the cloud is keeping her mostly covered."

"Yeah," he said, "I see it."

"Isn't mistress moon lovely tonight? Isn't she just the prettiest thing you've ever seen?" She squeezed his hand.

He felt his heart pump, felt blood dance to other parts of his body.

"And now she's shedding more of her cloud clothing. She's letting you see more of her—she's letting you know her."

"Sure," Drew said, and feeling something return to him below his waist, he added, "She's beautiful. She's beautiful and she's lonely."

"She isn't lonely now," Erica said. "She has you."

He couldn't say it was only or even mostly the moon and the star-speckled sky that made him feel what he was feeling. He felt Erica's blood throb against his palms; he felt how warm her hand was. He'd never known how sensual a woman's hand could be.

"She's beautiful, isn't she? She's splendid in all the darkness."

"Yes, beautiful," said Drew, thinking of the moon, thinking of Erica. "Beautiful."

Now the moon was fully revealed, clouds dispatched to the sides of her. The stars burned bright. He held Erica's hand as if he was about to fall. At the same time, he held himself, and he found himself growing. Her hand, the moon. He felt a rush of pleasure—more—of joy.

"Yes," he said, the word springing from somewhere primitive and essential within him.

"Yes," she echoed, her hand warming his, the moon burning in the black sky.

"Yes." Again: "Yes." As his body surged with sensation, as it rushed toward orgasm, he wondered if Erica was pleasing herself. He wanted to be part of her happiness, however small it was, however fleeting. He opened his mouth to speak to her, but his pleasure, as intense as any he'd ever felt, silenced him. In the delirious waves of his orgasm, he didn't feel her hand disengage from his.

A moment later, he heard feet strike across the grass. He looked up to see Erica racing toward the stands and, he was certain, the stadium's dark heights. He pictured her on one of the stadium's perilous edges, pictured her leaping into forever. "Erica!"

He sprang to his feet and chased after her, her bare ass brilliant and moon-white. He stumbled against a deflated ball or abandoned cleat, and for a second, he thought he was going to fall. He knew falling would mean losing her. But he righted himself and continued running.

She bounded up a set of wooden stairs from the field to the stands and climbed toward the right corner. Between the stands and the roof there wasn't even a guardrail but only sky and a fall of at least five stories onto concrete. She was two dozen stairs ahead of him, and he feared she would beat him to the edge. But he continued to chase her, and soon he halved the distance between them.

She was two steps from the unguarded corner when he caught her, his arms wrapped around her waist, his head pressed into her corkscrew curls. She resisted, slashing her elbows into his arms and the sides of his face, her strength surprising and scaring him. He thought she might break his hold, slip from his tiring arms. But at last, she relaxed. They were both hot and damp. From their breathing and nakedness, they might have just made the most intense love of their lives.

"Let me go, Drew," she said.

"I will," he answered, knowing there might be mercy in doing so. But he didn't let her go.

I RETURN

I'd always vowed that if I died young—any age shy of senility—I would return to earth as a ghost to look after my wife and children. My love was this strong, I was certain. Stronger than death. Strong enough to cross from the hereafter to the here.

I was forty-two years old when, having done my weekly part for the earth by dropping off at the Sherman Recycling Center a stack of newspapers, four cereal boxes, three tuna fish cans, a pair of plastic milk jugs, and the empty bottle of Circus Girl chardonnay Jennifer and I had downed Saturday night in a prelude to a higher order of merriment, I stepped into my Toyota Prius and was struck on the driver's side door by what my children (Elsa, fifteen, and Benjamin, thirteen) used to call the Crunch Truck. Who knew this mobile compactor reached speeds of up to seventy miles an hour—or up to sixty-eight, anyway, which was how fast the driver, a nineteen-year-old high on methamphetamines, was going when he plowed into me.

So I was dead. Which, although I'd spent a not inconsiderable amount of time thinking about such an eventuality, was a shock.

I considered myself a perfect candidate for neither heaven nor hell. In my later years, I had been more or less exemplary—a faithful husband, a good father, a solid citizen. As a younger man, however, I had, I feared, at least once crossed the line separating callowness from callousness. I didn't like to remember this time, although even unexamined, it left within me a residue of guilt, something my later good works, such as they were, didn't remove.

The hereafter as I first encountered it was neither heaven nor hell but a chat room in which a collection of the incorporeal dead blathered on, in a medley of languages, about their lost lives. Even when I couldn't understand what was being said, I could interpret tones; I knew who was bragging and who was spewing regret. I knew who wished to return to earth to redeem themselves and who wished to go back merely because they were curious to know what would happen next in the human story.

I heard talk about a portal to earth, and although I was tempted to dismiss it as wish and rumor, I committed to memory what I deemed the most trustworthy information on routes to it. At last satisfied with my road map, I set off, navigating through tunnels and mazes and, in one instance, what looked like a bowling alley with glowing orange pins. Months seemed to pass, but eventually I saw, in the black expanse below me, a hole the size of a manhole cover, opening on what looked like blue sky. It was guarded by a spirit who claimed to be a Sphinx, although he spoke in a Brooklyn accent and asked me no riddles. We chatted about the sense of smell, which, in addition to the sense of touch and taste, we had lost in transit to the hereafter. He said he missed the smell of his mother's fish stew. As he waxed nostalgic,

I floated over the open portal and focused all my thoughts on returning to what I'd left.

A moment later, I was in the men's room of a high-school football stadium. More specifically, I was suspended a foot above a urinal cake, which put me in the line of fire, so to speak. Before being doused, I levitated and floated out of the bathroom exit and into the stands. The stadium, situated, I eventually learned, in the depressed town of Hamlet, Montana, must have held five thousand people, and it was packed.

I discovered I had the ability to communicate with the living when, quickly bored with the game, I made my way to the concession stand and ordered two bags of popcorn. (Why two? For my children, I suspect. Or perhaps for me and my wife.) The boy behind the counter, whose acne and greasy bangs bespoke a miserable adolescence, offered my two bags to the air. We were in the north end of the stadium, about twenty yards beyond the goal post, and there was no one in the vicinity. A few moments passed as the boy glanced left and right. He even stared over the counter, as if whoever had placed the order might have collapsed. "Hello?" he whispered.

In retrospect, I should have withdrawn without another word. But I was as surprised to be speaking as he was surprised to be spoken to by a ghost. I said, "I used to put warm oatmeal on my face to help my acne. I'd lie on the kitchen floor like a mummy. One day my sister sprinkled brown sugar on me and threatened to pull out a spoon."

The boy whirled around, his hair flying like a cape. "What the fuck?" he said several times.

I had a vision of his future: In three years, he'd be a soldier, fighting on a distant frontier. It was possible I'd soon see—or, rather, soon hear—his soul in the hereafter.

Minutes later, I heard the churning of a freight train, and minutes after this, I was on board, headed back east, to my family in Sherman, Ohio.

— From the outside, my house looked the same as I remembered. On the inside, it was tidier, brighter. The newspapers I used to pile beside my armchair in the corner of the living room were gone. My old toothbrushes, which I had collected in a gray plastic cup on the left side of the sink in the first-floor bathroom, had been disposed of. None of my sweaters were hanging on the backs of the chairs around the dining room table. Indeed, I would have thought I'd entered the wrong house if I hadn't spied my wife in our bedroom, sitting in front of her vanity, combing her long, black hair.

I didn't know what time it was since the sky's grayness suggested anywhere from early morning to dusk, but by her outfit—a low-cut, cotton dress with a black-and-white checker pattern—I guessed it must be evening. She sprayed perfume on her neck. The gesture wasn't entirely foreign to me—I'd seen her apply perfume once or twice in the early days of our marriage—but I didn't immediately understand its implication. And when I did realize what it likely meant, I couldn't help but cry, "Are you going on a date?"

Immediately, my wife stopped combing her hair. Slowly, she craned her neck around. "Benjamin?" she asked.

It was a comfort to hear her speak my son's name. I was about to tell her so when she spoke another name, a name to which I couldn't attach a face or a history: "Peter?"

"Who's Peter?"

My wife shot bolt upright, clutching the comb like a billy club.

"Who are you?" she asked. "Who's here?"

She had thick lips I always thought sexy (although in my hereafter state I'd lost my libido), and the bottom one was trembling. She'd made herself up; her eyelashes looked like thin, black petals.

"It's me," I said.

She drew in a deep breath, and as she released it, her shoulders slumped, her breasts fell. She was, in short, relaxed. And a second later, she wasn't.

"Is this a joke?" she screamed.

"It's me," I said. "I've come back."

"Where?" she asked, surveying the room.

"You can't see me. I'm incorporeal. But I've made it back from the dead, to be with you again." With a measure of pride, I added, "Like I always said I would." It had been a long time since I'd told Lilly my love for her was so great that even death couldn't keep me from her. But it was on the record, and now I was fulfilling my promise.

She wasn't convinced I was who I claimed, and it took me a quarter of an hour, perhaps longer, to explain myself so she believed me.

"This is so strange, so strange," she muttered.

"Aren't you glad to see me?" I asked.

This was the wrong choice of words—she couldn't see me, after all—but I hoped it would draw a smile.

She looked down and fidgeted with her fingers. I noticed she'd removed her wedding ring. She looked up to where she supposed my invisible presence hovered. "Michael, I stood by your grave as they lowered your casket in. I cried. I sobbed. I was the perfect widow. And all my tears were genuine. But after a while, one tends to move on."

The doorbell rang, and Lilly recoiled. "Oh," she said, breathing heavily. "Listen, Michael, I have to answer that. I've got a . . . um . . ."

She sprang toward the bedroom door, but before leaving, she turned around. "I don't know if it's such a good idea for you to hang around here. We can't go to Peter's place because . . . well, there's the wife thing, and . . ."

"You're dating a married man?" I said with a mixture of incredulity and outrage.

"He's a transitional figure in my life—obviously." She patted her hair. "But he's kind and he's fun."

"Why don't you transition back to your husband instead?" There were a hundred things we needed to discuss, I believed, although I couldn't recall any in particular.

"Michael, I'm sorry. This is unexpected. It's awkward! Could you call next time . . . you know, to give me a heads up?"

"A heads up?" I repeated.

"In the meantime, you could stop in to say hi to the kids. They're at my parents' house. I'm sure they'd love to . . . uh . . . hear from you."

The doorbell rang again. "Coming!" she announced, and she disappeared down the steps without saying goodbye. I heard the door open; I heard a flurry of words. Then I heard the door shut followed by silence.

Our cat, Theodore, an overweight Persian, came in, sniffed the air, and jumped onto the warm vanity seat my wife had vacated. I called him a hundred times—I even attempted to imitate the electric can opener—but although he acknowledged me by perking up his ears, he soon settled into indifference. I suspect he knew I couldn't offer him anything he'd want.

I thought of what I might have said to Lilly had she stayed. Beyond a description of the hereafter and an account of my journey from Montana to Ohio, I couldn't say I had much to report. And Lilly clearly didn't deem it important to talk to me. When did Lilly and I stop having much to say to each other? I wondered. I might have shivered with the coldness of my revelation, but there was no longer a part of me that could shiver.

— I found my daughter chatting on her cell phone in her grandparents' basement. Elsa and I had once been close. She and I had shared an interest in magical creatures (I was once an aspiring fantasy writer, though my day job was high school physics teacher). The two of us would trade off being the narrator of our epic-in-progress, which bore a number of titles over the months we told the tale: The Purple Unicorn, The Pink Unicorn, The Pink Unicorn and Her Purple Baby. But this enchanted time of father-daughter closeness, I realized, must have ended half a decade ago, and the teenager sitting cross-legged on the floor and twirling her brown hair with her right index finger was, if not a stranger, then a mutation of the girl I'd known and understood.

Even the most skilled stenographer, I suspected, would have had difficulty recording every word Elsa spoke into the phone. I heard mention of boys and music and movies. I heard talk of girls and cliques and seasonal clothing. I heard nothing about unicorns, neither pink nor purple. Nor did she once mention me. But when, an hour or more later, she clicked off her phone, she wore such a look of despondence, I thought I knew the cause: She was missing me. Thinking I could console her, I spoke her name.

Her reaction was similar to her mother's, which made me think of Lilly, which reminded me of where Lilly was and with whom (and without whom—me). I would have felt profound sadness if, as was becoming apparent, my spirit state didn't preclude sadness.

After I had convinced Elsa I was her father, or at least her father's ghost, she and I fell immediately into an uncomfortable silence. For the life of me—oh, how those old phrases linger—I couldn't think of what to say. After a while, I began to grow angry or as angry, I suppose, as a hereafter being could. Didn't my daughter, a whisper away from being an adult, an adult who would become a geriatric, a geriatric who would die—didn't she care to know what might await her beyond this life? Didn't she want to talk with, converse with, rap with—whatever the latest, coolest expression was to describe communication—me? How lonely I might have felt if I could have felt anything.

Breaking the silence, my daughter looked up and said, "I'm glad you're okay, Dad." The briefest of pauses: "Do you mind if I make another call?"

"I won't linger," I said, but I doubt she heard me above the music her fingers made as they pounded numbers on her cell phone.

— I interrupted Benjamin in the guest bedroom, in the middle of a fantasy. At least, I assume he was in the middle of a fantasy (I always called on fantasies when engaged in solo flights under the covers).

What left his mouth was a series of expletives I'd never heard in the order he used them in. When, at last, he established who I was (which failed to remove the suspicion, even hostility, from his face), he said, "God, Dad . . . I mean, how rude. You never barged in on me when you were alive."

"When I was alive, I could knock," I said. "And, please, don't think the entire world—even the Pope, I'd bet, if I had anything to bet with—doesn't do what you were doing."

He had no response, and I was afraid we would lapse into the kind of silence Elsa and I had endured. It relieved me, therefore, when he said, "I have homework—about a week's worth."

"I'll help you," I said, which had always been my response. Doing Benjamin's homework had been my way of reliving, in his presence, my academic glory.

"Great," he said, and jutting his chin toward a corner of the room, he added, "My backpack's over there. The homework assignment's in the red folder. There's math, there's earth science, there's a reading passage I'm supposed to interpret."

"Sure, son," I said, and instinctively made my way toward the backpack. But I no longer had hands to open it. I had no fingers with which to squeeze a pencil, to print answers.

What will my son do without me? I wondered.

And I had an answer: *Learn to do for himself.*

I would be the stricter father—and the better teacher—in absentia.

"There should be a pencil somewhere in the backpack," he said. "If you can't find one, go ask Grandma."

He rolled over, falling quickly to sleep. His snores were light, childlike. If I was his future, they'd grow heavier over the years. When he was a freshman in college, his roommates would invest in earplugs—or have him exiled to off-campus housing.

Oh, the lessons he'd have to learn without me. But my absence, I was realizing, would guarantee he'd learn them.

If I could have, I would have kissed his tousled hair. I loved him—of course I loved him. I loved him enough to say goodbye.

— After such an unenthusiastic reception by my family, one might have suspected I'd be ready to hop a train west, to see if I could find the hole in the sky, the passage back to my eternal chattering place. I was confident I would find it more amenable, or at least less intolerable, than when I'd left it, since I had proved false the grand idea of my indispensability. But I had one more visit I wanted—I needed—to make.

I'd dated Katherine Peters during our senior year in high school. She was the first woman I'd loved who had ever reciprocated my love, and during the months we were together, everything I saw—from her lips to the tired bricks of our eighty-two-year-old high school building—seemed to blaze with color. We spent as much time together during the week as we could. On weekends, especially during warm weather, we sat on her front porch, sneaking an occasional cigarette, talking, kissing. We'd often stay up until two or three in the morning. After such nights, I'd walk the ten blocks back to my house singing to the stars.

Before long, our relationship began to run its course; our kisses, once so fiery and new, were becoming routine. We had been accepted to different colleges. She wanted to become a veterinarian; I wanted to become a best-selling author, J. R. R. Tolkien's heir. In short, we eventually would have parted ways. This is how I saw our lives, although I never exactly communicated this to Katherine.

Because Katherine and I had been dating for ten months, we didn't treat our high school's prom as an opportunity to hook up (in a phrase from my children's generation) or as one last chance to unleash the mischievous children in us by, say, spiking the punch or turning over the principal's Chevrolet in the parking lot. The prom was a dance, and we liked to dance.

When we returned to Katherine's house at two in the morning, I stood with her on her porch. The air was cool, even cold, although it was June. I was tired and ready to go home. I had something important to do the next day, which was an unfamiliar situation for me. Previously, everything important in my life had to do with Katherine. I was about to kiss her goodnight when she looked over my left shoulder and said, "You can't leave. We'd miss you too much."

Although grateful for the sentiment, I was about to plead my excuse, but I hesitated, tripped up by her use of the first person plural.

She stepped past me and shouted into the darkness, "You said you wouldn't leave and now you're leaving!"

She had awoken a dog, who barked furiously somewhere up the street. A moment later, I heard, or thought I heard, a window opening next door.

"Katherine," I said, pulling her to me. She pushed me away and began running down the street, screaming, "Don't leave me!" She'd run track until the eleventh grade, and as far as I could tell she'd lost none of her speed. I, no runner, huffed and puffed after her.

Fortunately, she did a loop around the block, finishing on her front porch, where she sobbed until her mother, with a cigarette in her mouth and a T-shirt down to her waist, collected her. Katherine staggered into her house without so much as a goodnight to me.

When I came to her house the next day, her sister, who had lived all her life as the bad girl to Katherine's good girl, told me Katherine had been admitted to the psychiatric ward of the Ohio Eastern University Hospital. She told me more: Katherine had had an abortion two months before we started dating. "I think she's talking to her dead baby," her sister confided. Katherine's diagnosis was schizophrenia. (Now, of course, I wonder if the phantoms Katherine saw were real.)

I had a job as a counselor at an overnight camp outside of Akron, and I left for it without once visiting Katherine in the hospital or speaking to her on the phone. Nor did I bother to write her. I was, anyway, soon off to college, in Maine. Sometimes I convinced myself that my behavior toward her wasn't cruel or heartless. I was only moving on.

A year after I graduated from college, I heard Katherine was working in her parents' pet supplies store, the Cat's Meow, in West Sherman and taking courses at Ohio Eastern. I thought about going to see her—to apologize for my behavior, my cowardice—but by this time I was dating Lilly. I had job interviews lined up all over Ohio, and I soon received an offer to teach at a high school on the far, and most rural, end of Sherman County. Lilly and I got married, bought an old farmhouse on the same dirt road the school was on, and, before long, welcomed Elsa into our lives.

Eight years later, my family and I moved back to town after I was offered a job at Sherman High School. Over the years, I probably saw Katherine a dozen times, always at a distance, the last time in the fruit section of Food World. She was holding a bunch of green grapes. She looked at me as she would a stranger. At the time, I assumed she didn't recognize me. This might have been wishful thinking.

Now I wanted to visit her in order to follow up on my long-ago intention to apologize. But the greater reason, I confess, was this: Because she wasn't married or attached (at least as far as I knew), I thought she would welcome the presence of an old lover, even if he was barely present.

I was aware, of course, of how my reappearance—or, anyway, my return to the scene—might exacerbate her mental illness. But after my rejection by my family, I was, I suppose, desperate to connect to someone who had once loved me. Even the dead, it seemed, could be selfish.

The Cat's Meow opened Sundays at ten, and it wasn't quite nine when I drifted in. Whereas the store's main competition, Pet Perfect, looked like its megastore cousin, Wal-Mart, the Cat's Meow resembled an overstuffed pantry. Cat food, dog food, bird food, leashes, catnip, collars—anything a pet owner could want—crowded the shelves of the narrow aisles.

The cash register was on a counter in the middle of the store's single, large room. Beside it were CDs with animal themes, or at least references to animals in their titles, including the Beach Boys' *Pet Sounds*. Katherine and I had often listened to the Beach Boys on her front porch, the cassette tape of *Pet Sounds* eventually becoming tangled and unusable, although by then one of us could merely hum the opening notes of a song and the rest of it would be in the other's head for days.

Behind the counter, sitting on the yellow-carpeted floor, was Katherine. She looked older than when I'd last seen her, of course, but I couldn't say she looked worse. Her brownish-orange hair fell in autumnal corkscrews onto her shoulders. There was silver in it, shimmering like fish in a sunlit creek. Sleeping in her lap was a puppy, copper colored and not much larger than her hand. I remembered Sundays at the Cat's Meow: It was the day a local animal shelter brought in stray cats and dogs in the hopes that the Cat's Meow's customers would want another pet.

The other animals were doubtless at the back of the store, in cages the shelter provided to show them off. Katherine had elected to spend the minutes before she opened the store in the company of this dog, who was sick or comatose or perhaps only sleeping. Something flared up in me, something unexpected but familiar: a desire to mock her charity, to ridicule the kindness she always extended to the world, especially to its most pathetic inhabitants. I remembered times she would cross Main Street to speak to her "friends"—I thought of them with quotation marks—sitting on benches in front of City Hall, stealing sips from bottles in bags. I'd stand apart from the scene until she finished saying hello, or I'd meet her later at the Book and Brew or at her house. I remembered, too, how two months or so after we'd begun dating, I found out she was writing to two prisoners, and I became as furious as if I'd discovered she'd been cheating on me. I wasn't consoled when she said, "They're in for life. No parole."

What was it, I wondered now, that I despised so much in her goodness? Just as I asked myself the question, I knew the answer: She was kinder than I was, more compassionate, and I resented the feelings of selfishness, even meanness, this engendered in me. So I had despised her for having what I lacked.

What a waste these emotions had been, I thought now, how destructive to the short, and mostly nice, time Katherine and I had had together. Contemplating their futility, I laughed.

Katherine's head had been bowed over the sleeping puppy, but she lifted it quickly, a disturbed look on her face. Freckles—I remembered how much I loved them—fanned in an upside down "V" from the top of her nose. Her lips moved, a jittery trembling, although no words left them.

I knew the power I had. It was nothing less than the power to destroy her. I could laugh in her ear now and whenever we were alone. I could whisper demonic suggestions, tease her insecurities. I was sure I could torment her into killing herself and so wipe from the earth the person I had hurt most in my life, a person who no doubt carried with her an impression of me as a selfish coward. I might once have been tempted.

But the hereafter seems to mute temptations. Or perhaps I'd grown as a person—or as a soul, a spirit—after my death.

I did not follow my laughter with more of the same. Instead, I flew toward the cages at the back of the room and gave, in the same register as my laugh, a happy bark. On my second bark, I was joined by the two adult dogs who lay in wire cages at either end of the wall and a golden retriever puppy in a glass cage in the center who might have been announcing himself for the first time. Meanwhile, the cats and kittens in the other cages scrambled around, alternately curious and cowering.

Katherine walked, smiling, to the back of the room, and facing the cages said, "Who started this?" She looked down at the puppy in her arms before staring at the tiny golden retriever, who released another howl. "Which one of you dogs has a bark like a laugh?"

I laughed again, but only after I had left the Cat's Meow. Outside, my laughter wasn't nearly as sonorous as it had been indoors, but it rang with some of the old joy, and with something else—something like the relief of the pardoned—as I was swept up, as with gentle hands, into the enormous blue sky.

CLASSMATES

You suspect the lawn hasn't been mowed since sometime in the summer; it is full of weeds and intrudes onto the concrete walkway from both sides. The house is in a similar state. Its gray vinyl siding was doubtless once white, and a section of gutter dangles from the roof like an arm over the side of a bed. You drop the knocker, shaped like a dragon or snarling dog, on the wooden door. A moment later, you knock again, three quick strikes. In your free hand, you hold six yellow roses.

Presently you hear a whine, the door's complaint as it swings inward. Standing in front of you is a woman with shoulder-length hair, its black conceding to gray. Her eyebrows, entirely black, are so thin they seem inked on. She is shorter than you imagined, the top of her head no higher than your shoulders.

After you introduce yourself, there is a silence, so you remind her of your phone call. She stands fixed in place, staring at you with neither irritation nor curiosity. Time passes, and you feel, as you sometimes have in the last year, like a phantom or dream figure, a shade shy of invisible. You are about to speak again when she says, “Come in.”

She accepts your roses without comment and leads you into the living room, painted baby blue. Against the near wall is a white couch, like a cloud, with matching armchairs on either side. Against the far wall is a stand-up piano, the dust on its keys exposed in the yellow-gray afternoon light.

You expect to see pictures on the wall or on the mantel above the fireplace or on top of the piano. In their absence, you recall the only picture of your classmate you have ever seen—the photo at the back of his lone book, in which he appears to have gained thirty pounds since your graduation. But you didn’t know him in college; he might have been overweight all of his life. In the same fifteen years, you have gained twenty-two pounds. The weight hasn’t altered your face, which preserves its hard angles; instead, it has settled around your belly, a beer gut on someone who drinks wine.

Your classmate’s wife has yet to invite you to sit down. You wonder if she is hoping you will leave. But you’ve driven five hundred miles to be here.

At last: “Sit down.” In a softer voice: “Please.”

You sit in one of the armchairs. After placing the roses on the coffee table in front of the couch, she sits in the other. “I’m sorry,” she says, “I didn’t ask if you wanted anything to drink.”

“I’m fine,” you say. “Thank you.”

“Oh,” she says. She has pulled herself to the front of her armchair. “Are you sure? All right.” She slides back.

You wonder if she has friends or family to help her. She must. But it has been two months since her husband’s death, and they probably have stopped calling and visiting as frequently. She is moving in a couple of weeks—she told you this on the phone—and doubtless she will feel better when she does.

"I've come because . . ." What you said to her during your brief phone conversation and repeated at her front door was: *I'd like to write a story about your husband for the alumni magazine.*

"You told me why you're here," she says. She adds, "Does anyone ever read the alumni magazine? Don and I used to stack them in a closet, saying we'd get to them when hell sold ice cream."

You smile at her joke; she doesn't. "I'm sorry never to have known either of you when we were in college," you say.

"Big school," she says.

"Did you meet in a class?"

"We met in a bathroom. In his sophomore year, he had a job cleaning dorm rooms. He was cleaning the bathroom in mine when I walked in." Her smile, though slight, is genuine. "We talked until dark. I don't think he ever finished cleaning the bathroom."

"It was love at first sight," you say, although you are thinking of the day you met your wife.

"I don't know," she says. "I can talk to anyone for hours." She looks at you. "It's probably hard for you to imagine, me being talkative. But it's true, I am." Her smile softens her. "Or was."

You offer her a smile as her smile fades. You wonder if she would have found you attractive in college. Your wife, during the early, easier days of your relationship, told you you looked like a movie star "in the age before the leading men grew goatees, before their skin glowed like tropical sunsets, before they depleted their mystique by thinking they could sing or save the world."

In the lingering silence, you imagine you are here to play the part of your classmate resurrected, to seduce his wife from her sadness. Yet all you see when you conjure her bed is a pair of pillows lined against the headboard like tombstones.

"Maybe it was love at first sight," she amends. "I've deleted the emotion from my memories of him. It's like watching someone else's home movies."

You wonder if your wife would have done the same. Or would she have grieved briefly, intensely, purging you in order to free herself to feel again? *Is this why I've come here?* you think. *To spy on the world I would have left behind?*

"He was a piano player," you say.

"We both played. But six months ago, he stopped playing. I should have distrusted the silence."

You remember your own estrangement from what you loved, how everything you enjoyed became torture, and how the gulf between the pleasure you once felt in such activities and the burden they became made your pain all the more acute. "I imagine this wasn't all he stopped doing," you say.

She frowns. "To go from being someone who lifts weights four days a week, who writes five hours a day—most of the time with the computer keys clicking ecstatically—who fucks like a freshman on spring break—to go from being this joyful person to being someone who has to be prodded into shaving and brushing his teeth . . ." She sighs or huffs, a sound of exasperation and something darker.

"This summer he was supposed to be working on his novel," she says. "I was teaching a couple of classes at State, which is an hour-and-fifteen-minute drive from here, so I couldn't keep a constant vigil over him. But he didn't look sick. It was like he was only under a spell and if I snapped my fingers, I could break it."

"How long had he been depressed?"

"It's hard to know. Maybe two and a half, three months."

"The same," you say.

Confusion crosses her face. "The same what?"

You hesitate. "The same with me."

"Oh," she says. "So you . . ."

You suppose you had always meant to tell her: "After three months with severe depression, I tried to kill myself. This was last year, ten months or so before your husband . . . before he . . ."

"Succeeded?"

"Succeeded." The word rings oddly triumphant in the small living room.

She sits up in her chair. "Why didn't you succeed?" Her tone is skeptical.

You tell her the story: At one thirty on a warm September night, you left the living-room couch, where you would often retreat when your restlessness threatened to disturb your wife's sleep, and stepped into your garage. After getting into your ancient Mustang, you turned on the engine, rolled down the windows, and waited to die. You were unconscious when a neighbor, a bartender returning from work, pulled you free of the fumes. *Five more minutes and you would have been dead,* the emergency room doctor declared. *Five minutes, no more.*

"You left yourself a chance to be saved," she says, her voice cool, almost accusatory.

"That wasn't my plan."

"But some part of you wanted to live. Otherwise you would have jumped off a bridge or blown your brains out."

You don't think this is true, but you don't want to argue with her.

"I wouldn't know," she says. "I'm sorry." She sighs, and her expression softens. "Don's psychiatrist was asking him to consider shock therapy. He shouldn't have been able to buy laundry detergent or Drano, much less a gun. But he drove half a mile down the road to a pawnshop and, a minute later, held his passport to eternity. Great fucking country. I'm glad the right to kill yourself with a semiautomatic pistol when you're so depressed you can't fix yourself a sandwich or read the sports page is constitutionally guaranteed." Her eyes meet yours. "He shot himself in the mouth, in the shed under the crabapple tree in our backyard." She pauses. "I found him, of course."

She looks at the piano again, as if expecting to see her husband seated on the bench. Your classmate had a widow's peak and an aquiline nose—like you do. Why are you seeking these similarities? You look at the flowers in front of you, laid as if on a grave. *Only one of us is alive.* The thought feels selfish and boastful, but it lingers.

"If I had been well enough to buy a gun, I would have," you tell her. "It was all I could do to leave the couch and stumble into the garage." You feel again what you felt the moment before you raced to your garage: dueling currents, hot and cold—extremes of discomfort—swirling inside you. The feeling passes, and you lean back in the armchair. "I was convinced my wife was going to leave me."

Her eyes catch yours. "Was she?"

You shake your head. "But frustration was an understandable part of her response."

"I'm sure she didn't think you would try to kill yourself."

"Even *I* didn't think I would try to kill myself—most of the time, anyway. And even in the worst of my depression, I had moments when I understood exactly what was happening to me, when I knew my suicide lust was death's seduction and not the right prescription to end my pain. But before long, I would return to thinking—to *knowing*—that suicide was the only way to stop my pain and end the humiliation I was causing myself and my wife and everyone who knew us."

You want to say more; there is so much more to tell. But you aren't here to unburden yourself of your story, although at the moment you can't remember why you've come.

"When you were depressed, did your wife have help—people to look in on you or take up the work around the house?" she asks.

Your memory of this period is imprecise; sometimes the months seem like a single, agonizing day. "Her sister lives in the area. She came by as often as she could." You lean forward. "And you?"

"Don's mother visited once, for a week. She fixed him chicken soup and told him if he'd only bother to bathe every so often, he'd feel better. After going home, she'd call him, and he'd tell her he was doing all right. It wasn't close to the truth."

"We lied to protect our egos," you say, "to spare ourselves from having people think we were weak and helpless and unmanly. We spared ourselves from having them think we couldn't overcome our sadness or the blues or whatever mild affliction they thought was troubling us. In the meantime, knives were being driven into our foreheads. Fires were raging in our brains."

She holds her gaze on you before putting her palms over her eyes. Time passes. You hear sounds outside: a dog bark, a siren. The house itself is silent. "I saw the receipt," she says.

"The receipt?"

She removes her palms and looks at you. "For the gun."

"When?" You try to sound unimpressed.

Her voice has a hollow quality, as if she is speaking over the mouth of an empty bottle. "The day he bought it? The day after?" She draws in a shallow breath, releases it. "I could probably figure out exactly when, but I'm afraid it would only . . ." She closes her eyes, holds them closed a moment, opens them. "I'm afraid it would only incriminate me more. If I saw it four days before he killed himself instead of three, I would be all the more guilty of aiding and abetting his murder."

"You didn't aid and abet."

She shakes her head. "When I found the receipt—a cash receipt, with the name of the pawn shop—I asked Don what it was for. And there was a moment, maybe half a second, when his face filled with worry. It happened so fast I couldn't swear I'd seen anything suspicious. The next moment, he said, 'It's for a fishing rod.' And I said, 'A fishing rod? You don't fish.' 'I'm trying everything,' he said. 'Maybe I just need to sit in a boat and listen to the mosquitoes and wait for a miracle to pull on my line.'"

She closes her eyes again. A few seconds pass before she opens them. "An hour later, he showed me a fishing rod. It wasn't much more than a stick and a string. The people who rented the house before us probably left it in the shed or in the storage space in the attic."

"He deceived you, the way I would have," you say, "the way I deceived my wife." You tell her: When your wife wasn't home, you listened obsessively to requiems—Brahms', Dvorak's, Mozart's, music you hadn't played in years—but before your wife returned, you hid the CDs under the couch, as if they might announce your intention.

If to be depressed was to show weakness, to consider committing suicide was weakness itself, you thought. So as you became obsessed with oblivion, you held your obsession private, like a secret you'd promised to guard with your life.

"I knew where the pawnshop was," she says. "I could have driven over and asked if they'd sold my husband a gun."

"You didn't want to believe he was so ill."

"Maybe. Or maybe I was so tired and frustrated I didn't care to know for sure." She bites her bottom lip. "Three months. He was sick for only three months. But each day was like walking a mile in quicksand."

Tears shimmer in her eyes before slipping down her cheeks. "I knew what the neon sign in the pawn shop window said: 'We sell guns'! What more did I need—a telegram? A message written across the sky?"

You leave the armchair and move to the end of the couch closest to her. Her face is a patchwork of white, pink, and red, and you notice the imperfect growth of skin over the piercing on her left ear. You smell cigarettes and wonder if she has resumed an old habit. "You didn't want him to die," you say. "You only wanted the pain to be over—for everyone."

"Isn't it the same thing?" she asks.

"No—because you're still in pain. In worse pain."

Presently, her crying ceases, and she stares past you. "Right," she says softly. "And for the rest of my life—the downhill, wrinkled, wretched second half of my life—I get to live with memories no one will be here to validate. I get to suffer the consequences of decisions two of us made—like the decision not to have children so we could pursue our fucking artistic dreams. I might as well be a nun married to the Holy fucking Ghost."

When her crying resumes, you reach across the arm of the couch for her hands, which are ringless, dry, and warm. She looks at you, and you are surprised to find her eyes hard and suspicious. "You've come back from the dead to tell me something," she says. "Well, what is it?"

When you can't think of anything to say, she continues, "Or did you come here to survey what the aftermath of your suicide would have been like? Did you come here to interview your wife's grieving double?" Her voice rises: "Did you come here to gloat?"

You release her hands and, using the arm of the couch as support, stand. For a moment, you feel dizzy, and you think you might fall. Slowly, the world reorders itself, although your stomach remains unsettled.

"If I've come here to gloat, or even if it seems I have, I'm sorry," you say, your voice uncertain, quivering. "And I am deeply sorry for your loss." This you say without equivocation. You turn toward the door.

"Wait," she says, standing. When you turn back to her, she steps into your arms. Her embrace surprises you with its fierceness. "I think you wanted to explain him so I would feel better," she says, her cheek against your thundering chest. "This is why you came—came without so much as a notebook and pen." She looks up at you. "Isn't it?"

Sobs threaten to rise from your throat. Meekly, you nod, although you aren't sure of anything.

She gives you a last hug and lets you go.

— You call your wife, but she isn't in. You leave a message saying you will be spending the night at a hotel and will be home sometime after noon the following day. Three hundred miles or so down the road, you pull into a Days Inn. Later, eating dinner at a Cracker Barrel, you think about your last exchange with your classmate's wife, as you stood outside her front door in the vanishing light. "I don't suppose you cured your depression by trying to kill yourself," she said from within her house.

You shook your head.

"What did make you better?" There was something hopeful in her voice, as if she might yet discover a remedy for her husband's pain.

You told her about your stay in a psychiatric hospital, the antidepressants you were prescribed, your twice-a-week talk-therapy sessions. "And time," you said, although she no longer seemed to be listening. "And luck."

You vow to call your classmate's wife, Jennifer—Jen—tomorrow, to thank her for seeing you, to see how she's doing.

You return to your hotel room and watch television until midnight, but even then you aren't tired. You read articles in the four alumni magazines you have brought with you. It is nearly two in the morning when you turn off the light, but after fifteen minutes, you know you won't be able to sleep. So you check out of the hotel and drive home.

You pull into your driveway at dawn. You don't have the garage opener, so you leave your car in the drive. You have crossed over from tiredness into numbness, a dreamlike sensation, what you might experience in the first few seconds after receiving anesthesia. It is like existing between two worlds, neither of them quite accessible through your five senses.

You walk around to the back of the house and stand outside the kitchen, in front of a window whose yellow curtains have been drawn back. As you anticipated, the kitchen light is on and your wife, her black hair in a ponytail, is at the table, the newspaper and a cup of coffee in front of her. Your eyes have trouble focusing, and the scene seems as much memory, or wish, as reality.

She reads for a few minutes before taking a sip. When she puts down her cup, she looks out the window. You want to acknowledge her, but you find yourself frozen in place. She continues to stare directly at you, her expression, if it holds any emotion, downcast. You remember the fume-filled garage and the blackness overwhelming your consciousness. *Five minutes, no more.*

You step forward and press your lips against the window, kissing its coolness. Your wife smiles and kisses you back.